IN DARKEST LONDON

D1388600

IN DARKEST LONDON

by

MARGARET HARKNESS

first published in 1889 as

CAPTAIN LOBE:
A STORY OF THE SALVATION ARMY

originally written under the pseudonym John Law

BLACK
APOLLO
PRESS

Published by Black Apollo Press, 2003
Reprinted in 2009
ISBN 9781900355636

Originally published by Hodder and Stoughton, 1889

CONTENTS

IN DARKEST LONDON

INTRODUCTION

Margaret Harkness was an extraordinary woman. Shrouded in mystery, she appears to us fleetingly from her books and articles, now mostly lost and forgotten, and somewhat obliquely through the journals of her cousin, Beatrice Potter. Yet despite this veil of mystery we get the notion of a strong and determined woman, with a unique vision, a tender heart and a passionate desire to address the horrors that surrounded her on the streets of late 19th century London.

What we actually know of her isn't all that much. She was born 28 February 1854 at Upton-on-Severn in Worcestershire where her father was a cleric. Coming to London in 1877, she briefly studied to become a nurse before realising her true career as a writer. She was soon attracted to the burgeoning reform movements led by the Social Democratic Party, quickly immersing herself in the ferment of intellectual excitement which was frothing with such effervescence in the 1880s.

Deciding to pursue a career as a journalist, Harkness took a room in the East End, in the poorest streets of Whitechapel, which she used as a perch to view the obverse side of Empire. It was here that she began her life's work as chronicler of the dispossessed. Unlike other social reformers of her day who gave second-hand accounts of life in the underbelly of the world's richest city, she wrote from everyday experience, gathering stories of those desperate souls trapped in the unrelenting despair of grinding poverty.

To Harkness it was incredibly obscene that just a stone's throw from the densely packed hovels where children grew up starving and babies were sold for a jigger of gin, just on the other side of Aldgate, the East-West dividing line, another London existed in dramatic counterpoint to the hellish lives which surrounded her in Whitechapel. It was to those affluent West Enders that she addressed her books and articles – those who refused to look, who refused to see the misery just minutes from their doorsteps.

Though she understood the direct relationship between brutality and environment and was actively supportive of the reform movements that challenged the notion that pauperism was simply an ugly reality – an unfortunate matter of fate – she soon became frustrated with those well-meaning but ineffective middle-class reformists who spoke fine words but saw poverty only in the abstract. Instead she found herself attracted to those she came to call the real heroes of the age – those dedicated slum workers (often young women) who gave their lives to the distressed, diseased and disabled festering in the dankest hovels of London's cancerous underclass.

Harkness's fascination with the recently formed Salvation Army led her to explore an amalgamation of Christianity and socialism. One can best see this in the pages of her work, *In Darkest London*, originally titled 'Captain Lobe: A Story of the Salvation Army' and written under her pen name of 'John Law'. Though clearly in awe of these selfless soldiers in the 'Army of the Lord', she portrays them as somewhat naïve in worldly affairs and questions their understanding of structural issues which might not pose a problem to the salvation of the soul but were necessary to the maintenance of the flesh and dignity of the earthly spirit.

Her hero, Captain Lobe, is an earnest young man who has come to religion through his childhood terror of hellfire and brimstone, flitting uncomfortably from church to church until finding a place for himself in Booth's Evangelistic militia, more from lack of alternative than true devotion to this drum-beating organisation of wide-eyed Salvationists. His friends, curiously, are mainly socialists and agnostics – the slum doctor who sees no hope but revolution and a mysterious woman, a wealthy, self-proclaimed unbeliever, who works with the Army's 'slum-lassies' because they, at least, are doing something to ease the burden of those wretched souls trapped in their hellish ghettos. (Lobe, himself, is thankful he's a man of faith rather than intellect as the burden of the mind, he feels, would be too much for him if he were always forced to analyse the wretchedness of others.)

In Darkest London is best read as a social documentary and a text in the history of ideas. Harkness is at her finest doing reportage inspired by a passionate desire to transmit the absolute squalor of poverty, the degradation of lives caused by the madness of Empire and unfettered Victorian capitalism. Of factory sweat-shops where girls waste their youth in dire servitude, of the horrendous workhouses with their prison-like regimentation, of the dark trade in children, the brutality of women, the nightly horrors of the East End slums – all these she has painted with a skilful brush. Even the likes of Frederich Engels was captivated by her past efforts enough to agree with her German translator that she had created a 'little work of art.'

There is one character in *In Darkest London* who truly stands out – that of Jane Hardy, the Labour Mistress. She is a complex and fascinating invention – a woman from the slums who has worked her way up to manage a candy factory sweated by young girls she looks after with the toughness of a no-nonsense mother; who hangs out at lending libraries lustful to read and goes to socialist meetings on Sundays instead of church; who is willing to emigrate to America or Australia as long as she is convinced they have a good position on the 'Women's Question;' who hates the idea of foreigners taking work away from her 'girls;' and who thinks that the best thing a slum mother could do to her offspring would be to apply 'a leetle pressure of the finger and thumb on the windpipe when they're just born' to save them from a life of unrelenting wretchedness. Jane Hardy hates Pember, the factory manager, and would murder him if given half a chance (she calls him 'the Capitalist!' – the worst expletive she can think of) but, at the same time, he remains the only man she ever loved. The only other man she half respects is Captain Lobe and she justifies that by thinking Lobe must really be a woman. Jane Hardy is not a standard 19th century literary figure, but she is a real 19th century working-class woman with all the anger, irony, sexual confusion, intellectual bewilderment, latent radicalism and misplaced chauvinism which was not at all uncommon as that century was coming to an end.

Harkness, like Jane Hardy, was a woman of deep emotions and intense contradictions. She, herself, was a unique creation – a writer, a social reformer, a spiritualist who was excluded from the pantheon of English literature for reasons that have more to do with power and prejudice than the value of her work. She deserves to be re-discovered and re-read. And so it is with pleasure that we begin our series of forgotten Victorian writers with *In Darkest London* by Margaret Harkness.

R. A. Biderman
Series Editor
Cambridge 2003

CHAPTER I

Captain Lobe

One Saturday night, just two years ago, a little man, with closely cropped hair and slight, neat figure, might have been seen walking quickly along the Whitechapel Road towards the London Hospital. His hands were in the pockets of a short jacket; and on his collar shone S, which proclaimed him to be a member of the Salvation Army.

When he reached the hospital gates the clock struck eight.

He nodded to the porter, and ran up the steps into the hall. Half a dozen women and men stood there by an open door. He looked at them for a minute, then went upstairs to a ward.

"Sister is in her room," a nurse said to him.

"I do not want sister," he answered, gravely; "I have come to see a patient."

He walked straight to the fireplace, beside which two girls were sitting. He laid his hand on the shoulder of the youngest, and asked:

"Patty, what brings *you* here?"

The girl was silent.

"Patty," he continued, "do you remember the night I took you to Mrs. Booth's home? Do you remember all you said then, all your promises?"

"I runned away," the girl said, sullenly.

"I have come to take you back again," said the little captain.

He shifted his position and stood facing the girl, with his back to the fireplace.

She looked a child in the distance, but on coming close one could see deep lines cut by Time in her forehead, and marks about her mouth that said before many more years had passed by she would be twenty.

"You are Sally," the captain continued, turning to her companion. "I know all about you. You nursed Patty last year through that bad illness. You went to your burial club and told them if they'd bury Patty instead of you, you'd begin paying again from the beginning."

"I wanted 'er to be buried like a lady," the girl said, apologetically. Then, seeing the captain's eyes fixed on her face, she blushed, and added, in tones full of defiance:

"I can't bide without Patty. Patty and me 've been together ever since mother died, and father turned me out on the streets. I can't bide without Patty. It's no good for you to take 'er to that Booth 'ome. It's so dull there; and if you make 'er go she'll run back to me. Won't you, Patty?"

As the words "Won't you, Patty?" left the speaker's lips, a titter ran through the ward.

The captain's attention had been entirely occupied by the two girls, so he had not noticed that he was a general object of interest. Now he found fifty eyes fastened on him, fifty ears listening to him with the keenest interest. This was not all. The door of the sisters' room stood half open, and leaning against the wall there were three or four young doctors.

"Do you remember, Patty, the night you came into barracks?" asked Captain Lobe, bending down, and speaking in an earnest voice. "You're ill, lass. Maybe you're dying. Come back with me, Patty."

Tears ran slowly down Patty's cheeks.

"I can't leave Sally," she said; "leastways, not till I'm well again."

"Good-night, lassies," said the captain.

He left the hospital, and went back to the Whitechapel Road.

That road is the most cosmopolitan place in London; and on a Saturday night its interest reaches a climax. There one sees all nationalities. A grinning Hottentot elbows his way through a crowd of long-eyed Jewesses. An Algerian merchant walks arm-in-arm with a native of Calcutta. A little Italian plays pitch-and-toss with a small Russian. A Polish Jew enjoys sauer-kraut with a German Gentile. And among the foreigners lounges the East End loafer, monarch of all he surveys, lord of the premises. It is amusing to see his British air of superiority. His hands are deep down in the pockets of his fustian trousers, round his neck is a bit of coloured rag or flannel, on his head is a tattered cap. He is looked upon as scum by his own nation, but he feels himself to be an Englishman, and able to kick the foreigner back to "his own dear native land" if only Government would believe in "England for the English," and give all foreigners "notice."

The loafer's mind is unknown as yet to psychologists. He has a mind, nevertheless, although he does his best to destroy it by narcotics and stimulants. Any one who cares to study it need not visit Whitechapel, but can find it in all parts of London. It is the mind of the parasite, the creature who is content to exist on other people. There are many such creatures among us. We used to put them into the army, but competitive examinations have made that impossible; so now we send them to land agents, give them family livings, or let them emigrate. Almost every family has a loafer somewhere – a cousin or son who is "good-for-nothing." In the West End they haunt the clubs; in the East End they hang around the public-houses. They are kept by their families, and almost always have some fond female relation upon whom they sponge, until death puts an end to their sponging.

Captain Lobe looked at more than one loafer as he hurried along the Whitechapel Road that evening; and of all the people he met, these men struck him as the most hopeless. He knew them well, for only too often they came into his barracks, bent on mischief. Then, if he could not find a policeman, he turned them out with the help of his lieutenant. They were worse than the roughs, more difficult to deal with, more hopeless. Only one had come once to the penitent-bench, and that one had given a false address.

The captain received many salutations as he passed between the booths and the public-houses. The flaring gas-lights showed him to vendors, and they stopped their "Buy, buy, buy" to wish him good-evening. An old woman who was selling pigs' feet pulled him by the jacket, and offered him a "pennorth" for nothing. Her head was wrapped in a shawl, and her wrinkled face was scarcely visible; but he recognized her, for he had picked her up dead drunk a few nights before, and had taken her to the place she called "home," a cellar which she shared with three old hags like herself.

At last he reached a penny gaff, outside the doors of which stood men brandishing swords, inviting people to see a skeleton arm, "a sight every mother ought to witness." A crowd of children flocked round the entrance, girls and boys without pennies, who were craning their necks to catch a glimpse of the skeleton arm, and watching the shining swords with breathless interest.

Captain Lobe passed the doorkeepers, and went into the large, low room used for penny entertainments. It was ornamented with pictures of fat girls, giants, acrobats, and other such things which uneducated minds delight in. Nutshells and bits of broken pipes covered the earthen floor, and on them stamped men, women, and children, while they pushed forward to see a half-naked youth, whose arm was withered from the shoulder to the wrist, but who could nevertheless use it for deeds of prowess, such as throwing knives and lifting hundred-weights.

At the farther end of the room hung a long red curtain. The captain raised it, stepped over a low stage, and opened a door that led into a small cupboard. There, lying on some old properties, was a dwarf. He held out his hand to Captain Lobe, and said:

"I'm glad to see you. It'll be time for me to get ready directly. I feel so ill this evening."

"Has the doctor been?" asked the captain.

"Yes."

"What did he say?"

"As he wasn't accustomed to midgets."

There was no chair in the cupboard, only a wooden stool, on which stood a candlestick. The dwarf's head rested on a bundle of properties, his small legs were stretched on an old sheep-skin. He told the captain to put the light on the floor, and then to sit down beside him. He added:

"I've something to ask of you, captain!"

"What is it, Midget?"

"Do you think I've got a soul, or do you think as there's no soul in midgets?"

He was about thirty-five, and his head was of normal size, rather too large if anything. His face was very pale. His dark eyes were full of mournfulness. He raised his hands to his thick black moustache – the hands of a child, with small fingers and wrists. His body and legs were only fit for a boy of six. He knew all this, so he asked:

"Do you think I've got a soul, or do you think as there's no soul in midgets?"

"To say you haven't a soul would be to go against the Almighty, seeing He's made you, and me, and everybody," said the captain.

"I ain't a man," answered the midget, sorrowfully. "I ain't nobody. Sometimes I says to myself as I'm 'the missing link,' as I'll come back again as a dog or something. Not but that I'd rather be a dog than a midget," he added, with bitterness. "I'm worse off than a dog now, for folks aren't afraid of dogs, but they won't come nigh me if they can help it. When I go out the boys pelt me with mud and sticks; and the women point at me and say, 'My, ain't he funny!' I've spent my life travelling about to be looked at. I'm tired of it, captain. I don't want to come back again. The world may be a good enough place for properly made folks, but it's just hell for midgets."

Captain Lobe took the dwarf's small hand in his, and sat silent.

"*You've* been good to me," said the midget. "It was a lucky day for me when I turned into your place. I like your face, captain. There's only one other face I'd care to see when I'm dying, that's a lady what came into gaff one night. When the manager told me to shake hands with the folks, she came straight up to me and held out her hand. She did, captain. The other folks was slinking away as they does always, but she held out her hand, and when I looked up at her I could see her eyes wet. She said nothing but I could tell she was sorry for me, and often as I lies awake I think of her!"

"I believe I know who you mean," said Captain Lobe, thoughtfully. "Was she tall, and dressed in black? Had she dark eyes, Midget?"

"I don't remember what colour her eyes was," said the dwarf. "I only know she had tears in 'em, captain."

Just then the cupboard door was opened, and the youth with a skeleton arm appeared, balancing a long spear on his chin. He was dressed á la Buffalo Bill, a costume greatly admired by East End young ladies.

"Look sharp, Midget," he said. "You're wanted."

When he had gone away the dwarf rose up slowly. He asked Captain Lobe to give him a small red coat and a black cocked hat, both of which were hanging on a nail near the old properties. After these had been adjusted, he buckled a small sword to his waist.

"Now I'm Napoleon," he said, raising his white face to a triangle of looking-glass. "I'm Napoleon, the midget."

The captain followed him out of the cupboard, and left him standing on the platform waiting for the red curtain to be lifted, ready to say:

"Ladies and gentlemen, I wish you good-evening."

About three hundred people were prepared to receive him, and among them walked "the sight that every mother ought to witness." He was evidently considered a masher by the female portion of his audience, and his skeleton arm made him all the more interesting. A little girl turned the handle of an organ close to the entrance, producing, as she did this, deafening music. Every now and then the men came in brandishing their swords; afterwards they walked back to attract fresh members for their audience. Mothers carrying market-baskets, old men, youths, girls, and children, all stood ready to greet the midget; and as Captain Lobe left the place, he heard a woman say:

"How could God Almighty make anything so ugly!"

It was a beautiful night, and on reaching the open air Captain Lobe looked up at the stars with a feeling of relief; they seemed so far away, so still, so restful. The words, "Shock–ing mur–der in White–chapel!" brought his thoughts back to the East End again.

It was the old story – a woman murdered by her drunken lover.

"Shock–ing mur–der in White–chapel!" echoed down the streets, and people flocked out to see who had been done to death, and who had done it.

The only things in which East End people take much interest are murders and funerals. Their lives are so dull, nothing else sets their sluggish blood in motion. But a murder gives them certainly two sensations; and a funeral has always some sensational features. Was the person poisoned, or was his throat cut? Did the corpse turn black, or did it keep until the nails were put into the coffin?

The thing that strikes one most about East End life is its soddenness; one is inclined to think that hunger and drink will in time produce a race of sensationless idiots.

Captain Lobe stopped to buy some hot roasted potatoes from a man with a weather-beaten, rugged face, who had been a sailor once, but who now picked up a living as a hawker in the streets.

"Do you want 'em peppered and salted?" the man asked, selecting some of the finest potatoes, "or will you have 'em in their dishabils, captain?"

"As they are, thank you," answered Captain Lobe.

He was putting the potatoes into his pocket, when the door of a public-house opened close behind him, and a bevy of girls and men came out, singing the chorus of a favourite East End song.

As they passed by, one of the men jerked the captain's hand up, and the potatoes fell into the gutter.

"Give it 'im, captain," a girl said. "'E's 'ad so much gin 'e can't see straight before 'im. At 'im, captain."

"Move on," said a policeman. "None of your nonsense; move on."

Captain Lobe bought some more potatoes, and then continued his way home. He reached the barracks, and went upstairs to the long, low room set apart for the Army's servants. The fire was out, and the room was dark. He did not wait for warmth or light; he sat down at once on an old horsehair sofa to eat his potatoes. He was hungry and tired, no uncommon thing with a Salvation Army captain. When the potatoes were finished, and the skins had been thrown under the grate, he lay flat on the sofa, thinking.

To live on a pound a week is difficult; but to give half away, and live on ten shillings, is a problem that would have baffled Euclid. Light suppers are ordered by Army regulations; and a lighter meal cannot well be conceived than one large potato, and two small potatoes in their "dishabils," neither peppered nor salted. Such meagre fare is apt to affect the spirits: and lying there on the sofa, the captain felt both mentally and physically exhausted.

He was slightly made, and delicate. The life he led took the strength out of him; for he felt every word that he said, and the sympathy which he showed to his fellow-men was a fire fed by self-sacrifice. He was no milk-and-water religionist, this little captain. He did not preach about hell, and then go home to enjoy a good meal of roast beef and plum-pudding. If he consigned a sinner to the burning pit, he gave the sinner half of his own dinner to eat on the journey, and recognized the fact that a man's soul has an intimate relationship with a man's stomach. He hated sin in the abstract; but he loved sinners, and most of all he loved his Whitechapel people. Even the loafers were dear to him. And the roughs were good lads, he said, lacking opportunities.

Presently he jumped off the sofa, and walked up and down the room with his arms folded. He was thinking of the girls he had seen in the London Hospital, wondering how he could persuade Patty to return home again. He could not conceive why the girl preferred a cheap, dirty lodging to Mrs. Booth's charitable institution, nor what her friend meant by "dullness". Girls like Patty were a puzzle to the captain. They seemed soft as wax in barracks; hard as brass out in the streets. No impression made on them lasted more than a few weeks. They gave promises with the greatest ease, and broke vows without any reluctance.

Walking up and down the long, low room he thought of a face, one as different from Patty's as light is from darkness. It was the face of a girl who sometimes came to his meetings with an old woman, her nurse. Her name was Ruth; and she lived not very far from the barracks.

CHAPTER II

Ruth

The next morning Captain Lobe went to headquarters directly after breakfast.

He had made his own bed before he started, swept out his rooms, and cleared away his breakfast. Tea, bread and butter, with an egg, were his morning rations. These never varied. When the egg-shell had been pitched under the grate, the tablecloth had been shaken out of the window, the cup and saucer had been put away in a cupboard, he was ready to begin the day.

He generally read the *War Cry* while eating his egg, or one of the few books that helped to form his meagre library.

People who *really* believe in hell do not indulge in the morning paper, or join a circulating library; they would imagine it un-Christlike to leave sinners to perish while they themselves enjoyed clubs, concerts, dinner-parties, crushes, and other entertainments. Moreover, a Salvation poke bonnet takes away from Satan his most subtle temptations for the female sex – shopping, and the looking-glass. A Salvation blood-red vest reminds men of other things than pipes and tennis.

Captain Lobe ran down the winding staircase, and out into the street. He passed by the butchers' shops nearly opposite Aldgate Station, and saw a herd of frightened sheep being driven over the sawdust into the slaughter-house. Their bleating was piteous! At their feet ran a dog, barking. Men in blue coats drove them along with sticks, callous of their terror and distress. Many people in the East End enjoy these sights. Some will climb up walls to see a bullock stunned with a spike, or a calf's throat cut. There is in every one of us a deeply seated love of cruelty for its own sake, although the refined only show it by stinging words and cutting remarks. So let no one think the scum worse than the rest. The scum is brutal, the refined is vicious.

Captain Lobe spat on the pavement and walked across the road. The smell of the meat made him feel sick after his light breakfast. Then he thought about the midget, and determined to visit the gaff that evening, after service.

Monstrosities were a trial to his faith.

"To turn away from them with disgust, just as one does from a butcher's shop, is to set oneself up above God Almighty," he said to himself. " Yet when I see creatures with two heads, or four legs, I feel all of a creep. I wonder if they're men or beasts! Now the midget's a man right enough, and yet *he* feels himself to be a missing link or something. I'll ask the general about it. The Army's got many queer soldiers, but none queerer than Napoleon the midget."

Soon he reached Victoria Street, and pushed through the doors.

"Here's a note for you," said the little girl behind the bookstall.

He broke the envelope and read:

"DEAR BROTHER, – I want to see you upstairs.

"Yours, in the service of the King,

"JAMES WARNER."

The writer was an older man than himself, one of the Army's best servants. This man had formerly been an employer of labour, a small capitalist. He had given up business because he felt (so he expressed it) "that somehow or other the devil was in it." Now he lived on £1 a week, and worked sixteen hours a day for the Army. He and Captain Lobe had fraternised from the day they met; and since then they had spent much time together; they had become very intimate.

Captain Lobe went upstairs to a narrow room that had six desks in it. By each desk sat a man in uniform, busy writing. The ex-manufacturer rose at Captain Lobe's entrance. He looked about forty-five, and his gaunt face had many lines upon it. His blue eyes smiled a welcome as he grasped the little captain's hand, but he proceeded at once to business.

"I took a woman to a doss-house not far from your place last night. Here's her name and address. She came to the penitent-bench, and we could not send her away without a penny."

"What is she?"

"A confirmed drunkard, I think."

"How old?"

"Fifty."

"I'll send one of the slum sisters to her. Those lassies know the way to deal with such women. We'd one of their 'saved' at our place last Sunday night, one of the worst drunkards in Whitechapel. A slum sister saved her."

"Praise the Lord!" said the ex-manufacturer.

"Praise the Lord!" said the men at the six desks, without looking up from their work.

Captain Lobe then went downstairs again.

He had come to headquarters for a special purpose. One of the inferior officers, a young man who was very fond of smoking, had determined to make a sacrifice. Captain Lobe had persuaded him to give up his pipe, because he spent more money on tobacco than anything else. The pipe was that day to be handed over to the Army, and placed among their trophies, with their flags and banners, in a place where every one could see it.

The assembly-room was full of people by the time Captain Lobe arrived in it. Men in red vests, women in poke bonnets, had formed a ring. They held banners and flags, and sang a hymn, while the young man produced his pipe. It was easy to see that he did not think the ceremony at all amusing. He seemed to realize what it meant to part with his special favourite, the symbol of pipes he had already sacrificed. He looked at it with great affection for a minute, then gave a sigh, and placed it in the hand of an old man whose duty it is to receive such trophies.

"If there is any one here who can smoke this pipe to the honour and glory of God, let him say so," said the old man, "and he shall have it."

"No, no!" cried the men and women.

"Then we will put it among the other things which have been given up by the Army's servants."

The men and women waved their flags, and cried, "Praise the Lord!"

in a frantic way, that would have been comic had they not looked so much in earnest. Then the pipe was placed on the wall among a strange collection of symbolic things, such as novels, ribbons, tankards, and photographs.

Captain Lobe left headquarters directly this ceremony was finished, and returned to the East End. His first work was to find a slum saviour, who lived with another girl on a block, whose business it was to visit in slums and alleys. But she was not at home, and her companion had taken a burnt child to the London Hospital. So he determined to seek the doss-house himself, and set out on his journey through some of the worst streets in the metropolis.

In order to reach the doss-house he was obliged to pass through the square in which lived the girl he had been thinking about the previous evening, after his visit to the girls in the London Hospital.

This square was quiet enough, except at mid-night. Then the public-houses that flanked its entrance vomited forth their cargoes of depravity and vice, and the air rang with the oaths of women who sell their babies for two shillings or eighteen pence, and with the curses of men lower than the beasts but for the gift of speech.

About those public-houses congregated the lowest dregs of the East End populace. Men from Shadwell and St. George's-in-the-East, women from Ratcliff Highway and the Dock back-streets, assembled there to rob the sailor. Directly a jolly Jack-tar came swinging past (the worse for drink), a vampire dressed in a gaudy skirt, with a string of blue beads about her neck, with a fringe of greasy hair on her forehead, had him by the elbow. Then a siren in a velvet jacket put her arm round his neck, and led him into the gin-pit, out of which he did not return, depend upon it, until he had been robbed of his very last sixpence.

That was bad enough!

But the Jack-tar was at least a full-grown individual, able to take care of himself. It was ten thousand times worse to see a drunken woman beating her baby because it *would* cry while she emptied pewter pot after pewter pot, hitting it on the back because it was sick to death, half-poisoned by spirits.

Such things do not allow themselves to be thought about.

The square was quiet, during the daytime, and the inhabitants had become so habituated to ghoulish cries and hideous noises as the clock struck half-past twelve, that no man, woman, or child woke up with a start when the law said, "Now it is time to close public-houses."

We grow accustomed to cawing rooks, ticking clocks, snoring relations, to everything that occurs over and over again, to every one who does the same thing without varying. "As it was in the beginning, is now, and ever shall be," we repeat like parrots. And we add "Amen" half snoring.

Legend says that years gone by the square was inhabited by "real gentry." "Middling folks" live in it at present – people who own small factories or large shops, who are in trades or business. These "middling folks" talk of the "lower classes," and it is difficult to say whereabouts in the social scale "middling folks" come exactly. Certainly the upper ten have nothing to do with them; although, if all the people who think themselves eligible to count as upper ten had their names entered in a book, not ten thousand, but ten million ladies and gentlemen would rank among the *élite* of society. It suffices to say that "middling folks" bestow old clothes and soup on "the poorer classes," just as "the real, gentry" visit "the deserving poor" when down in the country, and give donations to charities during the season in London.

In a house on the right-hand side of the square, in a room close to the roof, lived the girl Captain Lobe had contrasted so favourably with the girls in the London Hospital, the girl he had been thinking about while he walked up and down his small room above the Whitechapel Barracks the previous night.

She was the owner of a small cocoa-nut chip factory.

Her mother had (so Salvation Army people express it) "been taken away" when she was a baby.

Her father had died of small-pox in 1874, when she was only five years old, and no higher than the sitting-room table.

His will had made his foreman sole trustee of his property, on condition that the said foreman took charge of his little girl, and went to live with her, and her old nurse, in his house. If the foreman accepted these conditions, he was to draw a fixed salary from Weldon & Co.'s business, until Ruth reached the age of eighteen. Then she was to take possession of everything. Fifty pounds a year was bequeathed to the nurse, who was, however, to forfeit the money if she left her charge before 1886. But it was not likely that she would do this, for she had promised Ruth's dying mother that she would never leave "the little girl" among strangers. A stated sum was to be spent on Ruth's education and on household expenses; the rest of the money derived from Weldon & Co.'s cocoa-nut chip factory was to be invested in Ruth's interest. Everything was left to the care of the foreman, a man who had only been engaged to help in the factory when the junior partner went away in a hurry. (*Why* he had gone away people did not know exactly.) The foreman was named Pember, and was, no doubt, an excellent man of business.

It was a strange will, but no one could interfere after it had been read by the lawyer. The various uncles and aunts were obliged to acquiesce. They shook their heads, and called it "a bad business!"

The foreman gave notice at his lodgings, and went to live in Mr. Weldon's house with the little girl and the nurse. He was then about thirty-eight, and not married. He took possession of Mr. Weldon's office at the factory. He sat in Mr. Weldon's chair, and was called master.

This happened in 1874, and in 1886 he was considered by every one to be the owner of the business.

The East End is full of such small places in which "hands" number about thirty or thirty-five, all counted. In Weldon's factory three things were produced for the public: cocoa-nut chip (which was the chief business), sugar mice dipped in chocolate, and farthing surprise packets.

Ruth was the real owner of this place, but the manager made it appear as if the property belonged to himself, although in less than a year she would be entitled to turn him away, or to keep him on with a salary.

Captain Lobe did not like this man. He was inclined to think Ruth's guardian a hypocrite.

CHAPTER III

Ruth's History

He left the square and went down the Thieves' Alley. The place was quiet. Two little boys played tip-cat outside the door of a public house; and mangy dogs walked up and down, acting as scavengers.

"Nuts for Salvation crackers," cried a man who was standing at the foot of the alley, selling fruit to the public.

Captain Lobe took no notice. He walked quickly on, for he could see a few yards ahead someone carrying a basket. He recognized the neat print dress and the black bonnet. They belonged to Hester, the old woman who so often came with Ruth into barracks.

"Oh, captain!" she exclaimed, when he joined her, "you're the very person I want to see. I was coming to see you this evening."

"Well," inquired Captain Lobe, "what is it?"

"Ruth's made up her mind to become a slum saviour."

Captain Lobe drew in his breath, and said nothing.

"Why, you can't have nothing against it!"

The speaker had white hair that lay smoothly on her forehead. Soft grey eyes, and a broad mouth with thin pale lips, told their own story, for Nature had written on them, in unmistakable hieroglyphics, self-sacrifice. It was easy to see that the old woman lived so much for other people, and so little for herself, that she was scarcely conscious of her own existence.

"You can't have nothing against it," she repeated. "It's made me so happy, captain!"

Even Salvationists have prejudices. Captain Lobe conjured up a vision of Ruth working among the scum of London, with no other protection than an S on her collar, and a poke bonnet. Drunken men are not safe company for young women who go about at all hours of the day and night in the very lowest East End districts. Captain Lobe thought of this, and it made him hesitate. Yet he had given other girls who had become slum saviours every encouragement; he had not shrunk from seeing them put on the Salvation apron. Why did he say to himself that Ruth was too young for slum work, too delicate?

"I thought you'd be pleased to hear it, captain," continued the old woman, who looked disappointed. "When the little girl told me what she'd a mind to do, a weight just seemed to fall off me. I've often worried about whatever would become of her if I were to die; and I'd be quite happy if only I could see her safe in the Army."

"Has she no relations?" inquired Captain Lobe.

The old woman shook her head, and said:

"None as I'd like to see her take up with. If anything happened to me – and I'm getting an old woman, captain – she'd be left alone with Mr. Pember. I'm afraid of him, I am. He's got his foot in that factory, and sooner than give it up he'll do the little girl any mischief."

"Why did her father make a man like that sole trustee of his property?" asked Captain Lobe.

"Her father was one of those men who are always being taken in, and who know no forgiving," said the old woman, sorrowfully. "It's not for me to talk against the dead, but I'll tell you Ruth's history. You'll understand then why I want to see her safe in the Army. I took her from her dying mother, and I said as I wouldn't leave her among strangers. I've been with her all these years, and I've never known her do, or say, a thing she couldn't tell you, or anybody. She's that good and innocent it's difficult to see how she ever could go wrong exactly."

The old woman stopped for a minute, and a look of pain came across her face. Then she said: "You'd have thought the same thing of her mother. But her mother forgot herself. It came all of a sudden upon us. I was sitting in the kitchen one evening, waiting for 'em to come in, when I heard master open the front door with his key, and slam it as if he was angry. Then I heard words between 'em in the parlour, he talking loud and fast, and she saying a word sometimes, low-like. Presently master came to the top of the kitchen stairs, and called out, 'Hester.' I went to 'em all of a tremble, and I found 'em both standing in front of the fireplace. 'Hester,' says he, 'she was going to run away, and leave me and the baby.' 'Sir,' says I, 'there's some mistake.' She came to me then and put her arms round my neck, and I took her up to bed. She said nothing. She'd a strange look on her face, a look I've only seen in mad folks. She let me undress her like a thing past feeling. When I thought she was asleep I went downstairs to master. 'Sir,' says I, 'there's some mistake. She couldn't have so forgot herself.' But he shook his head, and told me to lock the front door, as he was going out, and wouldn't be in till morning. I went back to her, and I found her out of bed, standing by the baby's crib, in nothing but her nightdress. She looked at me like a mad thing, captain. I went down on my knees to pray; and while I was praying, God Almighty woke up the baby. I'd never have thought of doing that myself, but when the little girl began to cry, her mother took her out of the crib. She sat down with the little girl on her knee, and I covered 'em both up with a blanket. Then I got her into bed, and we lay there all night – she, me, and the baby. She didn't sleep, but she was still, and we both heard the hours striking. The little girl slept with her head close to her mother's neck, and her feet wrapt up in the blanket. Master came in for breakfast, and then he went to business, without speaking to me, or seeing her and the baby. It's my belief they never mentioned it again, unless, perhaps, he told her that the foreman had gone away and Mr. Pember was at the factory. It's a wonder we didn't guess what was going on! But we never so much as thought of it. That foreman stood in the dock not long after he carried on unbeknown to us. He was a bad man, captain. I know he'd *his* history; but because a man's unhappy himself, he's no right to spoil other folks' happiness."

The old woman stopped for a minute; then she said: "She sickened after that. There wasn't much the matter to speak of, but she couldn't sleep, and she couldn't eat, and nothing seemed to make her different. She went quietly about the place, looking after master and the baby, mending their clothes and minding their comforts. But she got worse every day. If master had forgiven her it might perhaps have been different. I've seen her look at him as much as to say, 'He'll *never* forgive me!' Then she'd go away to brush his hat, or fetch him something, just to show how sorry she was. But master took no notice. If he did see, he pretended to have his eyes somewhere else. So it went on for a year and a half. Then God Almighty took her from us. She gave me the little girl just before she died, and she said, 'Take care of her, Hester, and don't let her be ashamed of me. I'm sorry.' I said, 'Yes,' and I've kept my promise. The little girl thinks her dead mother perfect. So she is in the place she's gone to, depend upon it."

Tears rolled down the old woman's face, and fell on the market-basket.

"Didn't her husband forgive her at the end?" asked the captain.

The old woman shook her head. "He was never the same man from that evening. Folks used to say as he looked unhappy. He'd cause for it. He was one of those men who know no forgiving. He got that man Pember in the foreman's place, and left him to mind his business. I don't like Mr. Pember. He's no better than the man who carried on with Ruth's mother unbeknown to us, and sooner than give up the factory he'll do the little girl any mischief. The master was a weak man to be taken in by Pember, and, like all weak men, he suffered a deal of pain, captain. I'm going in here," the old woman said, stopping by a baker's shop. "Think of what I've told you, and if Ruth says to you as she's made up her mind to become a slum saviour, remember how glad I'll be to see her safe in the Army."

Captain Lobe walked on to the doss-house, thinking as he went about Ruth's mother, and the weak man who had "known no forgiving." Why should not Ruth join the Army? Girls had "calls" to do that every day. He had heard of a girl quite lately who had been offered by her father one thousand pounds if she would not put on the uniform. He knew another who had just said good-bye to her family, who had gone to India, knowing that she would never see England again, that she must spend her whole life on foreign soil as one of the Army's servants. These slum saviours were of all classes. They lived on ten shillings a week, and worked day and night among the scum of London.

He ought to rejoice that yet another girl was willing to accept a life of such complete self-sacrifice. Yet, when he thought of Ruth, he hesitated.

She was not pretty, perhaps; but her clear white forehead looked like an ivory tablet, upon which Time had written no false word, no evil thought, nothing but love and truthfulness. Her grey eyes were fearless and honest. Her voice was soft and sweet, an excellent thing in women! And her golden hair seemed to set her face in a halo of holiness. The captain thought of all this; for the Army has its saints. It has also its martyrs, and its evangelists.

Just then he reached the doss-house, and went in to find the woman who had come to the penitent bench, the confirmed drunkard for whom he must try to do something. The common room was almost empty. A long deal table was in the centre, and above it hung two lamps. Forms stood against the walls, and a few wooden chairs were by the fireplace.

"The deputy's in bed," a woman told him, "and the deputy's wife is in the back yard hanging out blankets!"

"Maybe she's upstairs," the woman continued, when the captain explained whom he wanted. "You can go and look for yourself. Here's a light. Take care you don't knock your head against the ceiling, for the steps twist in and out. Turn to the left when you come to the top, and go straight on till you come round again."

Captain Lobe took from the speaker a flickering dip, wrapped round with a bit of paper, and went up the narrow, spiral staircase. The dormitories were full of beds, and each bed was covered by a grey blanket. The atmosphere was nauseous, for no window was open, and the dormitories led one into the other, without any door between, or any partition. Here was a ward for men, there was a ward for women. Sometimes a cupboard showed a bed by itself, and on the door of this was written, "A slip is 6d."

In one or two beds people were still asleep, but most of the beds were empty. So Captain Lobe went downstairs again, and into the yard where the deputy's wife was hanging clothes on a line to dry, making the most of the bit of ground attached to the doss-house.

"No," she said, "I know nothing about such a woman. Perhaps my husband saw her. He's on night duty. I only do day work. The police fetched away a woman early this morning, who'd stolen a pewter pot at a public-house. If that's the party you want, you'll find her at Lower Thames Street Police Court!"

The captain wished the deputy's wife "good morning." He knew that the woman he wanted would not come to the Army again unless she required another night's lodging. Confirmed drunkards were almost hopeless. If such people were ever reclaimed, their salvation was generally achieved by a slum saviour.

No work in the Army requires more devotion and enthusiasm than slum work. A slum saviour lives among the filth and the vermin that surround the scum of London. Her work is ignored by the public, who think her either a fanatic or a lunatic. Yet she goes about from morning to night nursing the sick, and feeding the hungry with her own scanty rations, until an early death crowns her efforts. To a life like this Ruth meant to dedicate herself!

No wonder that Captain Lobe said to himself, "She is too young, too delicate!"

CHAPTER IV

"I Wish to Dedicate Myself to the Army's Service."

The following Sunday morning the Salvation drum was heard coming down the Whitechapel Road at eleven o'clock. Behind it followed Captain Lobe and his lieutenant. Next to them walked two women dressed in black. The faces of these women were worth looking at. One was a widow, aged fifty, perhaps, who worked all day to support herself, who gave her evenings to the Army's service. The other was an elderly spinster, whose face had a look of chastened sorrow upon it, as much as to say, "I've had my history." Then came a number of girls in Army dress, youths in red vests, and a small crowd of converts.

When the procession reached the doors of the penny gaff, Captain Lobe called out, "Stop!" He went to a side entrance, and disappeared for a minute. The people stared when he came back, for with him was Napoleon, the midget, wearing a red coat and a cocked hat. The midget looked very ill. His face was pale, and his little limbs trembled. Captain Lobe and the lieutenant held him up, and so he went towards the barracks.

The Salvationists entered the hall singing:

> "When the roll is called in heaven,
>   And the host shall muster there,
> I will take my place among them,
>   And their joys and triumphs share.
>
> "Angels call the roll up yonder,
>   Muster roll in heaven proclaim;
> Call the roll, and at the summons
>   I will answer to my name."

The hall was almost empty. Only one hundred men and women sat on the benches reading the *War Cry*, waiting for the Salvationists. Yet that morning one of the most interesting men in the Army had come down to take part in the proceedings, a stockbroker who had given up money-making in order to save sinners from the burning pit. He *really* believed in it. He was a fair specimen of "properly-made folks." He had a handsome face, and a well-knit, muscular body. He could have lifted "the missing link" between, a finger and thumb, could have held Napoleon suspended in the air on one finger. The midget looked at him with a sickly smile, and turned away. It was hard to see this strong young man, and to feel a missing link, or something! The feathers of the cocked hat shook, and the breast of the red coat moved up and down as the stockbroker smiled from his superior height upon a monstrosity (to turn away from which he would have thought a sin, a "setting-up of himself" above "the God who made you, me, and everybody"), and helped Captain Lobe to place Napoleon on a form near the table.

A man's face on the body of a child *is* pathetic; how pathetic only those know who visit penny gaffs, who are intimate with the unfortunates that travel about to be looked at. Even in the Salvation hall people stared and laughed, because a dwarf had come there to sing and pray, because a midget had joined the Army! Napoleon hid his pale face in the cocked hat; so no one guessed that he was saying to himself, "This world's just hell for midgets."

Captain Lobe told the people to "gather in," and the small congregation drew nearer to the table, behind which stood, or sat, the men and women whose duty it was to sing and pray, also the stockbroker, who had come down to say *why* he had joined the Army.

General Booth thinks that nothing carries so much weight as the history of a man's conversion related by himself. Such histories are not calculated to make people conceited, at any rate. A man has to confess how very depraved he was before his conversion took place, and he must take no credit to himself for the garb of holiness which he is supposed to have put on with the Army uniform. The worse he makes out his state of sin to have been, the greater credit he gives to "the saving blood of Jesus." "The wages of sin," says the Salvationist, "is death." Satan is sin, and Satan binds the sinner fast. But sinners can escape from the snares of the devil by making a mental effort. Salvationists do not attempt to reason; they appeal to a man's heart, and think the intellect a little thing that requires wheedling. Consequently, few educated men and women join their ranks, and they cannot point to one scholar in their camp of any importance. But in slums and alleys their work is a real force, for the inhabitants of these places recognize their sincerity of purpose, and do not approach them in a critical spirit. Such people feel sin, and fear to sink into the burning pit by reason of it; such people are not educated enough to find hell in an uneasy conscience.

"To get saved" is a phrase that forever haunts the lips of Salvationists. How this process takes place they cannot tell us. They merely point to its results. The conversion of the captain who led the Buddhist Salvation Army in India, a rival force with a drum, and a procession of white elephants, is one of their latest achievements. It has encouraged them to think that the Church Army will before long surrender to General Booth, will one day adopt the Salvation red vest, and the poke bonnet.

Another hymn was sung, with the help of a small harmonium. Then the ex-stockbroker stood up to say why he had joined the Army.

"This is a very memorable day for me," he said, looking at the little company of men and women. "This day, a year ago, I walked into a hall like this, and I went out of it saying to myself, 'I will join the Salvation Army.' I was then possessed of all that this world thinks necessary for happiness. I had health, money, friends, and a pretty wife. I was making money on the Stock Exchange at a rate I could not understand myself. The money-fever was upon me. I was almost delirious with success. Yet, even then, I thirsted after the waters of holiness. I seemed to see them far away, in a deep green valley, while I stool on a hill worshipping the golden calf. I hugged my wealth, but it did not give me happiness. In my delirium I cried out for something to quench my thirst. It was just then, one Sunday morning, I walked into a place like this, and found out what it is to be in earnest. All my life I had been regularly to church, but this had not satisfied me. On every side, among the members of our congregation, I had seen worldliness. The men and women who knelt beside me at the communion rails pursued money-making and amusements like myself; they had the same ambitions, and self was their principal object of interest. The clergyman spoke of doctrine, and said nothing about sacrifice. One Sunday morning I fell asleep in church while this clergyman was preaching. In my dream I seemed to see a luxuriously furnished room, in which this clergyman lay dying. His wife stood beside him, and his curate was administering to him the Sacrament. Above his bed hovered two spirits, an angel of light, and a demon of darkness. 'He is mine,' said the demon. ' The Lord rebuke thee,' said the other, raising his eyes from the dying man; 'he is a clergyman.' 'He is a hypocrite,' said the demon. 'His aim has been to please his congregation, and to do this he has avoided saying anything in his sermons, that might jar upon their feelings. His church has been crowded by ladies in satins and silks, by gentlemen wearing diamond rings, while hungry men and women have filled the streets, and one-fifth of the population of London has died in the hospital or the workhouse. He has made men and women sceptics by his want of earnestness. He is mine. He belongs to the father of hypocrites. It is too late for repentance.' 'Repent! Be quick! Humble yourself!' cried the angel of light to the man who was dying. 'Quick! Quick! It is written, "If any man love the world, the love of the Father is not in him." Don't you see how you loved the world? You could not vex those rich ladies by saying that three times as many children of the working class die, as of the upper classes. You could not offend those titled men by telling them that 35,000 London children go to school every day without breakfast. You had the mind of the world. Repent! Be quick!' The dying man stretched out his hand to the curate, and I heard him say, 'I do not think I was worldly. I never went to theatres and dances, only to harmless social gatherings. If I forgot the poor it was a mistake. I had collections for charities and missionaries. God will forgive me. God is –' At that moment the life left his body, and I saw him carried shrieking away by the evil spirit. 'What has he seen? Why is he shrieking?' I asked the angel of light. 'He has seen the souls which he sent to hell by his want of earnestness.' 'Follow him,' I cried. 'He is a clergyman. I have heard him talk of heaven as though he had seen it. The word "hell" has fallen glibly from his lips. He is our parish priest.' 'I dare not follow,' answered the angel of light,' God would spew him out of His mouth. He is a hypocrite.' I woke up just as the clergyman reached the end of his sermon. His voice had sent me to sleep. It was soft and pleasant. It fell like music on the ears of drowsy men and women. 'Now to God the Father, God the Son, and God the Holy Ghost, be all honour and glory,' he said. The rustling silks of the ladies made it impossible for me to hear the end of the sentence. Then I said to myself, 'I will search all over London until I find a place in which there is real earnestness. What good will my money do me when I am dying? I profess to believe the Gospel of Christ, yet I make no sacrifice.' After that I visited many chapels and churches. It did not occur to me that I should find what I wanted in the Salvation Army. I was prejudiced against it. I knew that Salvationists are always in a row, and I forgot that there are at least thirty rows recorded in the New Testament. I had seen a man with an S on his collar being led through a street with a halter round his neck; and I had thought it a rowdy sort of advertisement. I did not know then that we must make ourselves fools in order to win the foolish. I went from chapel to church, and church to chapel, and still I seemed to see those waters of holiness far away in the deep green valley. At last, one Sunday morning, this day twelve-month, when I was on my way to hear Mr. Nevile Sherbrooke at Portman Chapel, I was stopped a little way past Oxford Circus by a girl in a plain blue dress and a white apron. She was a slum saviour. I will not tell you her name, but you will guess who I mean when I say that she brought to the penitents'-bench Swearing Bill and Drunken Sally. She put a handbill into my hand, and invited me to come into a hall close by, a place that belongs to the Salvation Army. On this handbill I found a summary of the work which had been done by the 5,000 officers of the Salvation Army during the previous year. They had held 1,810,380 meetings, visited 2,717,880 homes, sold 12,740,000 *War Crys*, and made 148,905 converts. A good year's work! I followed the slum saviour into the hall, and sat down near the door. General Booth was preaching on the text, 'What have you done with your stewardship?' He spoke about avarice and covetousness, and every word he said seemed meant for me. The money-fever must have showed itself on my face, I think, and he must have noticed it. When he had finished speaking, I said to myself, 'These people shall be my people, and their

God shall be my God. They are in earnest.' But when I told General Booth this, he said, 'You must show us that you are in earnest.' 'What shall I do to satisfy you?' I asked. 'Go down to the Stock Exchange to-morrow in Army dress. *Then* we will believe that you are in earnest.' Six weeks later I joined the Salvation Army. My friends, from that day to this I have known nothing but happiness. I have given up my 'prospects' in life, and accepted 'a miserable pittance.' My wife has put on the uniform. We daily expect orders to go to India, and if they come we shall obey them, although we must leave our child behind us. In the Covenant of War we promised 'to accept any position, do any work, or fulfil any commission that may be given to us, in view of the wicked and wretched condition of the men and women around us, and the danger to which they are every hour exposed of being lost for ever in hell.' Before we go our child will be given up to the Army's service.

"Did I hear some one ask what it means to dedicate a child to God in public?

"It means that we are willing it should spend all its life in Salvation War, wherever God may choose to send it; that it shall be despised, hated, cursed, beaten, kicked, imprisoned, or killed for Christ's sake. It means that we desire it shall be kept away from intoxicating drink, finery, wealth, hurtful books, and worldly acquaintances. It means that we accept the wishes of our superior officers with regard to it. It means that we shall probably never see it again until we meet it in heaven. My brothers and sisters, it is easier to accept the War Covenant for oneself than to dedicate a child to the Army's service. Yet I would rather give up my child like this than see it exposed to the dangers which beset me before I joined the Army. I was brought up by Christian parents, I learnt the Catechism. I attended church. But until I joined the Army I did not know what it meant to be in earnest. That dream saved me. But for that dream I should have gone on with my moneymaking, athirst for holiness, perhaps, but unable to get cured of my money-fever. When I came into a place like this a year ago, I said to myself, 'If Jesus of Nazareth were on earth this morning. He would come here. He would walk straight in here and sit down among the publicans and sinners. Clergymen would not like to see the Son of a carpenter in their fashionable pulpits, for He might say things that ladies and gentlemen would not find pleasant. Jesus of Nazareth must come to a place like this, unless He put on broad-cloth, and said agreeable things in smooth sentences.' Oh, my brothers, my sisters, think of this, and you will be ashamed to live in a half-hearted way, to play at Christianity. Give up that sickly religion which avoids the Cross, and prates in kid gloves about sacrifice. Come to Christ this morning, you poor, tired men and women. Drink of the waters of holiness which now seem so far away in that deep green valley. Beside those still waters are paths of peace, and He whose voice is like many waters calls you to happiness."

The officers began to sing a hymn called "The Great Physician."

While they were singing, a girl with golden hair, and a face made beautiful by its expression of childlike confidence, walked up to the table, and said in a low voice:

"I wish to dedicate myself to the Army's service."

CHAPTER V

Slumdom

Half an hour later, Ruth was walking towards Seven Dials, between two slum saviours, girls a little older than herself, dressed in slum uniform.

The face of the eldest girl was very pale and thin. Large, prominent eyes shone like lamps of fire beneath her broad forehead. She seldom smiled, and she seldom spoke. She seemed to be looking at something she could see far away in the distance.

The other girl had a bright colour in her cheeks. *Her* tongue never stopped. She talked incessantly to Ruth, and related all sorts of things about herself and other people. One item of news she repeated twice, namely, that the day before she had ransacked Booksellers' Row in vain to find a Bible; and that the shopkeepers had laughed when they heard what she wanted.

Both girls wore short blue skirts, white aprons, black hats, and vests with "Salvation" embroidered in red letters on the breast.

No time is wasted by the Salvation Army's servants. They believe that each minute a soul passes to heaven, or to hell; that on their efforts depend the eternal happiness or the everlasting woe of men and women.

So directly after Ruth walked up to the table, and said, "I wish to dedicate myself to the Army's service," she was confided to the care of two slum saviours, in order that she might see their work, and judge of her own fitness for it. And as that morning the Whitechapel slum saviours did not happen to be in barracks, Captain Lobe handed her over to two girls who work in Seven Dials, saying, "These lassies work in the worst slum in London, so if you go with them you will see what it means to say, 'I wish to dedicate myself to the service of the Salvation Army.'"

The three girls walked through the City to Drury Lane, and then turned into a narrow street not far from Covent Garden Market. In the middle of this place was a large heap of refuse, a sort of general dust-bin, into which the people of the neighbourhood threw rags, cabbage-stalks, and other things which were not wanted. Half a dozen hens were trying to find their dinner there that Sunday morning, and a cock stood close by, flapping his wings while he pecked at a broken basket.

Women sat on most of the doorsteps, gossiping to neighbours, or watching the children that swarmed about the pavement. Occasionally a mother opened her mouth, and from her lips fell "the universal adjective," Sometimes a baby tumbled into the gutter, and was picked up by a child not much bigger than itself, who swore at it.

"Holloa, Salvation!" cried the women, when the slum saviours came amongst them. "Where have you been to this morning?"

"Bless your golden hair," said a big boy to Ruth. "If I want saving I'll come to you, miss."

So the girls passed on, amidst good-natured chaff, until they arrived at an open door, beside which stood a child whose eye was bound up with a dirty pocket-handkerchief.

"I was looking out for you, sister," the child said to the eldest slum saviour. "Mother's come to herself, and she's given me these flowers for you. Mother's right down ashamed of herself."

"Did mother hurt you much?" the child continued. "She was dead drunk, sister, or she wouldn't have done it."

The slum saviour turned up her sleeve and showed a large bruise above her wrist.

"Mother's right down ashamed of herself," the child repeated, apologetically. "It's only Saturday nights she gets like that. Deed it is, sister. She never lays on me with a poker lest she's been drinking. She was dead drunk last night. I can't see out of my right eye this morning from the way she banged me about afore you came up and stopped her. Sometimes I think she'll kill me or the baby when she's had too much.

Then she'll swing for it. There was a murder last night, leastways the man's dying – I mean the one that was knocked over nigh us. Did you hear him screaming, sister?"

The slum saviour took the flowers which the drunken woman had sent to her as a peace-offering; and then she unlocked a door just inside the entrance of the house.

"We heard screams overhead last night," she explained to Ruth, "so we went up to see what was happening. We found the child on the floor and her mother beating her with a poker. The woman turned on us directly we tried to interfere, and she gave me a blow on the wrist."

"Do they often treat you like that?" inquired Ruth, who felt a cold shudder running through her veins; for she had never come in close contact with slumdom, although she lived in its precincts.

"Some of the people are very rough," was the answer. "When we visit from house to house we get the worst treatment. We don't mind going to common lodging-houses and public-houses, for then we have only men to deal with; but the women pinch us, and throw things at our heads; they are more like demons than human beings. One ran after us yesterday with a kettle full of boiling water, and threatened to scald us. Another said she would fetch some pals to help her throw us out of the window. We go straight up to the top of each house we visit, and work down. If we began at the bottom and tried to work up we should never get beyond the first landing. It does not do to let the people see that we are afraid of them. If the women thought that they could frighten us we might as well give up the work at once. We pretend that we are not afraid of anything, yet we are trembling all the time from head to foot. It's human nature to be afraid of women like those we work amongst. The men are lambs compared to the women."

"They are a terrible lot about here," chimed in the other slum saviour. "An old woman came to us last night and asked if we would take her to the doctor. Her little grandchild led her in. Her husband had knocked her eye out. She is stone blind now; for he knocked out her right eye when she was fifty, and last night he knocked her left eye out of its socket. I know six women close by this house whose husbands have knocked their eyes out."

"The people about here are worse than those in the East End," the eldest slum saviour said to Ruth. "I have worked in Whitechapel, but I have never seen anything to equal what I see in these streets. And what makes it so terrible to me is the fact that, not a mile away, people are enjoying every luxury. This whole slum could be cleared away in a fortnight if people had a mind to do it. Depend upon it, on the Day of Judgment God will say to the rich men and women who lived near Drury Lane and Seven Dials: '*I* was hungry, and ye gave Me no meat: *I* was thirsty, and ye gave Me no drink: naked, and ye clothed *Me* not: in prison, and ye visited *Me* not.'"

"Animals could teach the people about here many a lesson," remarked the younger slum saviour. "But, then, how can one tell these people that they ought to keep clean when they are starving? We visited a woman yesterday who had just had a baby. She was lying on a sack, and had nothing to cover her up but an old blanket. The baby's face was like that of an old man, although it had only been born two weeks. Its arms and legs were like sticks. The rooms beat anything I have ever seen for filth; but the husband was out of work, and while the poor thing lay ill he pawned the washtub. I say, 'Praise the Lord,' when He takes away a baby from a place like that. It can grow up to nothing but sin, and live to see nothing but misery."

The slum saviours then set to work to prepare their dinner.

Their room was neat and clean. The walls were whitewashed. General Booth's picture, an almanack, and a few texts were its only ornaments. Above the fireplace were the rules for slum work, relating to hours of work, food, sleep, knee-drill, and Army meetings.

Directly after dinner they set out to visit the common lodging-houses of the district. They put shawls over their Salvation vests, and carried large bundles of *War Crys* to distribute. Everywhere people greeted them, Sometimes a woman begged them to visit a sick relation, or a man asked for a paper. Again and again they were stopped by women who had a tale of misery to relate, by children whose mothers wanted "to see sister for a minute."

At last they reached a thieves' kitchen, and went down a steep flight of steps to an underground place at the end of a long passage.

They walked in.

Half a dozen men sat there by a fire, doing nothing. If they had had any dinner, the remains of the feast had been cleared away. Not a plate nor a crust stood upon the table. Only a black cat licked its paws and purred as it looked at the slum saviours. (However hungry such men may be, they never let the pet of their establishment remain famished.)

They were a savage-looking set of men. No policeman ever entered alone into their kitchen. A clergyman found his way in one Sunday evening. He was stripped, in order that the men might see if he was a detective. Finding all his linen marked with the same name, and nothing in his pockets, they kicked him out, advising him never to come there again unless he was plentifully supplied with soup tickets.

There they sat, doing nothing, when the slum saviours opened the door. Bits of pipes, ginger-beer bottles, pots, and refuse lay upon the earthen floor. A lamp hung from the ceiling. They were glad to have a *War Cry* to break the monotony of their Sunday afternoon; and they greeted the slum saviours with a hearty:

"Well how *are* you?"

The eldest slum saviour walked straight up to an old man, who was sitting by the fire, and asked, Have you made a start yet?"

"Where to, my lass?"

"Heaven, daddy. The time. is short. You are getting an old man. It's time to make a start."

The thieves laughed; and daddy hid his face, in order that the girls might not see that he, too, was laughing. They sang a hymn, and the thieves joined in the chorus. Even daddy's cracked voice came in at the end among the rest.

"Let's have another," the men said.

So the girls kept singing until it was time to go away. Then they wished the thieves good-bye and "God bless you!"

The next kitchen they visited was the resort of those people who make up as deaf and dumb, lame, blind, and infirm objects of interest. Here fifty men were sitting on forms and by tables finishing their dinner. One man was eating cheese and red cabbage pickle off a cracked plate; another had cold bacon and bread in his fingers; a third was devouring a red herring-head, bones, tail, everything; a fourth was enjoying cold sausages.

When the slum saviours came in the men laughed and shouted. They declared that they did not care for sing-songing, and that they knew "a deal more" than the Salvation Army.

"Six foot under the clay, that's where I'm going to," one man said. "Don't talk to me about heaven. You haven't seen it, nor have I, nor has nobody. It's no good for you to come here with your hymns and papers; we know all you've got to say, and more, most likely."

In vain the slum saviours talked about "the saving blood of Jesus." One man declared that Christ was a clever fellow, who had known how to impose on people; another vowed that "any one could see through that Christ business;" a third said that he had travelled all over the world, and as he had found out that Buddha had more disciples than Christ he thought he would be a Buddhist; a fourth wanted to know how much the slum saviours made a week by their preaching; a fifth told them to "clear out," as they took away his appetite.

At last, in despair, they went away, after shaking hands with the man who acted as deputy.

So they visited lodging-house after lodging-house and in all they found the same sort of people – men who from some cause or other had fallen out of the ranks of that great army-civilization, who were sinking into the scum of London.

The men smoked, played cards, and gambled in low, dark rooms, into which not a breath of fresh air could enter. Shutters and pieces of brown paper covered the broken windows; so no one could see in, unless a child lay flat on the pavement, and craned its neck to peep through a hole at what was going on in a lodging-house kitchen. Directly a man came downstairs, he threw off his coat, and turned up his shirt sleeves; then he sat down with the rest, to smoke, play cards, and gamble for halfpence.

From kitchen to kitchen the slum saviours went, heedless of rebuffs. Once or twice they brought a man to his knees, one who was recovering from a fit of drinking. Some people seemed to think that the slum saviours could give them something. Some jeered at the Salvation Army, not a few stopped to argue about religion.

Materialists, pure and simple, were these men in the common lodging-houses.

But the slum saviours said, "They are given over to Satan."

"Are you saved, brother?" they asked a man with a white face and bloodless lips, whose clothes hung loosely on his emaciated body.

"If starving will save me, I ought to have been saved long before this," the man answered.

"You must give up your sins; then God will send you food," was the reply.

The man shook his head, and said, "The Bible calls God a father, and no father would starve his son for sinning. He would give him food first, and speak about his sin afterwards."

"God is merciful and just," said the slum saviour, whose eyes seemed fixed on something in the distance.

"Let Him send me work," the man said; "then I'll believe in Him."

"Every breath you draw is a gift from God. He has let you live so long. He might have cast you into hell years ago, brother. Give up your sin. Come to Him."

"It's hell to live in a place like this," the man answered, looking round the dark room, and at the faces of the lodgers. "Have you any money? Give me food first. I'll attend to salvation afterwards."

"Gold and silver have I none," was the girl's reply; "but what I have, that I give unto you."

"Then, my lass, you can carry your preaching somewhere else. Don't come here to talk of salvation to a man like me. I'm hungry."

CHAPTER VI

Slumdom (continued)

The girls returned home at five o'clock, and while they were having their tea the youngest girl related her history.

The elder girl listened, with a quiet smile on her face. *Her* history is a secret. It is ticketed "Slum Saviour No_," in Captain Cooke's desk. No one else knows anything about it.

"The people next door had a wake last night," the youngest girl said to Ruth. "I went in there to see what was the matter, for they were making such a noise that I thought some one was being murdered. I found the room full of Irish. They looked as if a wedding had taken place, not a death. The corpse was standing upright in its coffin, and round it the women were dancing and groaning, while a number of men sat by the fire drinking and smoking. I have never seen a more ghastly sight in my life, not even while I was a Roman Catholic."

"A Roman Catholic!" exclaimed Ruth. "Yes; I spent two years in a convent."

"Where?"

"Near Glasgow."

"How did you get in?"

"How I got out is more to the purpose," the girl said, laughing. "I ran away and joined the Army. They used to beat their drum under the convent wall; and we younger nuns often climbed up to have a look at them. We could not think why they wore red vests, or what they meant by their services. If the drum came while we had recreation, and the older nuns were in chapel, we twisted our veils round our necks, and danced to the Salvation music. At last I determined to attend a Salvation

Army meeting. So one night I pretended to have a headache. I was sent to bed; and while the other novices were at vespers, I slipped out of the convent and went to the Salvation Army. I got saved that night, and offered myself for the work. But they would not have me then. They sent me back to Glasgow, where my poor old father was a city missionary. He is dead now. He died just before Christmas. Directly after his funeral I volunteered for slum work. He was a very religious man, and he brought me up in Scotch fashion. I was not allowed to go anywhere on Sunday except to church; I might not even look out of the window. I hated the Bible then, for he forced me to learn long chapters of it, and to say texts even while I was eating my breakfast. These things made me a Roman Catholic. I found a little chapel in Glasgow, where they had beautiful music, and I went there without telling my father. One day while I was in this place a priest came to me and said that the devil would fetch me to hell if I did not follow him directly. I was so frightened that I let him take me to a convent a few miles away in the country. He promised to tell my father where I had gone to, but he did not keep his promise. My poor old father searched for me all over Glasgow, and it was three weeks before he found out that I was in the convent. I believe the fright he was in helped to kill him, for I was his only child, and he had lost my mother while I was a baby. When I think of all he went through during those three weeks, I cannot forgive myself. *I* was wretched, too. I hoped every day to get a letter from him. A scolding would, I thought, be better than nothing. But no letter came. At last I went to the Rev. Mother, and said that I should run away if she did not let me see him directly. I was obliged to go down on my knees while I said this, for no novice was allowed to speak to the Rev. Mother standing. She listened to what I had to say in silence. Then she opened a drawer, and took out of it a letter from my father. I jumped up when I saw his handwriting, and begged her to give me the letter. At first she hesitated. Then she let me carry it away to the dormitory. I shall never forget what he said in it. He told me that his heart was broken, and he begged me to come away from 'the scarlet woman.' I carried the letter about inside my dress, and I often cried over it. At last he paid me a visit. But the Rev. Mother was in the room all the time, so I could only say that I was very happy. I stayed two years in the convent; and if the Salvation drum had not come under the wall, I should be there now, most likely."

"Did you ever see your father again?" inquired Ruth.

"Yes. After I was saved I went back to Glasgow. I walked all the way home in my novice's dress. He opened the door for me. His hair had become quite white while I was in the convent. On his death-bed he said to me, 'I would rather have gone to hell myself than have left you in the scarlet woman's service.'"

The girl rose up to clear away the tea-things, and Ruth could see that she was crying. The memory of the old missionary brought painful thoughts with it; for he lay under the sod in the Scotch churchyard.

"We shall meet beyond the river," sang the elder girl, while she put on her bonnet.

Then the lassies set out to bombard the public houses, of which there are no less than eighteen in __, which place they call "our little parish." All of these seem to be doing a good business. They take the place of clubs to poor men, of drawing rooms to poor women. Let no one think that people frequent public-houses solely for the sake of drink; they go there to enjoy each other's company, to hear some new thing, to joke and to gossip.

The streets were almost empty that Sunday evening. The shops were shut; and there was little traffic. But outside public-houses stood women and men, also children. Girls in short petticoats carried babies. Boys played "shove a halfpenny" on the pavement.

"Do you want to buy a baby?" a woman asked, as the slum saviours stopped for a minute beside a gin shop. "You can have this one for a shilling. Look at it, sister. It's a nice little thing. You can make it into a Salvation captain."

"I believe you would sell your child for a glass of beer," said the eldest slum saviour, looking at the woman's face, on which was written a thirst for spirits.

"'Deed I would," was the mother's reply. "I'd sell my very soul for a glass of gin. Come, you shall have it for sixpence, if you won't give a shilling."

The slum saviour turned away, saying, as if to herself: "Men's hearts hardened, and the tender lips of women loud in laughter, and the sobs of children helpless, and the sighs of slaves, and priests with dead lies for the living truth."

"Surely," said Ruth, "that woman is not in earnest."

"Oh yes, she is," replied the slum lassie. "The people about here often ask us to buy their babies; sometimes they offer them to us for nothing. They know that we have a Home for children at Clapton ; so they think that we will make their boys and girls into soldiers. They say, 'You. can bring them up to earn a decent living. We have nothing for them to eat, and with us they must see a deal of wickedness. Take them to your Home, and give them a proper start. They'll do nicely for the Salvation Army.'"

Just then they passed by a common lodging-house, outside which stood a bevy of young women, gossiping and laughing.

"I'd like to know what you make by your preaching," said a girl who was dressed in shabby black silk. "No one in this world takes trouble for nothing. Come, tell us what you get. Maybe I'll join your business."

"Board and lodging are promised," replied the slum saviour, "nothing else."

"Come, now, tell the truth. It's not likely that you would give your time for nothing. How much is it? Ten shillings a week?"

"I say that only board and lodging are promised."

"But you get paid. That's the point," said the young woman. "The work's hard, but the pay's certain. If it wasn't for the bonnet and the knee ache, I'd join the Salvation Army. I'm sick of my life I am; I'd just as soon be a happy Eliza as myself. I know that the Salvation Army is a paying business."

The slum lassies said that they would gladly receive her into their ranks, but that she must get "saved" first. Then they pushed open the doors of a public-house, and went in to distribute *War Crys* among the men and women. Half a dozen people stood at the bar, and more sat beside the tables. Men played dominoes and cards; women gossiped to neighbours. A girl with an untidy dress, and hair cut in a heavy fringe across her forehead, leant against a wall, talking to the publican. She had a baby under her shawl, and as the slum saviours came in, she cried out,

"Here are the sisters come to the christening." So saying, she dipped her finger in gin, and made the sign of the cross on the child's forehead. Its eyes were shut, and it took no notice, although its mother tried to wake it up by shouting at it.

"Do you wonder that we say 'Thank God' when He calls away a baby?" whispered a slum lassie to Ruth. "What good can come of a child that is christened in a public-house? If I had money, I would like to buy all these slum babies."

Ruth looked from one person to another, and thought that they were a more miserable set of men and women than those she was accustomed to see in East End districts. They were casuals of the worst type, people who have given up all hope of regular employment.

Such men hang about Covent Garden Market and those who watch their faces can see them deteriorating daily. They come there hoping to earn a few shillings, and wait outside the market for jobs all day long. Gradually they sink into the scum of London, and become paupers, gaol-birds, and vagrants. It is a pitiable thing to see them deteriorating! First they grow reckless, then they become hopeless, finally they take to drinking. Starvation prevents them from doing mischief at present; but they add to the seething mass of discontent that is even now undermining the whole of society. Only those who go amongst them, who know them intimately, are aware of the bitter hatred which they express for "the upper classes," the angry feelings which they smother while ladies and gentlemen roll by in carriages. People will not listen to the warning voice which is again and again lifted up by those who associate with starving men and women; they refuse to hear the truth because it is unpleasant. Yet truth raps loudly at the door, and says that although starvation saps the energies of the unemployed and undermines their health, nevertheless to let thousands of men and women remain in enforced idleness is dangerous. People think, "We have soldiers and policemen to protect us." They are ignorant that policemen went in the dark hours of the night to a well-known Socialist, and begged him to take part in their last demonstration. They forget that soldiers are beginning to ask, "What will become of *me* when my short period of service is over and I leave the army?" Go to the dock gates before breakfast. Watch the scenes enacted there every morning. Look at the thousands of men who fight for work, who struggle like wild beasts for the contractors' tickets. Remember that a million men throughout the United Kingdom are out of work; and then think what your fate will be if the police take the part of the unemployed, if the military say, "We cannot shoot these men, for they are our brethren." Every generation stones its prophets; but for the sake of the children we say, "Take warning."

Huge barrels of beer half filled the narrow room in which the slum lassies were standing, and behind a cask sat an old woman who attracted Ruth's notice. She held out her hand for a paper, and said:

"It's no good to speak to me. I'm stone deaf, my dear. I'm seventy-two, and I haven't been able to hear nothing this ten years. Give me a paper; It's dull sitting here, and my beer is finished."

Ruth held out a *War Cry*, and, as she approached the old woman, she heard some one say:

"Ain't her hair lovely?"

Half a dozen men had climbed up the partition to see what was going on, and Ruth's golden hair had been pointed out to them by the publican.

"If you become one of us you will have to dye your hair," the slum lassies said to Ruth. "It attracts too much notice."

They visited twelve public-houses, and everywhere they found men and women playing cards, gossiping, and drinking. Church bells echoed through the open windows, and mixed with ribald songs that rose from the lips of young girls and children. The air was thick with smoke, and heavy with the stench of spirits.

"Go home! Where shall I go to?" asked a woman, whose dress was in rags, and whose feet were wrapped in old pocket-hankerchiefs. "I've no home to go to. This is my home, and a doorstep is my sleeping-place. Mind your own business."

"Keep a civil tongue in your head when you speak to the lassies," said a man; "they are the only folks that come among us. They have been good to my missus."

"You are like my daughter," a woman told Ruth. "She's dead now. This is her little baby."

"Oh, mother," one of the slum lassies pleaded, come out of this place.

Come with us. Listen to the church bells. Don't they make you think of that daughter you have lost? You want to see her again. Come out of this dreadful place."

But the woman shook her head.

"My dear," she said, "I share a room with another woman. She's in it now. It won't be mine till bed-time. It's better here than in the streets."

The only well-dressed people in these dens were the publicans and the barmaids. Warmth and light attracted customers inside the doors, and the sight of women in satin and velvet, of men with diamond rings on their fingers, enlivened the scene after people had said what they wanted. Coloured glasses stood on the shelves; red, blue, and yellow bottles were reflected in the looking-glasses. Sleek men in broadcloth took pence at the bar, well-fed women handed gin and beer across the counter.

"You can stay here as long as you like," these people said to the slum lassies. "We've no objection. But if you make a draught, out you will go; remember that, and keep the door shut."

It was nearly nine o'clock by the time they left the public-houses and turned towards home. Not far up the street they were stopped by a little girl, who ran up to them and said:

"There's a party in our house that wants to see you. She's had nothing to eat all day, and her little children are so hungry. She was taken ill last night, and I don't think she will live long. She's lying in the dark, without a bit of fire, and no blanket."

The slum lassies told the girl to lead the way, and followed her into a narrow alley. This place is lined on either side by dark-looking houses. The postman seldom pays it a visit. If he arrives there boys and girls hail his advent, and the person for whom he has brought a letter is fetched down to meet him. Policemen are little known there. They prefer to keep away when a fight is going on, for the people are rough, and more than once boiling water has been thrown over constables by intoxicated women.

The girl darted into a house and up a dark staircase. Eight families live in that place. They rent rooms at five shillings, four shillings, and three shillings a week, unfurnished apartments with broken windows and smoking chimneys. The landlord makes quite a nice little fortune, for he can go to bed although his houses are overcrowded, and he can sleep knowing that his tenants have empty pockets. He sends an agent to collect the rents, and salves his conscience by giving a donation to some charity when he hears that So-and-so has been evicted. His wife begs him not to talk about the poor things, because their sorrows are quite too much for her feelings, and she entreats him not to go near the place for fear that he should bring home small-pox.

The clergy read prayers in church for their absent parishioners.

Policemen say, "Such places are only safe for a slum lassie."

The girl opened a door at the top of the house, and went into a room that was wrapped in darkness.

"Who is there?" asked a weak voice. "Who is it?"

"It's the sisters," the girl said. " You told me to bring them in, if they came along this evening."

"I wish I could see their faces," the voice continued. "There's a box of lucifers on the fireplace. Strike a light, Polly, and take care you don't fall over the baby. It's asleep now, I think; anyhow, it's stopped crying."

Presently a flickering light let the slum lassies see the woman they had come to visit. She lay on the bare boards, and was covered over by some old sacks. The room did not contain one single bit of furniture. Four walls and the floor were there, nothing more but the human beings who were "so hungry."

On the woman's face was the look which all who have watched the approach of death know how to interpret. She was not dying, but inch by inch the waters of dissolution were creeping nearer to her, and even then she had touched the brink of the river. Her thin white hands lay on an old sack. By-and-by they would take fast hold of it. Her white sunken cheeks had red spots beneath the eyes and her parched lips had grown brown with thirst. Sweat lay thick upon her forehead.

"Sister," she said, in a hoarse voice, "I want you to take my little baby. I can't leave it here without a mother."

So saying, she lifted a corner of the sack to let the slum lassies see a little child, with its fist in its mouth, and its feet curled under its tattered petticoats. Two other children sat close by, with wide-open eyes and hungry faces. And at the window stood a man in rags, with a desperate look on his face, and his hands in his pockets.

The match went out, and the room was once more wrapped in darkness.

"Fetch a candle," the elder slum lassie whispered to her companion. "And bring a loaf of bread. These people are starving."

Few words were said while the girl was away, but the dying woman tried to explain *why* they were all so hungry.

She had been taken ill the day before, after buying flowers at the market; and she had been obliged to come home to the children. Her husband had been out of work for nine months, and during that time they had sunk gradually lower and lower. One thing had followed another to the pawnshop, until at last nothing was left – not even a blanket.

"You ought to go into the workhouse," the slum lassie said to the man. "It is cruel to hold out like this. You have no right to do it."

"It's all my fault," the dying woman said, faintly. "I couldn't bear to part with him and the children. Don't be hard on him. He'd have gone in before this if I'd have let him. It's not his independence; it's me. I've been so ill that I wanted to stay with him."

They could not do much for her. They fetched some milk to moisten her lips, and promised to look after the baby when she had gone over to "the great majority." They fed the children, and gave the man some bread; but the woman was too ill to swallow anything. She lay on the bare boards waiting for death; and when they went away, she said, "God bless you!" very faintly.

"Come with us, and we will give you a pillow," the slum lassies told the man; and he followed them in silence, with a dogged look on his face that meant hopelessness.

Ruth went back to Whitechapel in an omnibus that put her down at the door of the barracks. She thought of all she had witnessed: of the poverty, the sin, the hopelessness, and the drinking. When she entered the room Captain Lobe came up to her, and asked, "Do you still wish to become a slum saviour?"

She looked at the men and women who were just going home from the meeting, and at Hester, who was waiting for her. Then she said, "Yes."

CHAPTER VII

What it is to be an Agnostic

The following evening Captain Lobe returned home tired and depressed, after a long day spent in the lowest East End districts. His Sunday work exhausted him so much that he always required two or three days afterwards to recruit his strength, and on a Monday he generally suffered from an attack of low spirits. He opened the window, and looked down into the street. Presently he heard a voice behind him say, "Good-evening." Looking round, he saw a lady standing by the door of his sitting-room. "May I come in?" she asked.

Captain Lobe came to her and shook hands, with a look on his face that said plainly enough how glad he was to receive her visit.

"No, I will not sit down," she continued, refusing to take a chair. "I like to look out of your window. I always think that you have a better view of the Whitechapel Road than any one else. What were you thinking about when I came in?"

"It is sickening to see all this misery," Captain Lobe said, looking at her. "I ought not to say so, perhaps; but you know what I mean, and sometimes it is a relief to say what one is feeling."

"I agree with you," she told him; "it is sickening."

"'Ye have the poor always with you,'" Captain Lobe continued, with a sigh. "But things seem to get no better, only worse. Every day more men fall out of work, more women must support the men, more children are starving."

"You make a mistake," was the reply. "To put that interpretation on those Bible words is ridiculous. Disease will not be stamped out for centuries, and while the children suffer for the sins of their parents, the poor will remain among us. Death and accident will always be upon earth; and they will cause poor men and women to need our help. But to say that some people will, as long as the world lasts, be hungry and homeless, is to put an interpretation on those Bible words that is quite ridiculous. Poverty of that sort is the outcome of social conditions; it is not a Divine fiat."

"I had not looked at it in that way," said Captain Lobe, slowly.

"I do not mean to say that the law could at the present time give every man and every woman enough to eat and a decent place to live in," she continued; "but I am certain that these things could very quickly be done by public opinion. Supposing, for instance, that Christianity had continued to be what it was at first, that the followers of Christ had not grown callous, why then there would be no hungry men or starving women in England to-day. The world would have seen the Millennium before the nineteenth century. But instead of that, Christians have hidden Christ so deep in doctrine, that, search how we will, it is difficult to find Him; instead of giving us the Sermon on the Mount, they have placed before us intellectual stumbling-blocks. If Christ were to walk down the Whitechapel Road this evening, do you think that He would stop to discourse about doctrine? No; He would feed the hungry men and women; He would gather round Him the little starving children, and then –"

"What then?"

"He would be run in by a policeman."

"Why?"

"Because He would walk into a church, and say, 'While My brethren are starving, I do not care to see Myself upon a gold crucifix;' and clergymen would say, 'He has spoken blasphemy.' He would bid ladies take off their ornaments, and gentlemen take off their rings; and congregations would say,

'He interferes with the rights of private property.'"

"I wish He *would* come," said Captain Lobe. "He tarries so long that people ask, 'Where is the sign of His coming?'"

"Perhaps He cannot come until the world is ready to receive Him," she said. "I sometimes think that God puts a veil between the eyes of

Agnostics, because if they could see His face they would be so blinded by the glory of His presence, that they could not do His work on earth, which is to prepare for His Second Advent. Christians have grown callous. Just look what London is at present. It is divided into two nations, East and West; one nation is starving, the other nation is rolling in luxury. Depend upon it, if Christ were to come again, the West End would crucify Him."

"There is some truth in what you say," Captain Lobe said, thoughtfully. "But a great deal is being done by religious people."

"Oh yes! Look at the Destitute Workmen's Aid Society! It has the names of the greatest people in the land on its circulars; and when a sermon for it was preached in Westminster Abbey, £15 was handed in to divide amongst 10,000 starving men and women!"

Captain Lobe made no reply.

"I must be going now," she said. "Is there any one you want me to visit?"

"Yes, there is a little dwarf near here," he told her, "who would like to see you very much. You went into his gaff one night, and shook hands with him. He says that you are the only person he would care to see when he is dying. He is very ill. Will you come this evening?"

"Let us go at once," she said. "I remember him perfectly well. He had such a pained look on his face when I walked up to him, for the people were shrinking away, and calling him 'a monstrosity.'"

She left the room, followed by Captain Lobe. When they reached the street, she began to talk again about Agnostics. "I was at your place in Victoria Street the other day," she said, "doing some work with the staff. At half-past twelve o'clock a bell rang, and one of the officers said, 'This is the hour at which we pray for converts.' I wanted to leave the room, but they begged me to stay, and told me that I could sit still while they were praying. Then they all dropped down on their knees, and I said to myself, 'They are going to thank God that they are not Agnostics.' Instead of that, man after man prayed that God would point out *why* I did not join the Salvation Army. Here I was doing the same work as themselves, only under another name. Would the Almighty say what prevented me from joining the Salvation Army?"

"You *will* belong to us some day," Captain Lobe told her.

But she shook her head. "The difference lies in the fact that you believe in immortality and I do not. That is why I say that social conditions must, and *shall* be altered, in order that all may have, during their short span of life, a chance of happiness. You can afford to see human beings suffering here, because you think that they will be happy hereafter."

"If they are saved," said Captain Lobe.

"Ah yes! You believe in hell! That is a terrible doctrine."

They reached the gaff, and passed through the crowd towards the red curtain. The room was full of people, and a little girl turned the handle of the organ to keep the audience amused until a man without arms appeared on the platform. This man could shave himself, play a violin, and do many other things with his toes instead of his fingers. He was advertised at the entrance of the gaff as "A credit to his Maker."

Captain Lobe lifted the curtain, and then opened the cupboard door. It was quite dark there, so he stopped to say, "Midget, I'm here, and I've brought a lady."

Presently the light of a candle showed them the dwarf, who was lying on the old properties. He was dressed in his red coat, and the cocked hat lay beside him. But that night he would not say, "Ladies and gentlemen, I wish you good-evening," for the doctor had told the manager that he was very ill, perhaps dying.

"This is the lady who shook hands with you the other night," explained Captain Lobe. "You said that you would like to see her again, so I have brought her this evening."

"Come *here* to see *me*!" the midget said, slowly.

"Yes," she said, kneeling down beside him. "I wanted to see you very much. How are you?"

"Come *here* to see *me*!" he repeated.

"What are you reading?" she asked, seeing a book open on the floor beside the candlestick.

"It's a story," the dwarf answered. "A love story," he continued, while a faint blush came over his face, "about two people who got married."

"Do you read many love stories?"

"I like them best. But I read the *War Cry*, now that I belong to the Salvation Army. I want to find out what I am. I'm so afraid of coming here again as a dog or something. I've travelled about all my life to be looked at; and I've seen all sorts of 'missing links,' as the gov'nor calls us. We often talk among ourselves, and wonder what will become of us. We don't go to church because we're afraid of being laughed at, and no clergyman ever comes near us. Do you think I've got a soul, lady?" he asked, gazing wistfully into her face. "I don't want to come back again. Do you think I've got a soul, or do you think I'm nothing?"

She hesitated. Then she said, "You need not be afraid to come back again. Things are changing fast. Social conditions are becoming different. Barriers are breaking down, and classes are amalgamating. By the time you come back all men will be brethren. Young men will be ashamed of their strength, if it makes them despise midgets; young women will not shrink away, if it makes you look unhappy. People will put you first then, if you come into the world handicapped. For love will be strong, even down here in Whitechapel; and this earth will be heaven."

"When will that time be?" the midget asked, eagerly.

"I cannot tell, but you will find the world like that if you come back again."

Then she kissed him. As she left the room Captain Lobe heard him say, "She'd never have done that if I'd been a missing link. I'm a man, captain!"

After they reached the Whitechapel Road, Captain Lobe asked, "Does that future you talk about satisfy you?"

"No. But I work on. The Bible says that if a man does the will of the Father he shall know of the doctrine. You remember the old allegory. St. Christopher wanted to find Christ; so he was told to carry little children across a stream to school, and to carry them back again. He went patiently on at that work until, at last, he carried over the child Jesus."

"Well, what then?" inquired the captain.

"Oh, he fell down dead, or, as the old version has it, 'he was translated.'"

CHAPTER VIII

An East End Doctor

They parted outside the Aldgate Station. The lady went West; the Salvation Army captain returned to his East End quarters. On the way home he thought about the conversation that had taken place between the lady and the midget. It is wonderful what queer people I meet down here," he said to himself. "Roman Catholics and infidels, High Church and Low Church, all trying to do good in their own fashion. Why, at Toynbee Hall there are quite a colony of men busy at something; and at Oxford House a few men seem busy, too. I wonder why one sees so little result from so much effort! I suppose it is because people don't go the right way to work. One must get these men and women saved first. If salvation does not bring food and work along with it, a saved person knows how to put up with starvation. But it's hard to tell a starving man, 'bread shall be given him, his water shall be sure,' day after day, and yet to see the cupboards empty!" He thought of a woman who had said to him that morning, "If the Almighty did as right by me as I do by Him, it would be a good thing for me, captain."

That woman had been out at daybreak to search among the dust heaps. She had brought home a few old boots for fuel, and some bits of paper. A smell of leather had pervaded the atmosphere when Captain Lobe payed her a visit; and on the burning boots he had seen a saucepan full of old tea leaves that a neighbour had given to her. She was sitting on the floor when he opened the door, preparing the paper for the nearest rag shop. Her children had gone to school without any breakfast; and when they came home again she would only have the boiled tea to give them, and perhaps a bit of bread if the paper fetched a few farthings. Captain Lobe had offered up a prayer for patience; and at the end she had expressed a wish that the Almighty would give her work, just as she gave Him prayers and praises. Her words had sounded blasphemous to the little captain, but he had not been able to say so, because he knew how hard it is to see one's children starving. "Thank God the winter is over at last," he said to himself. "As the warm weather comes on the people will feel less hungry."

A church clock struck eight, and while it was striking he thought, with some relief, "The day's work is finished." But he made a mistake. At his door he found a woman. She was fidgeting with her apron, and swaying her head backwards and forwards. Directly he drew near she began to speak, or rather to ejaculate. "It's you I want. You must come at once. Mrs. Rhodes, she's gone off. She's taken the baby. When her husband came home last night, he found the two children crying, and he couldn't see her nowhere. He thought she'd gone to her mother in the country. But I knew better. His behaviour's been shocking." She paused, out of breath.

Well, what can I do?" inquired Captain Lobe.

"You must come with me. He's threatening to murder the children. Her sister's come up to say as she's not been down in the country. She said she'd do away with herself; and it's my belief she's done it, for she'd never have left the children and taken only the baby if she'd meant to come back again. He's just mad, he is, and I've come to fetch you instead of a policeman."

Captain Lobe followed the woman, listening as they went to her statement. "She's left the room that neat, you could eat your supper off the floor, and she's washed the sheets on the bed, a thing she's not done since her illness. I says when I come in the room, 'She's done away with herself,' for the bed's fit to lay a corpse out on it. He treated her just shameful; and she was the quietest creature that ever lived. She's showed me the characters she had in service, and often she's said to me as it was a bad day for her when she took up with such a queer-tempered feller. He'll never see her again, I'll lay my solemn oath, and serves him right if he doesn't."

"I think I remember the woman," Captain Lobe said. "She lives on the third floor of your block, does she not?"

"Yes, her room is just opposite to me. She's been my neighbour this two years, and I wouldn't ask for a better. She's never grumbled when it's been her turn to clean the passage, and she's helped me more than once in the washhouse. Her husband's always been going on at her for having so many children. As if the poor thing wanted 'em any more than he do! The way he's gone on at her has been something shocking!"

They reached a large human bee-hive, where five or six hundred people have cells to live in, and went up some dark stairs to find the room of the unfortunate woman whose fate it had been to have too many children. On the third floor they stopped to enter a place about which buzzed an angry crowd of human insects. "Make way," said the woman. "I've brought Salvation to see what can be done for them poor children."

As Captain Lobe went into the room the buzzing stopped for a minute; so it was possible for him to hear the voice of a man who stood by a table, and the sobs of a girl who sat beside the fireplace, with her arms round two small children. "It's no good for you to go on at me," the man was saying to the girl. "You can take the children away to-night. If you leave them here, they won't be alive to-morrow. I'm tired of them, I am. Why, I'd like to know, has your sister given me all these brats to keep? Now she's run away, and taken nothing but the baby. Does she think I'll put up with it? When she comes back she'll find 'em dead, I say."

"She'll never come back again," answered the young woman. "She's dead, I know she is. You've been a cruel man, and if you kill these blessed children you'll swing for it. Thank God I'm not married." The women at the door joined in a chorus of abuse, and the man stamped his foot, bidding them go away, as the children belonged to him, and he would do as he liked with them, regardless of women or policemen.

The room was clean and neat. It contained little furniture, but the few chairs had been scrubbed, and the deal table had received careful attention. A white quilt covered the bed, and a white quilt was spread over the empty cradle. On the mantelpiece stood shining brass candlesticks, and a bright tin teapot. The place had been swept and garnished by the woman before she went away with her baby. Captain Lobe glanced at the room for a minute, then he walked up to the man and asked, "Have you been to the police station?"

"I've been nowhere, and I'm not going nowhere," the husband said. "If she likes to go away she can. It's nothing to me. I wish she'd taken all the brats along with her instead of leaving them here. They won't see the light to-morrow so you'd best take 'em back to your mother down in the country," he continued, looking at the girl. "You're not the only one, I guess, who's said, 'Thank God I ain't married.'"

But in spite of his violence, it was not difficult to see that the man was anxious about his wife. He fumbled in his waistcoat pocket, and then slipped into Captain Lobe's hand a dirty bit of paper. Afterwards he turned round to slam the door in the face of the buzzing insects. The girl by the fireplace sobbed. The children whined. The woman who had been to fetch Captain Lobe ejaculated. Every sob, every whine, every ejaculation seemed to exasperate the man. He swore and cursed the day on which he had been married. "If those twins had lived there would have been five of 'em," he said, shaking his fist at the children. "Now there's them two and the baby. If it's not enough to anger a man, I'd like to know what is. I've been married four years, and but for the whooping cough I'd have five children now to keep besides myself and the missus."

"She's dead, and you'll never see her again," said the girl, who was sobbing.

"A good thing if I doesn't," he answered.

Captain Lobe read the bit of' dirty paper while the man was swearing. "Dear Husband, – I can't put up with you any longer, coming in and talking as you do, and going on about the baby. I think you will be sorry when you read this, for then I'll be in the water, and the baby along with me. I hope the Lord will have mercy on my soul, as you are always swearing about the baby. My body may be brought home to you, so I've put clean sheets on the bed ready for me, and clean sheets in the cradle for the baby. I was drove to it."

"If you have not been to the police-station we had better go there together," Captain Lobe said, after he had returned the dirty bit of paper.

"I have been," the man told him in a low voice; "but I wasn't going to let those women know it."

"Then," said Captain Lobe, "we must go at once to the London Hospital."

The man reached down a hat from a peg on the door, and followed "Salvation" out of the room. When they reached the street he began to make excuses for his wife's letter, and said that she had been "a bit queer in her head lately." Captain Lobe was silent. The man mumbled on to himself until they came to a dark street, where a red lamp shone like a beacon above a dispensary. "We'd best go in here," he said then to the little captain. "Maybe the doctor's seen her."

The door was ajar, and as the man pushed through Captain Lobe heard a voice saying, "I'm too young to die; make me well again."

The speaker was leaning against a long counter, looking up at a tall, broad-shouldered man. Captain Lobe could not see her face, only the face of the doctor, who stood with his back to the wall. Shelves were arranged round the room, and on these were bottles and glasses. A pair of scales stood on the counter, also a board for making pills, and a bottle full of dark-coloured physic.

"Too young to die?" the doctor said. "Well, yes. But disease is like a sickle, child, it cuts down the corn and the flowers alike; and it's as well to be cut down young as to wither, isn't it? You will die loving life, and that is better than to live loving death. Go home, and take this physic."

"I'm too young to die," the girl pleaded.

"Well, come again another evening. I'll do all I can. Here's a shilling!"

The girl thanked him. As she turned away Captain Lobe thought of the woman who had been "drove to death," whose letter lay in the man's pocket.

"Well, what do you want with me?" the doctor asked, after the girl had left the dispensary.

"I want to know if you've seen my wife, sir?" the man said.

"Who is she?"

"She lives at No. 201 on the Block, in ____ Street."

"What, the woman who had a baby six weeks ago?"

"Yes."

"No, I've not seen her for a month. Is she ill again?"

"She has gone away, and I thought maybe you'd seen her."

"Gone! Where?"

"I don't know."

"You had better show the doctor the letter," said Captain Lobe.

The man hesitated. Then he brought out of his pocket another dirty bit of paper, and handed it across the counter, saying, in a sheepish way, "That's what she left for her mother."

The doctor took up the letter, and read aloud, "I am drove to it. God help my poor baby. Mother, look after the children. I have always done my best by him, but I can't put up with the way he swears at me for having so many babies. I didn't make myself, God knows it."

The doctor brought his fist down on the counter with so much force that the bottles and glasses shook, and the pill-boxes danced. "You men down here in Shoreditch are brutes," he said, throwing the bit of paper down before the man; "the way you treat your wives is shameful. Now look here," he continued, turning to Captain Lobe, "I attended that poor thing in her confinement. I found her up two days after the child was born, and she told me that fellow had wanted to know if it was 'fashionable' to lie in bed, if those were the sort of manners she had seen in service. She was ill last time I saw her; and if he has driven her to death, he deserves to be hanged for it. Go at once to the London Hospital," he said to the man. "You will probably find her in the dead-house. If not, come back to me. No, don't go with him," he told Captain Lobe. "Stop here, I've something to say to you. Come into my room." So saying, he raised the door of the counter, and led the way into a small place in which he is accustomed to see his patients.

The doctor pointed to a chair, and then drew a pipe out of his pocket. After Captain Lobe had taken the proffered seat, he placed himself with his back to the fireplace, and smoked silently for a minute.

"I know it's no good to offer you a cigar," he said, presently; "it's against your regulations."

Captain Lobe answered, "Yes."

Again there was a minute of silence.

At last the doctor said, "That little girl in ____ Square tells me that she is going to join the Salvation Army."

Captain Lobe acquiesced.

"Now I've a theory that people only do things like that when they are below par for some reason or other," the doctor said, taking the pipe from his mouth and looking critically at it. "I mean when they are in love, or after they have lost a relation. If a man is in a normal condition, he thinks of nothing but himself; the troubles of others slip from his memory like water off a duck's back. But if he is below par for some reason or other, the disease of caring about the sorrows of the world creeps in upon him. That was my case, at any rate. I lost my father, sister, and some one else within six months. There's no pillow so hard as the lid of a coffin; and if three times within half a year a man's head lies there he becomes sleepless. While I was in that abnormal condition the disease took hold of me; and ever since then I have been unable to shake it off. That is why I am here to-night, instead of in the West End, where I could make a decent living."

"So you were completely bowled over once," the little captain said, in a sympathetic voice.

"Yes. My father died first. My sister followed him. Last of all *she* went. She gave me this," he continued, taking a black ring from his waistcoat pocket. "Sometimes I put it on, but sometimes I try to think that I have forgotten it."

He put the ring back in his pocket.

"How long ago is that?" Captain Lobe asked.

"Ten years. I was at the London Hospital then, in the out-patients' department. I had done well at the examinations, and I was keen about science. If she had lived I should have been something by this time; as it is, here I am, fighting a hopeless battle against starvation. The whole of the East End is starving. What the people want is food, not physic. Yet I cannot go away, for the disease has taken such a hold of me."

"If I could do anything, I would not grumble," he continued. "But here I fight, day after day, against an overwhelming mass of misery. I dare not give the people drugs that are used by West End physicians; for if I did the poor wretches would be killed outright. They have no constitution, only flabby flesh and blood with scarcely any oxygen in it. All I can do is to colour water with something or other, and hand it over the counter. The poor things drink it directly they get outside the dispensary, and they call it 'comforting.'"

"The whole of the East End is starving?" Captain Lobe interrogated.

"I do not mean to say that they have no bread," the doctor said. "But they are all underfed. Why, it is brutal to make children go to school without a proper breakfast, to force the brains of boys and girls who have empty stomachs. If the poor were not so wonderfully generous to one another, the result would be a generation of idiots. It is this cardinal virtue of theirs which makes them so attractive. And their misery binds one to them with a heavy chain, if the sorrows of the world once take hold of a human being."

He stopped for a minute. Then he said: "The disease would never have taken hold of me if I had not been bowled over, as you call it. I returned from her funeral in an abnormal condition. They say that I stretched out my hand across her grave to the man I hated most. If I did, it must have been in a dream, for it seemed such a little thing to forgive him. After I came back, the faces of the patients haunted me. Her eyes met me again and again in the starving men and women. I could not go away to the West End. I stayed on here as a parish doctor. Here I have been for ten years, knowing all the time the people had better die than live on in this state of semi-starvation. I am at it still. I bring into the world scrofulous children; I bolster up diseased patients; I let people down easily into the grave; I do no good, but I cannot go away. The misery I see binds me here as a parish doctor."

He stretched out his long arms on the mantelpiece, a modern Prometheus, bound to the rock by the woes of his fellow-men. And he could do nothing.

Captain Lobe glanced at the little room, and seemed to see the tide of human misery that rose and fell there every day, the waves of starvation that broke against the chair of the doctor. An open book lay on the professional table, a book full of cases; debility was written there, also scrofula, and the other complaints that come from want of oxygen and from inanition. The floor had no carpet; it was marked by the weary feet of unemployed men and overworked women. One door opened into the dispensary, another into a small room that was fitted up as a laboratory. A lamp let Captain Lobe see this private workshop, in which the parish doctor indulged his love of science. Yet by working night and day in that place the modern Prometheus could not find a remedy for the misery he was called upon to witness, unless he could discover some chemical secret that would prevent men and women from wanting bread, that would enable children to thrive without food and raiment. The room was plentifully supplied with works of science, but not a book on the shelves could say what drug had power to counteract the evil effects of being hungry.

"Sometimes I go to the West End," the doctor said, "and I wonder if the people there are mad or wicked. They talk such rubbish. They do not seem to recognize the fact that drink is a phenomenon of the people's wretched condition. They say 'The poor should not have so many children.' Listen to what Frederick Engels says on the subject."

He took a book from the shelf, and read:

"'All conceivable evils are heaped upon the heads of the poor. If the population of great cities is too dense in general, it is they in particular who are packed into the least space. As though the vitiated atmosphere of the streets were not enough, they are penned in dozens into single rooms, so that the air which they breathe at night is enough in itself to stifle them. They are given damp dwellings – cellar dens that are not waterproof from below, or garrets that leak from above. Their houses are so built that the clammy air cannot escape. They are supplied with bad, tattered, or rotten clothing, adulterated and indigestible food. They are exposed to the most exciting changes of mental condition, the most violent vibrations between hope and fear; they are stirred up like game, and not permitted to attain peace of mind and quiet enjoyment, of life. They are worked every day to the point of complete exhaustion of their mental and physical energies, and are thus constantly spurred on to the maddest excess in the only two enjoyments at their command.'

"That is a truthful statement of the case. But those who are stupid, or wilfully ignorant, say, 'The poor in a lŏomp is bad.' They cannot, or will not, see that while the environment of these people remains what it is, these people will indulge in the only two enjoyments they can command.

I get angry with the poor things down here sometimes, as I did with that man this evening; but I generally feel for them nothing but pity, because they are the victims of a state of barbarism which some people call 'civilization.'"

"What do you think can be done?"

"That is a large question. If I were a younger man I would give up medicine and go into politics. I would teach the people to use their votes, to send their own men into Parliament; and I would agitate myself in St. Stephen's for measures that would make the proletariat master of the situation. In fact, I would be a constitutional socialist, using all lawful means to improve the condition of the working man. God knows that it wants improving!"

A bell rang in the dispensary, and the doctor said, "That man has come back again."

"Why did you bring me in here?" Captain Lobe asked, rising up, and preparing to leave the room. "What did you want to say to me?"

"Oh, it was about that little girl in _____Square. She has taken the complaint – I mean to say she wants to go into the Salvation Army. I knew her mother, and I have known her ever since she was born. She ought not to try slum work; she is too delicate."

"Well," said Captain Lobe, "it isn't my fault."

So saying, "Salvation" put on his cap, and returned to the dispensary.

"Have you found your wife?" he asked the man.

"No. She's not at the London Hospital."

"Then we must go to St. Bartholomew's."

They left the dispensary, and walked towards the City. Captain Lobe trudged along with his hands in his pockets. The man shuffled on beside him, mumbling indistinct sentences. Those dirty bits of paper were like lead in his pocket. He did not throw them away. He was too frightened now to be angry. He was thinking of the days when he went courting, before he took to himself a wife, and children began to multiply in that small, dismal room, at the door of which always buzzed a crowd of human insects. His wife had been a neat little thing when he married her, and the room had presented at first a tidy appearance. But each year had brought a fresh "brat" along with it! Thus his wife had been ill, too weak to keep the room clean, or to prevent the children from squalling. The place had become a hell, out of which he had made his escape into the nearest gin-shop. His wages had been low enough to begin with, and they had dwindled to almost nothing after the publican had begun to take tribute from them. But what could a man do whose home was a pandemonium? How could a man come home at night to a dirty place, at the door of which always stood a crowd of buzzing human insects? Then he thought of a certain evening, and remembered how ashamed he had been to see his wife walking up the street in an untidy dress, with a grimy infant in her arms, and two dirty children clinging to her apron. He had followed her at some distance, and had sworn when he reached the room which contained all his possibilities of happiness. It was then that she had threatened for the first time to destroy herself; and he had said, with an oath, that she had better drown the children first, and herself afterwards.

He looked at Captain Lobe, and wondered why "Salvation" did not "let out" at him. It would have been a relief if the little captain had said something; for then he could have defended himself. "Salvation's" silence was even worse to bear than the dirty bits of paper.

At last they reached St. Bartholomew's Hospital, and passed through the gates to find the steward's office. It was dark, but the lamps showed the irregular buildings, and the plots of grass, which are designated, for want of a better name, the garden. Their dim light fell on the pond in which every year men are said to duck a medical student whose hands have been discovered in other people's pockets; and on the seats where sit convalescent patients, young doctors, nurses, all those people who make up the sum of a hospital.

"Wait here," Captain Lobe said; "I will see the steward."

He went into the office. Presently he came back, followed by an enormous man, who was carrying a lantern.

"Is she here?" the man asked.

"Yes."

"Where?"

"In the dead-house."

The man fell back against the wall.

"Do you want to see her?" inquired the porter.

"The baby?" said the man, looking at Salvation.

"You had better come with me," Captain Lobe said.

"Perhaps it is not your wife, but some one else."

Salvation linked his arm in that of the man, and they followed the porter, who was carrying the lantern. It was almost dark in the mortuary, but a jet of gas let them see some black coffins covered with white sheets. Each coffin had a number on it.

"Is this she?" the porter asked, lifting a sheet.

This woman was found in the river along of her baby, and brought here to see if any one would claim her. Is this your wife, mister?"

The man could not look for a minute.

Captain Lobe led him up to the coffin.

Then his head fell on the hardest pillow human hands ever make, and he knew that his wife would never have another infant.

CHAPTER IX

He fascinates me

People seem to think that men and women have only to say, "I wish to join the Salvation Army," and then General Booth opens his arms at once to the applicants. People are mistaken. Many questions have to be answered before applicants can even set about slum work. They must get a medical certificate as to the condition of their heart, throat, and chest; and say if they have any tendency to epilepsy, if they have had small-pox, if they are strong enough to stand the strain of frequent singing and public speaking. Afterwards they are obliged to answer at least fifty questions, varying from age and height to where they intend to live and die; they must make a number of promises, such as that they will not publish any books, songs, or music except for the benefit of the Salvation Army. General Booth, is, in fact, a benevolent despot; but he works with such good-will, and he is so facetious that attempts to split the Army up have hitherto proved insignificant.

After Ruth had sent in her application to the superintendent of the slum work, she received a foolscap sheet of paper, headed "Candidate's Personal Experience."

On this she was requested to give "a brief account of your life and experience since your conversion."

She carried the sheet of paper to Hester, who was in the kitchen, with the maid-of-all-work.

The old woman put on her spectacles to look at it, and then said in a puzzled way:

"But you've never been converted, darling."

"No," said Ruth, "unless it was the day when I made up my mind not to hate Mr. Pember. I am not sure," she continued, lowering her voice, "that I ever hated him exactly. But I often came down late for breakfast because I was afraid to meet him, and sometimes I ran away when I heard him open the door at night. It was a sin to feel like that, I think; and ever since that day I have not hated anybody."

Then Ruth sat down by the kitchen table to write her "personal experience." An old Dutch clock ticked thirty minutes while she did it. The maid-of-all-work came and went with saucepans and plates, looking sometimes at the golden hair of the would-be slum saviour. Old Hester watched the girl with an indescribable look of love on her face, and thought about her dead mistress.

Ruth found her personal experience difficult to put down on paper. It would have been easy to speak of sin that had rolled off her conscience like a heavy load, and of peace that had come to her afterwards through "the saving blood of Jesus." But she had never experienced anything of the sort.

She had said her prayers to Hester as a child, and to herself after she could read and write. Her great aim in life had been to become like her dead mother, for Hester had taught her to think her dead mother perfect. "Your mother would not have done this," "Your mother would have done that," Hester had said to her again and again, ever since she could remember anything. So she had grown up with her mother's likeness for a fetish, surrounded on all sides by the watchful care of Hester. She had called herself a miserable sinner Sunday after Sunday, but until she became conscious of a vague fear with regard to Mr. Pember[1], she had not felt any guilt on her conscience.

---

1 As some people – for instance, General Booth, Mr. Barnett, and Captain Cooke – are mentioned by name in this book, readers may perhaps think that all of the characters represent living men and women. This is not the case. The people whose names are given occupy an unimportant place in the story; consequently there has been no attempt to disguise their personalities. But the principal characters, such as Mr. Pember, are all types, not real men and women. Captain Lobe is a type of a Salvation Army captain; Jane Hardy is a typical nineteenth-century Proletarian spinster; Ruth and Hester do not exist in East London. I hope that my English readers will understand this; also my translators, who are introducing "Captain Lobe" into Sweden, France, Russia, and Germany.

At last the paper was filled in and put into an envelope. The superintendent of the slum work received it that night, also a letter from Captain Lobe, in which he said "Yes" to the following question:

"After speaking to the candidate on the subject, and with such knowledge as you possess as to character, do you back this candidate as a person likely to succeed in the slum work, and make a true blood and fire slum saviour?"

But Captain Lobe had qualified his affirmative with the words, "If not too delicate;" and he had added, "You had better see her yourself."

So shortly afterwards the post brought to Ruth a second communication from the slum superintendent, in which she was desired to call at New Cross "Tomorrow morning, ten sharp."

She had no difficulty in finding the house, for a bright red text ornamented the window, and by the open door stood two girls wearing poke bonnets. A minute later she was seated in a small office, opposite a good-looking young man, who wore the usual dress of Salvationists. Captain Cooke took out of his drawer a long sheet of paper, and while he asked Ruth a variety of questions he watched her face. Every day he received applications from girls of all sorts – daughters of rich men, nieces of noblemen, servants, dressmakers, and others, who were ready to work in the slums at a moment's notice.

Never since the world began has there been seen such an attempt as these girls are making at present. They go to the slummers with a Bible in the one hand, with the other free to nurse the sick and help the helpless. No room is too filthy for them to work and pray in; no man or woman is too vile for them to call brother or sister. They penetrate into cellars where no clergyman or priest has ever ventured, and spend hours among people who frighten policemen. Directly they see any danger ahead, instead of running away they fall down on their knees and begin to pray. So it comes to pass that not a single slum lassie has been hurt anywhere, for the slummers say "They are so plucky." Whatever we may think about the doctrines which they preach, we must recognize the fact that these girls are a civilizing force of no mean import. Thank God slumming can never become fashionable. No girl will ever go into these slums in order to wile away the time or to win admiration. No princess will ever patronize slum saviours, so these girls will carry on their crusade against poverty until the slummers begin to see more clearly, for even in these dark corners of the earth a light is breaking at present.

At last Captain Cooke said, "If you join us you will find the work very laborious. Look here," he continued turning round his head, and showing her a wound on his neck, "this is what they did to me in the slums yesterday. If you go into this work you must be prepared for rough treatment. A murder took place last week close to where two of our slum saviours live, and no one could find out who did it. The girl's throat was cut from ear to ear because she had offended her neighbours. The same thing may happen to you if by any chance you give offence; and as you will have to speak to these people about their sins, and visit all sorts of places, you will carry your life in your hand from day to day you will live in a state of perpetual anxiety. All this will be hard to bear, remember."

"I am not afraid of any one, except Mr. Pember," Ruth said, looking at the superintendent.

"Who is he?"

Then she told Captain Cooke about the man who looked after her factory.

"Why are you afraid of him?" the superintendent asked, after she had finished.

"I do not know," she answered, while a scarlet flush came over her face, and mounted up to her forehead. "But when he is in the house I want him to go away; and if he goes out, I listen for him to come in again. I did not put that on the paper," she continued, seeing Captain Cooke take up her "Personal experience," "but that is how I feel about him. I used to think that I hated him, and ever since the day on which I made up my mind to join the Salvation Army I have tried to feel different. I do not know that I ever hated him very much, but–but–" she hesitated.

"Well, what?"

"Have you ever been to the Zoological Gardens?"

"Yes."

"Have you ever seen them feeding the serpents?"

"No."

"Well, I have watched little yellow ducks given to the serpents, and I have seen the poor things shaking with fear, but they couldn't go away. I don't know how it is, but I feel like that; he – he fascinates me."

Captain Cooke looked at the girl, and seeing that her eyes were full of tears, and that every trace of colour had left her face, he asked gently:

"How old is this Mr. Pember?"

"I do not know. He has grey hair, quite grey. Perhaps he is fifty."

"Is he kind to you?"

"Very."

"Do you see much of him?"

"No, not much. He goes to the factory directly after breakfast, and sometimes he does not come home all day."

"Have you ever been to the factory?"

"Never."

"Yet it belongs to you, I think?"

"Yes."

"And Mr. Pember is only your agent?"

Ruth did not see what he was driving at.

At last he said, "I think you ought to stay where you are and fight this man, instead of running away to the Salvation Army. Charity begins at home, and until you have done your duty there it is not right for you to become a slum saviour. How many people work in this factory?"

"I do not know," Ruth told him. "But last Christmas Day thirty girls came to fetch dinners from our house. They always fetch dinners at Christmas."

"Well, it seems to me," said the superintendent, "that your duty is clear enough. You ought to fight this man, and look after those young women. I will think it over and let you know, but I fancy we shall wish to see some stronger reason before we consent to take you into the slum work. Don't be afraid but that a reason will be 'sent along' if you are to come. I will talk it over with the general." Every religious organization has its peculiar phraseology, and to "send along" is a very common expression among the Salvation Army's servants. Thus they pray that the Lord will "send along" a Bible, a dinner, a bed, anything that is wanted; and when the things do not "come along," they declare that more faith is needed to bring them. They have a wonderful list of men to whom work has been "sent along" after conversion; and they forget that not only faith, but also hope and charity, visited these men when the Salvation Army made them brethren.

Ruth looked very much disappointed and a good deal perplexed where she heard the words of the superintendent. They pointed in a direction directly opposite to the one she had expected; and on the road she seemed to see a formidable array of difficulties, not the least of which was the shadow of the man who reigned supreme at the factory.

"But what can I do for the girls?" she asked. "I have never spoken to them except at Christmas."

"Then get to know them at once. Go and work amongst them as one of themselves, not as their mistress. So you will gain an influence over them, and you will see what this man Pember is doing in the factory."

"But he will object."

"Perhaps. How old are you?"

"Eighteen in a few months!"

"Well, then you will be his mistress. He knows that, and he is aware that when you are twenty-one you can take legal action. He cannot keep you out of your own factory."

Ruth rose up to go away, and she sighed rather heavily. It seemed to her so much easier to become a slum saviour.

The superintendent looked up at the picture of his wife, which hangs above the fireplace, and then his eyes fell on this girl, who had neither father nor mother, who had compared herself to a yellow duck fascinated by a serpent.

"You shall hear from me in the course of a week," he told her; "and remember that if you are to join us a reason is sure to 'come along.' Neither I nor any one else can keep you away, supposing that you are really wanted in slumdom."

It was a great disappointment to Hester. The old woman had made up her mind that she was to see Ruth safe in the Army. For a whole week she waited patiently, in order to hear what the superintendent would say after he had laid the matter before General Booth, and during that time she hoped against hope that Ruth would be received as a slum saviour. Once or twice she put on her bonnet, thinking that she would pay the superintendent a visit; for she said to herself:

"If he knew about the little girl's mother it would make a difference."

But she did not get further than the doorstep. The dead are sacred. Only to people like Captain Lobe do human beings tell such secrets as Hester carried in her breast about her mistress. She consoled herself with the thought, "Perhaps Captain Lobe has told the superintendent."

But at the end of the week Ruth received the following letter:

"Headquarters Slum Work, New Cross,
"*May 6th*, 1886.

"My Dear Comrade, Your request to become a slum saviour has been carefully considered, and I have decided that it will be better for you to remain where you are, and work for God and souls in connection with the corps of which you are now a member.

"Do not be discouraged at this decision, but go on more than ever you have done in the past in helping to pull down the strongholds of Satan in your own neighbourhood. The Army needs faithful Holy Ghost servants, as well as slum saviours, and you do not know until you put God to the test how much He will use you where you are. God abundantly bless you.

"Yours affectionately in the service,
"James Cooke
"*Superintendent*"

CHAPTER X

The Factory

A few days after Ruth received the superintendent's refusal to let her become a slum saviour, Mr. Pember might have been seen at half-past seven o'clock one morning shaving himself before a looking-glass. He belonged to the class of men who go grey prematurely. His moustache was black; but his hair had changed its original colour in order to correspond with his varied experiences. He had lived his life before he settled down as manager of the factory in Whitechapel. Now he meant to end his days in comfort. Neither for Ruth nor any one else would he exert himself. His father had died of paralysis, and a touch of the same complaint made him apathetic. He liked his pipe, plenty of wine and beer, and a good dinner. He enjoyed the routine of business. To get up, eat his breakfast, work at the factory, and then end his day at an East End club suited him exactly. He said to himself:

"Nothing shall interfere with me, certainly not the Salvation Army." He had listened to the idea that Ruth should become a slum saviour with complacence; but her request to work in the factory had made him twist his black moustache between his finger and thumb without speaking. Then he had asked for time to consider the question, saying to himself:

"They have put her up to this. They have an eye to business."

That morning he was to give her a decided answer, and while shaving he thought:

"I shall have to marry Ruth. There's no doubt of it. She's getting into mischief."

He had often contemplated this marriage as a thing that might be his fate some day, and the idea had never spoilt his dinner. She was a nice little thing, with golden hair and a good temper. Rather than give up the factory he would marry its mistress. So he had said to himself more than once, while Ruth was a little girl. But marriage was an awful nuisance.

"Well, directly Ruth is Mrs. Pember I shall send Hester about her business," he continued. "I hate that old woman's face, and her cant is enough to sicken any man of religion. But she would have saved me a great deal of trouble if she had persuaded Ruth to become a nun or something. I wonder who has put the girl up to this idea of working in her own factory! General Booth, I bet. He's an eye to business. I shall have to marry Ruth; it's the only way to keep her out of mischief. If those red vests think to get a penny out of *my* factory, they are very much mistaken. They had better try it on. But it's an awful nuisance to begin this love-making. I wish the little girl had become a nun. These Salvation Army people have an eye to the main chance. Give me a simple nun, who will pray all day, and think nothing about money."

Then he went downstairs to breakfast.

Ruth met him at the foot of the staircase, and held out her hand, with a shy "Good-morning."

"Would you like to come with me to-day, and see over the factory?" he asked, looking down on her.

"I want to work myself," said Ruth. "I do not care to see the people working."

"The girls were all taken on an hour ago," he told her. "They begin at seven in the morning and leave off at eight in the evening. Don't you think this idea of yours rather foolish?"

"I wish it," said Ruth.

"Very well. Then I will tell the labour-mistress to expect a new hand tomorrow." He added to himself, "Your father was the most pig-headed fool of my acquaintance; but I managed him, and I'll manage you, young woman."

Then they had breakfast.

Hester poured out the tea; Ruth cut the bread; Mr. Pember helped himself to some bacon. Certainly he was very good-looking. He had grey hair, and he was not young, but he was one of the devil's own children. If it had not been for the taint of paralysis in his blood he would still have walked the earth doing a lot of mischief. The disease which he had inherited made him lazy; so he coiled himself up like a serpent, and only fascinated the yellow ducks thrown in his way when he was hungry.

"So I am to tell the labour-mistress that you will come tomorrow morning?" said he, after he had finished his breakfast.

"Tomorrow is Sunday," remarked Hester from behind the teacups.

"Well, then, Monday morning."

"Yes."

At seven o'clock the following Monday morning Ruth went to the factory, where she found a little herd of girls gathered together. The doors were shut, and the girls pushed up against them, jabbering and scolding like young magpies. A more miserable set of girls it would be difficult to find anywhere. They had only just escaped from the Board school; but many of them had faces wise with wickedness, and eyes out of which all traces of maidenhood had vanished. Their language astonished Ruth, for "the universal adjective" fell from their lips as a term of endearment, while the foulest names were given to girls they did not like, also blows and kicks by way of emphasis. The only girl who received any attention was a small, puny, lame creature. They helped her to a place near the entrance, and stowed her basket safely away on the doorstep. Of Ruth they took little notice, for she stood some way off from the rest, waiting for the door to be opened by the labour-mistress. She watched the fighting, and listened to the jabbering voices, thinking, "How different these girls were when they came to fetch their Christmas dinner." At last the doors were thrown open, and a tall, strong woman, in a clean white apron, appeared on the threshold. A dozen girls rushed past her; another dozen followed them. Then the labour-mistress stopped the way, and said:

"I only want eight more – six old and two new ones."

"Me! me! me!" cried fifty voices, while the girls pressed in upon her. But she threw them back like a female Hercules, and barred the entrance.

"Six old ones, I said. Now then, Mary Grey, and you, Susan Murphy, and you, you, you, and you. Two new ones. I'll have that girl with the clean apron. Let her through directly."

She beckoned to Ruth.

"It's no good to slang me," she told the girls, who were clamouring for work. "I never take on for less than two shillings a week. I know you'd come for eighteenpence. But then you'd be no use to me, you'd be fainting all day. You can't work without food. 'Taint likely. My price is two shillings and sixpence – two shillings for work, sixpence for good conduct. That's fivepence a day, and enough to buy bread with. Go and try somewhere else, and don't slang me. 'Tisn't my money."

She slammed the door in their faces, and as it closed upon them Ruth heard an angry roar of voices. The labour-mistress took no notice, but stood watching the girls who were hanging up their hats and jackets. Turning round, she said to Ruth:

"I say that the feathers working-girls wear in their hats ought to be put down by Act of Parliament."

Afterwards she led Ruth into a small room and shut the door.

"What made you think to come here like this?" she asked. "Mr. Pember's told me all about you. Why, the place belongs to you, doesn't it?"

"I came here because I could not become a slum saviour," said Ruth.

"My!" exclaimed the labour-mistress, "you're religious."

"I belong to the Salvation Army."

"Do you, now? Well, I've no doubt they have good and bad amongst 'em, like the rest. I don't go in for religion myself. You see I'm a bit of a scholar; I belong to a circulating library. I've not always been a labour-mistress. Time was when I studied, and somehow I thought you might be one of the new sort – I mean one of them that takes an interest in us."

"What do you mean?" inquired Ruth.

"Well, one as says that we're all equals. That's my doctrine, though I *do* stay on here grinding work out of poor girls for the capitalist. I've a mother to keep, so I have to put my principles in my pocket. But I believe in combination, fighting the upper classes, and justice. You shall come along with me some Sunday night and hear all about it."

"Where?"

At a Socialist meeting. I thought maybe you were a Socialist, as you've come down here like this to work among the girls, instead of looking on like a mistress. There's a deal could be done to help 'em. Mr. Pember, he just grinds 'em down to nothing. He won't give 'em a cup of tea even. I've spoken to him till I'm tired of speaking. It's no good to talk to the girls about combination, they're so down-trodden and mean-spirited. The best thing that could happen to girls just now would be a leetle pressure of the finger and thumb on the windpipe when they're just born, and don't feel any more than young kittens. Maybe later on it will be different but now there's too many of 'em, and they only add to competition, which, as the Socialists say, is playing the devil with us at present."

"But they have immortal souls," said Ruth, looking with wondering eyes at the labour-mistress.

"No one can say when the soul comes into the body," the woman answered, coolly. "Anyhow, I wish as some one had drowned me as a baby, for I've never had a minute to call my own since I was born, nothing but hard labour. I'm sorry for the girls, I am. Just a leetle pressure of the finger and thumb on the windpipe would be so good for 'em; it would save 'em from starvation."

The labour-mistress pressed her thumb against her finger, and seemed to see the girl babies vanishing by a heathen Chinee process, which we are taught to think barbaric. But who can say if the heathen behave so very badly? Day by day girls starve in the London streets, and live lives worse than death, while money is sent to teach the heathen not to murder their innocents.

"A leetle pressure of the finger and thumb on the windpipes of the girl babies would be so good for 'em," said the labour-mistress, "and so bad for the capitalist," she added, shaking her fist. "They use the girls to cut the throats of the men, and they say it isn't murdering."

"God is their judge," said Ruth, who was getting frightened.

"Yes, He is," said the labour-mistress, "for God is justice."

The labour-mistress looked about thirty. She was strongly built, and the muscles of her arms were well developed. Those arms had seen good service. With them she had lifted many a heavy burden in order to support herself and her mother. They often ached so much at night that she found it difficult to do household work, such as scrubbing, washing, cooking, mending, and carrying her bedridden mother to a chair near the window or the fireplace.

Stiff little curls were arranged on her forehead, across which Time had ruled lines to say how many years had passed by since she first saw daylight. High cheek bones and a narrow jaw proclaimed her to be "north country." The mouth gave a clue to her character; for lips cannot lie when shut: it is only when open that they deceive us. Eyes tell fibs, and smiles are hypocrites; but closed lips reveal secrets. The lips of the labour-mistress were almost colourless, and very thin. They quivered, even when they were drawn closely together, thus indicating an emotional nature kept in check by a great deal of determination. She was the sort of woman that a mouse sends into hysterics, but that buries her dead tearless.

Ruth formed a great contrast to this strong-minded spinster.

She had taken off her hat, so the labour-mistress could see the smooth, white forehead that lay below her golden hair, and the clear skin beneath which the red blood was coming and going. She raised her eyes to the face of the labour-mistress in a guileless way that the woman thought "silly."

"She's just the sort that goes into the Salvation Army," said the labour-mistress to herself; I wonder why they've sent her here like this?"

"Do you mean to preach?" she asked Ruth.

"Whom to?"

"The girls. If you do, they won't listen. They've no time for religion. It's work, work, work, with them from the time they get up till they go to bed, except on Sundays. I'll take you to see some of their homes, if you like. The places they live in aren't any better than pigsties. What can you expect of girls who only earn fivepence a day? And that fivepence sometimes has to go to keep the family. But they're good to one another, they are. You'd be surprised to see what they'll do to help a girl that's ill, and how they'll put themselves about to buy crape when a girl is dead and has to be buried. I couldn't keep the lame girl you saw on the doorstep if they didn't do some of her work; but sooner than see her turned away, they'll give up a penny. They have kind hearts, they have. I'm fond of them, though I'm obliged to keep them steady at work, as

I'm the labour-mistress. I've been a girl myself, and I know how hard it is to go on day after day doing the same thing without varying."

"But surely they get holidays," said Ruth, "in the summer and at Christmas?"

"Not they. Drilling's the only holiday they ever get – I mean being sent home because they come late, and kept a day or a week doing nothing. They don't like that, for it's better to work twelve hours a day than to go hungry."

"How many are there here altogether?"

"We've thirty-five on the books. Sometimes we take on a few extra, but that's our number. I like to get them straight from the Board school, for then I know what I've got to deal with. I do all I can for them if they're good girls; if not, I send them about their business. I don't mind their being cheeky. Cheeky girls generally have something in them. I never take on a Jewess. The East End is just overrun with foreign people, and that makes matters worse for us English. Last year I went to Hamburg in a sailing vessel, and I'll never forget the hold of the ship when I came back in it. It was full of Polish Jews and Russian beggars, with bundles of rags for luggage, and enough babies to fill a cabin. They'd have starved on the way if a lady hadn't given the steward money to make them pea soup; for they'd only enough money to pay themselves over here. You never in your life did see such a miserable set of men and women as those foreign wretches in the hold of that ship. They were all huddled together, hungry and sea-sick, with babies crying and husbands scolding, just a mass of rags and wretchedness. When we got to London it was Sunday morning, and a lot of little boats came to take us ashore. Well, we couldn't land for ever so long, because of those foreigners. They hadn't a penny to pay for landing, so the boatmen wouldn't let them go ashore, and the captain said he wouldn't have them back on his ship, because he'd got to clean it. Such a noise as they made with their foreign gibberish! And all the while the boatmen were swearing and growling, so that we couldn't get to land for a good ten minutes. I says to a policeman, 'Whatever will you do with these poor creatures?' 'Lock 'em up,' says he, 'till to-morrow morning.' 'What will become of them then?' says I. 'The Jewish Board of Guardians will fetch 'em,' says he, 'and some sweater will take 'em into his shop to undersell us English.'"

She stopped, out of breath.

"No," she continued, shaking her fist to give her words emphasis, "I never take on a foreigner. It's bad enough for us English, and I won't help to make it worse by giving work to a Jewess."

"Then *you* get a holiday sometimes?" Ruth said.

"I'll tell you how it is. I take the place of a stewardess, and she comes here as labour-mistress; so I get a trip for nothing. I'm going again this year; but wouldn't you like to look over the factory before you begin to work? I won't tell any one that you're the mistress."

So Ruth was taken to see her factory, which is like the hundred-and-one small factories that lie in the neighbourhood of ___ Square, by the river. It is a four-storied house, about fifty years old, built of yellow brick. It has large cellars below the ground floor, which are used as kitchens. At its entrance is a small office in which sits Mr. Pember's factotum, a youth of nineteen, who is forever changing. Behind this youth's sentry-box is Mr. Pember's sanctum, into which readers shall enter by-and-by, when they have been shown over the factory.

Ruth followed the labour-mistress up some steep stairs to the top of the house, and into a room where the slanting roof left little space for "hands" to move about. Long deal tables stood against the walls, and beside these were a dozen girls making farthing surprise pockets. Tubs full of cheap wooden toys, and boxes holding broken sweetmeats, were placed beside the workers, also pots of paste and piles of coloured paper. When they went in two of the girls were kissing, and this sight roused the ire of the labour-mistress, who said:

"Kisses between women mean nothing. I've seen women kiss that have longed to scratch each other's eyes out. Go on with your work, and keep your kisses for your sweethearts."

The girls were all standing up. There was neither stool nor chair in the place. The lame girl sat on a tub full of cheap toys and jewellery, with her feet on an old box. She turned her sickly face towards Ruth for a minute. Then she went on with her work.

"These are made in Paris," said the labour-mistress, taking a handful of small toys from a tub, and showing them to Ruth. "It's wonderful how they can make the things so cheap! Someone must starve to supply children with farthing surprise packets, and as the girls here get fivepence a day, I suppose the people that make these starve in France or Germany. It's just the same with the sugar-plums."

"I've heard Mr. Pember say that sugar is very cheap," Ruth suggested.

"It's not the sugar that's cheap, it's the labour," the woman said, diving her hand into a box of broken sugar-plums. "One reason the girls like to come here is that they can eat this stuff till they're sick. I tell them it's bad for their complexion. But they don't listen to me. Eating sweets keeps them from feeling hungry."

Then she conducted Ruth to the next landing, and introduced her to a dozen girls who were dipping white sugar mice in chocolate. Vats of chocolate were arranged against the walls of the room, and into these the white mice were dipped by small maidens who had just left the Board school. Girls brought the mice on trays from the kitchen, and gave them to "hands" who were mere children. These puny things stood by the vats, inhaling the sickly smell of the chocolate, dipping a finger into a vat and afterwards sucking it. They looked up when the labour-mistress opened the door, then continued their work of dipping and ornamenting, drying and packing, as though they had been bits of machinery.

"They must get very tired standing all day," Ruth said to the labour-mistress.

"Yes," the woman answered. "But Mr. Pember thinks that sitting down makes them lazy. He has let me put a form in the back yard when they have their dinner, but he won't have a chair in the working-rooms, not even in the kitchen."

"No holiday all the year, and standing all day, with half a crown a week for wages!" Ruth said to herself.

"How long do they work?" she asked the labour-mistress.

"From seven till seven, with an extra penny an hour when we keep them on in the evening. Come down into the kitchen."

They went into the cellars. There they found a dozen girls and two men, cooking. All were covered with powdered sugar from head to foot.

The whole place had a snowy appearance. Powdered sugar was on the floor, the tables, and cupboards. Powdered sugar ornamented the rafters of the ceiling. Some of the girls had wrapped their heads in pocket-handkerchiefs, the rest had hair like snow. On the oven stood large open saucepans full of boiling syrup, which the men were stirring, also small pots and pans holding condiments to make cocoa-nut chip, chocolate, and cheap sugar-plums, such as one is wont to see in the shops of pastry-cooks. Girls cut cocoa-nuts into shavings, and threw the shells into heaps to be sent away to another manufactory. Syrup was poured into tins, and set to cool in places a little less hot than a furnace. Balls and bars of sweetstuff were broken up and stowed in bottles. Hot cocoa-nut shavings were thrown upon crystallized sugar to give them a shiny appearance, and chocolate was put into moulds with cream in the middle. The place was so hot that Ruth felt the perspiration streaming from her face. There was not a window to ventilate the room, only one or two doors which led into other cellars. Powdered sugar filled the air, also the smell of cocoa-nut, mixed with half a dozen other scents, such as vanilla and chocolate.

"You look faint," said the labour-mistress; come and see the yard I've made Mr. Pember give the girls for their dinner. They've made it into a bit of a garden. It's hot here now the summer's coming on, but in the winter all the girls want to work in the kitchen.

The "bit of a garden" was about eight feet square, and surrounded by four yellow walls. It contained a mound of earth, surrounded by oyster shells, and planted with creeping jenny, which was the "hands" attempt at a green-house (so it was designated by the labour-mistress). A long form stood opposite the mound of earth, for the girls to sit on while they had their dinner. And in the centre was an Aunt Sally made of cocoa-nut, with a hideous grin on her face, and two arms which held in their grim embrace a surprise packet. This prize fell to the lot of the girl who could knock it down with a stone or a stick, which missiles were kept beneath the seat ready for the only fun these girls might indulge in.

"You've seen everything now," said the labour-mistress. "I must begin my work, or I shall have the girls getting into mischief. But perhaps you would like to have a look at the guv'nor's office."

Ruth followed her past the factotum's box into a room which was fitted up with every possible comfort. For a moment she stood still. This had been her father's room. She did not know the bitter hours he had spent in that place, but she was aware that he had sat there before Mr. Pember.

While she was looking at a card above the fireplace, which tells people to call in business hours, transact their business, and then go about their business, she heard the labour-mistress say:

"Here's the guv'nor himself! Whatever will he think of us?"

Turning round, she saw Mr. Pember at the door of the office.

CHAPTER XI

The Labour-Mistress

The labour-mistress now appears for the first time before the public; so readers must pardon rather a lengthy sketch of her character. She is living in this year of grace 1888, and is a fair specimen of a strong-minded proletarian spinster. She would attend women's-rights meetings if she knew where they take place, and agitate for the enfranchisement of her sex if she knew how to agitate. Her ideas about Socialism are vague, for she has no time to study, and little time to think; but she believes in justice, and she hates the capitalist. A string of words and phrases, such as "exploitation," "bloated aristocrat," "white slavery," and "the emancipation of labour," dangle like charms before her eyes. She sees the words, but they elude her grasp, for they were not written in her School Board lesson book, and she has no money to buy a new-fashioned dictionary. On Sundays she tries to "improve her mind," with the help of a circulating library, which contains many three-volumed novels and a few standard works. The latter she has long since "finished." Such libraries are not meant for strong-minded proletarian spinsters, but for clerks and young ladies in business. She lives far away from the British Museum Reading-room, where she might graze among a herd of like-minded ladies.

She would rejoice the hearts of the learned gentlemen who sit there in the Centre, who declare that too many readers like fiction for their mental pabulum.

"Bring me Weeds," she might hear an official there say to an attendant, while gazing severely down on a fair reader who has asked him if Ouida can be found in the catalogue.

As to the young men who inquire why Zola's "Piping Hot" and "How jolly life is" have no place in catalogue Z, they are sternly told that the reading-room is meant for students. Among these students strong-minded spinsters form a large percentage; and to the credit of the Centre, it may be said, that such people are seldom sent back to their seats empty-handed.

The labour-mistress will soon be made familiar to readers of fiction, for directly a new character appears on the boards of romance, she or he becomes the property of novelists.

The strong-minded proletarian spinster will come before us half a year hence in a variety of garments. She will be put in the novelists' character-box, and be made to dance with their other puppets. Before she becomes common property, readers are invited to look at her once again, standing outside Mr. Pember's sanctum, shaking her fist at the capitalist.

She has drawn back to let Mr. Pember pass into the room, and has closed the door upon Ruth and the serpent. The expression of her face cannot be seen, for the passage is dark, but the action of her arm and fist is sufficient. To the glory of the sex, it shall be said what a woman has invented! Look at the arm of the labour-mistress. Who will wonder, then, that a woman taught men round-hand bowling? What could not that arm perform if it were emancipated from merino and print, if it had better things to do than box the ears of factory girls, and shake an impotent fist at the capitalist!

Men have (so they say) a surplus of muscle, and women a surplus supply of nervous energy. Hence the second great invention of the sex, typical of suppressed strength which is evanescent. Sodawater was given to the world by a woman; and yet men say "women have no inventive faculty."

"Show me a woman who can climb the mast of a ship and shoulder a gun – then I will believe in the equality of men and women," says a well-known cardinal, before whom nuns bend the knee in great humility.

The reign of muscular force is said to be well-nigh finished, and men, having prepared the rough ground for women, are now, we are told, making way for the gentler sex in all places, even in politics. Untamed instincts are being trampled underfoot, and we are about to see "a glorified humanity."

This being so, women must begin to emulate the few virtues which men have left; they must no longer indulge in eaves-dropping and gossip. Alas for the cause of the strong-minded spinsterhood! The labour-mistress dropped her fist, and put her ear to the keyhole of the capitalist's sanctum in order that she might hear what was going on there between Ruth and her master. When Satan wished to lead our first mother into mischief, he traded on his knowledge of the female character. He knew that the rib of Adam had been infused with subtle stuff of which curiosity formed a strong ingredient. So he whispered in Eve's ear a variety of things, while his evil head lay close beside the fruit she was coveting. And ever since that time women have inherited our first mother's weakness. Curiosity has made them lovers of eaves-dropping and gossip.

The labour-mistress crouched down with her ear to the keyhole, and was so intent on listening to the voices inside the room that she quite forgot Mr. Pember's factotum. This youth rustled his newspaper and chuckled with masculine contentment.

"So like a woman!" he said to himself. "Nice sort they'd be to manage the country."

He thought of the many disputes he had had with the labour-mistress on the subject of politics. Then he began to read the Parliamentary summary, saying to himself, "Women are so foolish!"

The labour-mistress put her right eye to the keyhole, and screwed her left eye into the smallest possible compass. At first she could not see anything, but presently her efforts were rewarded. She saw Ruth sitting on a sofa almost opposite the door, and Mr. Pember standing close by, with his arm on the mantelpiece. The girl's face was very pale, and her hands were crossed on her knee,

"Poor little thing!" ejaculated the labour-mistress.

Then she heard Mr. Pember say, in a low voice, while he looked down on Ruth:

"'For you to come here like this is quite ridiculous. Of course I cannot say you shall not do it, but you must know that I feel for you a fatherly

– a more than fatherly interest. If I have not shown this in words, it is because I think deeds of greater importance. Anyone can talk. A girl who has money is sure to hear a lot of talking. Men will make love to you for your money. Even now they are beginning to do so; I happen to know one man who has an eye to more than your golden hair, a fancy for this place, which he thinks is a good business. Well, the factory is doing well now, but when I took it up your father had muddled the books, and it was a poor look-out. He made me your guardian, and I did not thank him. If I had not felt an interest in the little orphan consigned to my care I should not have stayed in a place like this. But I considered you a sacred trust, left to me by – ah – ah – by Providence. You may have thought me indifferent, but I had my eye on Hester while she brought you up, and I did not interfere because I could see that she was doing her best, that she was – ah – ah! shaping the ways of the Almighty. I do not talk much about religion myself; but I have taken care that you should have what is called 'a religious training.' And I have looked after your interests in this place, I have served you faithfully, and I have asked for no reward except the gratitude which I felt sure you would give me later on, when you were old enough to understand what I had been doing. Sometimes I have been anxious. I have said to myself, ' She will not accept your faithful service, she will prove an ungrateful mistress.' But again I have fancied from time to time that you were not indifferent to me, that I was becoming to you something more than a guardian. I did not speak sooner because I felt that you were too young to make a decision; but in a year you will be mistress of this place, and then you can send me away or keep me. If I stay it will be on one condition, and that is, that you recognize my services. Money is nothing to me; I do not care for money. What I ask is the reward of long years devoted to your interests. Only one reward is possible, and you can guess, I think, what I mean without making me speak more plainly."

"I do not understand," said Ruth, casting a frightened glance towards the door, feeling that she would like to escape from this man, but fascinated by him. "I am very grateful for all you have done; but I am sorry you stayed here, Mr. Pember."

"Sorry?" he asked, in a reproachful voice, bending down so near that his breath moved her hair, and made her shudder. "Oh, Ruth, if you knew how I love you!" he said, drawing closer, "if you could have an idea of the anxious years I have spent in your service!"

He sat down beside her, but when his arm touched her waist, she gave a shriek that made the labour-mistress hastily leave the keyhole, and the factotum drop his newspaper.

A minute later she was in the passage, having slammed the door of Mr. Pember's sanctum in the face of that astonished gentleman. She put her hands out in the dark as if to protect herself from some unseen presence, and she walked straight into the arms of the labour-mistress. Her head fell on the shoulder of the strong-minded spinster, who folded one arm round the girl's waist, while she extended the other towards Mr. Pember's door, and said, shaking her fist, "*The capitalist!*"

It is the age of personalities. Weekly papers chronicle the deeds of remarkable men and women, and the *Star* has a whole column every day "mainly about people." Novels have ceased to revolve round a plot, or to be philosophical treatises. The mental history of a man, the emotional nature of a woman, absorb the novelist. People are flayed alive to please a personality-loving public. No one is safe from the interviewer's visits, not even a royal princess who devotes her time to art-needlework and the distribution of soup-tickets.

Those of us who are compassed in by coffins, who walk the earth surrounded by the faces of dead friends and relations, shrink from the reviewer's pen as if it were dipped in caustic. We plead not to be noticed. But the interviewer drags the skeleton out of our cupboard by main force, rattles the bones in our face, and is surprised to see us getting angry.

A notice in the *World*, a paragraph in *Truth*, what greater glory can mortal desire, unless it be a place in the *Star*'s galaxy of fixed planets? Reviewers do not wait for people to be dead and decently laid in a coffin, before they bring the scalpel out of their pocket. They dissect living men and women in broad daylight. They call all this "legitimate curiosity," and are astonished to hear that their scalpel gives pain to sensitive men and women. Alive or dead, a man's personal history should be respected; and no reviewer has any right to tear away the veil which shields him from the gaze of the public. It is just as unlawful to display a man's inner life to a gaping audience as it would be to seize his clothes and leave him to walk about stark naked. Adam and Eve made to themselves aprons of fig-leaves after they had tasted the forbidden fruit, and at the same time they devised a covering for their thoughts and feelings, the warp of which is speech and the woof of which is silence.

All this is *à propos* of the labour-mistress, who stands with one arm about Ruth, and the other stretched towards the door that hides Mr. Pember. In order to interpret the expression of her face it would be necessary to take the skeleton from her cupboard and rattle before her the bones of a ghost laid some years before – the ghost of a man who was dear to her then, although he happened to be a capitalist.

"'I know him well,'" she said to Ruth, in tones of suppressed fear and anger. "I know him well, and I hate him."

Then she led the girl into her little office, and threw open the window. She had despised the would-be slum saviour at first, but a revulsion of feeling had begun to set while she watched Ruth sitting on the sofa in Mr. Pember's room; and when that shriek made the factotum drop his newspaper, she swore inwardly that she would protect the factory's mistress.

"Let us shake hands," she said to Ruth. "You've got one friend in this place, at any rate, and that's me, Jane Hardy."

CHAPTER XII

The Factory Girls

From that day the labour-mistress devoted herself to Ruth's interests. She would not let the girl work with the "hands," saying that as her "help" Ruth would be in a better position to render them assistance.

"A great deal can be done to improve their condition," she said, briskly; and she added, in a lower voice, "Don't give in. Stay on here. I'll help you to fight Mr. Pember."

That same evening she took Ruth to see the homes of some of the girls who worked in the factory. "You can't form an opinion about the hands," she said, "until you have witnessed their environment."

"Environment" was one of the words she had picked up at Socialist meetings; and she did not quite understand it. When Ruth asked her for an explanation, she hesitated, and then said, "It means the filthy places they live in, where there's nothing to lift 'em up, and a great deal to pull 'em down; where they see nothing but wretchedness, and become old women before they've been children."

The first house they visited was the home of the lame girl, the one who could not have been admitted into the factory, or "kept on," but for the generosity of her fellow-workers. She lived in a little alley not far from Aldgate, a narrow place, into which Ruth followed the labour-mistress. The houses there were not numbered, but each door had a hieroglyphic upon it, unless it was known by an old boot in the first-floor window, or by a coloured rag that waved on a stick above the entrance. The alley was paved with large, uneven flag-stones, between which sprouted weeds and grass that had a sickly appearance. On the stones were scores of ragged children. Some scooped up the dirt with oyster shells to make mud-pies of it; some lay on their backs, catching the water that dripped into their dirty hands from an old pump. Three small boys sat on the pump-handle, regardless of angry voices that issued from the surrounding windows; and half-a-dozen girls craned their necks to see a thrush in a cage near the entrance. By-and-by the poor captive would cease to beat its head against its "environment," and chant a country dirge in cockney language. Then a lean cat would begin to prowl about near it, looking down on it with glittering eyes that seemed to say, "I am watching for my opportunity," and if the cat escaped stones thrown by boys bent on mischief, it would one day furnish a "tit bit," and there would be nothing to pay for it.

The labour-mistress pushed through a door that had neither latch nor key, and led the way up a dark staircase. It was a two-storied house, with a loft at the top, and cellars at the bottom. Two old women lived in the cellars, the labour-mistress told Ruth, or rather one old woman, for the other was just dead, and would have to be buried. "I went yesterday to see the one that's left," the labour-mistress continued, "and I found her broken-hearted. She was sitting beside the coffin, and she said to me, 'Who'll pray for the living now she's gone; who'll pray for the living when she is buried?'

"I couldn't make out what she meant for a minute, but she explained herself 'Sally used to say, "God help the living," night and morning; and I always said, "God help the dead."' Then she began to cry again, and she wouldn't look at the bit of crape I'd brought along with me, although poor people like her generally find comfort in mourning. You see those two were sisters; and now the one's gone the other feels as if a bit of herself was going to be buried."

"What did she die of?" inquired Ruth.

"Old age," answered the labour-mistress. "At least that was the name the doctor gave to her complaint. He was a clever young man from the London Hospital."

Then she knocked at a door on the top landing.

It was cautiously opened by a woman with a very pale, thin face, who said in a relieved tone of voice, "Oh, it's only the labour-mistress."

"Whom did you expect to see?" inquired the strong-minded spinster, while she beckoned to Ruth, and followed the pale-faced woman into a dark, low room. "Why did you look at me in that frightened way?"

"I thought you was the landlady," the woman said; "you'll excuse this untidy place, but I've no time to look after it. I'm out scavengering if I've got no work at home. But I've just got in a lot of match-boxes, and if I can get them done they'll pay the rent. I thought it was the landlady come to say as she must have the money."

Half the room was filled by a large, low bedstead, and there lay the lame girl asleep, with her crutches resting against the bundle of rags that served for a pillow. A dirty blanket covered her feet, and across her breast was the little coloured triangular shawl that the factory girl buys so cheap, and which she rejoices to wear with a smart-coloured feather. One arm was stretched across her face to keep out the daylight, the other lay on the bed. Her untidy hair fell about her head and neck, looking as if neither brush nor comb had ever come near it.

"She's had no tea," the mother said, apologetically. "I fetch the leaves from a tea shop where they taste samples, but today these match-boxes came in to be done, and I've had no time to go after 'em. Sara fell on the bed when she came in, as you see her now, labour-mistress. Her hip has been painful lately, and I think I'll have to let her see the parish doctor. But for her four shillings we'd all have been in the Bastile long before this, so I hope you'll not turn her away from the factory. She's a good girl, and she gives me all the money, but she's not strong. You see she was born on the workhouse doorstep, for they wouldn't take me in until I was ill, and then I fainted at the door of the Bastile. The other children are right enough, but Sara can't expect to be different."

Meanwhile the woman's hands were busy with the match-boxes. Strips of magenta paper and thin pieces of wood came together with the help of a paste-brush. They were then thrown on the ground to dry, forming pyramids of trays and lids which would presently be made into match-boxes, tied up with string, and sent back to factories which give $2\frac{1}{4}d$ per gross for match-boxes. Two little children stood on the floor amidst the trays and lids, and an older boy chopped wood in a corner of the room with a look on his face of hungry impatience. The babies, who had on apologies for petticoats, were quarrelling over a jam-pot full of water, and seemed hungry enough to devour their own naked toes if their mother did not make haste to finish the matchboxes. The room showed that poverty reigned supreme among the inhabitants, for it had no furniture but the table, the bed, and a few old hampers; a heap of coke was near the fireplace with which to dry the woman's work, also some cabbage leaves and onion stalks. This refuse the children would eat later on if nothing else was forthcoming. It had been thrown in as fuel by the vendor of the coke, and a dog would scarcely have swallowed it. But in these days animals are better off than slum children. (The owner of that alley has been heard to say, "My dog turns tail when I go in; it's so disgusting.")

"Has your husband found any work yet?" the labour-mistress asked, after she had glanced at the girl on the bed.

"None, labour-mistress. He's been out selling lighters at public-houses, them bits of sticks the boy's cutting there in the corner. But yesterday he went almost to Woolwich before he took a farthing, for matches are getting so cheap, publicans don't care to buy old-fashioned lighters, and he's losing the business. If it wasn't for Sara we'd have to go into the Bastile, so you won't turn her away, will you? She does her best, labour-mistress."

"I couldn't keep her on if the other girls didn't do her work," answered the strong-minded spinster.

"I know that. But they'd do anything for my girl, they're so tender-hearted. They often give her a bit of dinner middle day, and take her home to tea of an evening."

"It's wonderful how the girls about here stick together," the labour-mistress told Ruth while they went down the dark staircase. "I often think when I hear people talk about communism at Socialist meetings they'd be surprised to see the way girls go on in factories. I don't mean to say that their language isn't filthy, and they don't fight and push when there's a lot of them together, but for generosity I'll back them against any set of men, let alone women. And if you once touch their feelings you can twist them round your little finger. They'd be a fine set if only their homes were decent. I'll take you to see one that's ill. She came to me as a little thing from the Board school, and now she's got what the doctor calls a complication, that is, a lot of diseases without any name in particular, the sort of thing that carries off many of our girls before they become women. I think it's brought on from want of proper food while they're growing, for most of them have someone at home to help, and fivepence a day isn't much to keep a girl, let alone her family."

They went into a house not far from the alley, and mounted the staircase. No one said "Come in" when the labour-mistress knocked at the door of the room she wanted, so they walked into the place without waiting for an invitation. It was getting late, and the room was dark, but they could see the face of the girl by the light of a small lamp, and the figure of a woman who was sitting on the bed beside her. This was her mother. The poor thing seemed stupefied with grief, unable to do anything but gaze at the face, and listen to the laboured breath of her child, who was quietly sinking down into the dark valley. A cup, half full of milk, was on the table beside the bed, also a crucifix. Some pictures of saints on the walls showed that the women were Roman Catholics, and a rosary that lay in the girl's hands proved that she had said her beads during her last moments of consciousness. Her mother did not cry, but mute suffering is terrible to witness, and the labour-mistress turned away to look out of the window before she attempted to say anything. Then she asked in her quick, practical way

"Do you need money?"

The mother hesitated; afterwards she said, "There's only one thing, labour-mistress."

"What's that?"

"She *did* say as she'd like to meet the Almighty like a lady. I've got her white muslin dress, in which she made her first communion, to lay her out in. I'd like to think as she'd stand up before the Almighty in a pair of white silk stockings."

The woman's face showed so much dumb distress that the labour-mistress suppressed her thoughts, which were to the effect that to believe in the resurrection of the body in white muslin and silk was a sort of realism with which she had no patience. She knew that death is *the* great event in the lives of poor people, so she stopped to meditate over the mother's request, instead of giving the abrupt reply that rose to her lips, "You are a silly Papist."

Below in the street carts rattled, men shouted, and children cried – all was confusion and noise. Here in the little dark room the factory girl lay unconscious, with a mother who would soon be exceedingly lonely. The labour-mistress knew what it meant to come back after the funeral, and see the empty bed, "the bits of things" that would never more be wanted, and the rosary that the factory girl's lips had pressed before death sealed unconsciousness. She looked at Ruth, who whispered:

"How much?"

"Three shillings and sixpence."

Ruth took the money out of her purse, and gave it to the labour-mistress. Then they went away, softly. Neither spoke for some time, for Ruth was thinking of the dying girl's face, and her companion was pondering over the mother's strange request.

"To meet the Almighty like a lady," said the strong-minded spinster to herself, "a hand who has lived in the slums of Whitechapel on four shillings a week. It's ridiculous!"

The lamps had been lighted in the streets, and seeing them, Ruth suggested that it was getting late.

"Hester will be looking out for me," the girl said. "If she goes to the factory and finds it shut up, she will be anxious."

"I will take you safely home in a few minutes," answered the labour-mistress. "I must just inquire after a girl who left me six weeks ago through illness. Her father is out of work, and I have heard that she is getting into mischief. I will tell you where the difference lies between the work of men and women," she continued, putting her arm round Ruth for a minute, and then drawing back as though anxious not to appear demonstrative. "Men must labour or beg. Women can always earn money. *Earn* it, I say, and so help their family."

Ruth looked at her with puzzled eyes, while she continued to discourse about the female labour market. She seemed to know all about it, and she expressed a wish that the upper classes might one day suffer for the way in which they encourage white slavery.

"Don't tell me they are ignorant of what they do," she said, in an angry voice. "Human nature is the same in a garret as in a palace, and a royal princess can, if she chooses, put herself in the place of a factory hand who is obliged to live on fivepence a day and help the family. Virtue is easy enough when a woman has plenty to eat, and a character to keep, but it's quite a different thing when a girl is starving."

They reached the house she wanted before her sermon was finished, and went to a door on the first floor. There was an attempt at order and cleanliness about this place. The boards were covered with sand, and the walls had lately been whitewashed. Two little children sat on the staircase sucking their thumbs. It was an artisan's dwelling, and its inhabitants were removed from the slummers by as many degrees as exist between a duchess and the wife of a man who is pushing his way into London society.

"Does Fanny Smart live here?" the labour-mistress asked one of the babies.

The child took a small red thumb from his mouth, and pointed to an open door. Then they went in without knocking.

Squalor is less painful to see than respectable poverty. That room, from which thing after thing had been sent to the pawn-shop, told a piteous tale to the labour-mistress. The girl she wanted was not there, only the father and the mother. When these two people saw the strong-minded spinster their faces took on a guilty appearance. The man did not rise up from his chair. He laid his arms on the table, and buried his head in his shirt-sleeves. The woman began to cry, and to wipe her eyes with an apron made of sackcloth. No one spoke, but the babies came in, and took their place in front of the labour-mistress. They could not tell what it all meant, and Ruth was equally astonished. The youngest boy went to his father, and tried to push a small fist between the shirt-sleeves. The man drew the child on to his knee, but did not raise his head from the table. He could hear his wife sobbing, and he knew without looking up what was taking place. At last he heard the labour-mistress say:

"Where is Fanny?"

A long story was told by the mother. Fanny had not been able to get a place after she was turned away from the factory. Her father was out of work, but he hoped to find a job every day, and if he went into the Bastile he was a ruined man, for employers never take on a pauper when other men are forthcoming. The home must have been broken up but for Fanny, and she had said herself that she would not go into the workhouse. It would not be for long. Her father was a hard-working man, and he *must* find employment in a few weeks, for he was out all day looking for work. And, after all, it wasn't anybody's business to come and interfere. Fanny had been turned away from the factory.

"I've tried my best to get charing," the mother said. "But work is slack for men and women, and we have to depend on Fanny for our living."

The labour-mistress did not attempt to argue; she accepted the inevitable with a sigh, and turned to leave the place.

The man got up from his seat to open the door for her, and she saw on his face a look of anguish. He bent his head down to whisper, in an apologetic voice:

"It's ten shillings a week, labour-mistress."

CHAPTER XIII

A Penny Gaff

After Jane Hardy had taken Ruth to see the "environment" of the hands, she wished the girl to visit their places of amusement. Ruth said "no" at first, for the Salvation Army does not approve of music-halls and penny gaffs. It classes such places among the pomps and vanities of this wicked world, and says that they should be avoided. But at last she persuaded Ruth to accompany her, and she called for the girl at the house of the Whitechapel slum saviours (those who live in Angel Alley) one evening, just as the clocks were striking seven. Ruth had gone there to fortify herself against that insidious enemy of all religious denominations, *the World*, that many-headed beast which they all fight against, but which obtrudes its head, nevertheless, even in charities and pulpits. She opened the door when the labour-mistress knocked, and introduced the strong-minded spinster to the slum lassies, who were counting *War Crys* at a long table.

"God bless you," said the eldest, without looking up from her work.

"Come in," said the other. "Ruth, give her a chair. We shall have finished these *Crys* in a few minutes."

The labour-mistress looked about her rather suspiciously. Although she believed that the Army contained good, bad, and indifferent people, like every other organization, she thought that poke bonnets and red vests probably cover a good many hypocrites. This was her first introduction to real Salvationists. Ruth was but a neophyte. These girls worked night and day, and lived in Angel Alley. So she made a mental inventory of their "environment," and the first thing that attracted her attention was General Booth's likeness, in the centre of an almanack.

"Who's that?" she asked Ruth.

"The Chief."

"Who's he?"

"The head of the Salvation Army."

She gave a sniff. Then she looked at the texts on the walls, and at the list of rules for slum lassies.

"Knee-drill at six o'clock!" she exclaimed. "What does that mean?"

"Praying."

The room was small and narrow. A long table stood beneath the front window. Forms and chairs were piled up at the further end, under a window that looked out on the St. Jude's playground.

"What are *they* for?" she asked Ruth, pointing to the seats.

"Meetings," Ruth answered. The people come in here to get saved. Sometimes they are invited to tea, but generally they come in to be made holy."

"We had a woman beautifully saved here last night," remarked a slum lassie. "She had been a great drunkard, and her husband is an infidel. We mean to get him fully saved before we have finished. It is wonderful how the Lord helps us. Souls seem to fall into the Salvation net wherever we spread it."

The labour-mistress walked up to the table, and looked critically at the speaker.

"What are you going to do with these?" she inquired, laying her hand on the *War Crys*.

"Give them away in the doss-houses and the publics. We must have some excuse for going into these places, so we carry *Crys*, and the Lord goes with us."

The speaker looked about twenty. She was dressed in a short skirt made of some dark blue stuff, and, a blue vest with Salvation embroidered on the breast. Her smooth brown hair was plaited about a head that would have been dismissed without any comment by the professional phrenologist. Her grey eyes were facsimiles of those which look out from beneath the veils of nuns in convents. But her eyes were wide awake, while those of nuns are generally quiescent.

"Are you not afraid to go into dosses and publics?" the labour-mistress asked.

"I have never been afraid of anything since I came into the slum-work," was the answer. "You see, the Lord protects us. He knows that we have no one else to take care of us."

"He has just given us a Jewess," said the other slum lassie, "a woman near here who couldn't get any peace in churches and chapels after she gave up her own religion. She has suffered a great deal of persecution; but now, praise the Lord! she is wholly converted."

Just then a fife-and-drum band was heard in St. Jude's playground, and a herd of children swarmed into the yard at the back of the slum lassies' house.

"It's sad to see the things that go on in that place," said one of the slum saviours, "and to think that a clergyman is at the bottom of it! They hang up lanterns sometimes across the yard, and the people dance for hours to the music. I don't know what they're up to in that St. Jude's parish, but I hear that their goings-on are meant to advertise the church, and bring it into notice."

"You don't mean to say that you are speaking of Mr. Barnett!" exclaimed the labour-mistress.

"I don't know who he may be," said the slum lassie, "but I think it's a sin to spend money on music and lamps while people are starving, and that a clergyman should try to save souls instead of letting sinners dance straight from Whitechapel into hell. There's sorrow and sin enough about here to make Christians mourn in sackcloth, especially when they think that some of the poor creatures must burn forever. A lot of money is spent on the Church of England, so it seems queer to me that we never meet clergymen in the doss-houses and the publics – only sometimes a city missionary. If General Booth had the money that's paid to clergymen he'd storm the whole of London; there would not be a man or a woman then that could say on the judgment Day, 'I never heard the Gospel.'"

"But Mr. Barnett is one of the best men living," said the labour-mistress. "He's brought happiness into the lives of people like me – people that have no chance of seeing the world and of knowing what is going on in it. He's started lectures and classes, and all sorts of things to improve the minds of the working classes; and his church is a sight to see, with its flowers and pictures on Sunday. It's not every one can be satisfied with your Salvation drums and hymns. Some folks, like myself, want other things to satisfy us."

"Lectures and classes won't help you much on the Day of Judgment," the slum lassie said, solemnly. "There's a dear woman lying dead not far from this house. She talked just as you do about flowers and pictures when she was well; but she sent for us on her death-bed, not for Mr. Barnett or his curates. That sort of religion may be right enough for those who understand it, but I say that for an East End clergyman to countenance it is to place a stumbling-block in the way of ignorant men and women. I daresay that Mr. Barnett is a good man, but he should go to the West End, where people can understand him."

"It would be a bad day for people like me if he went away," remarked the labour-mistress. "People can't all think alike, and his sort of religion suits a lot of men and women who laugh at the Salvation Army. I don't laugh myself, but I know others that think you very foolish."

"Are you saved?" inquired the slum lassie.

"What do you mean?"

A knock at the door prevented the girl from explaining. The visitor was a woman, bent almost double by age, and wrapped in rags from head to foot. Her costume would not have fetched twopence in the Old Clothes market. As she came in the labour-mistress moved away, but the slum lassie greeted her with a "God bless you, granny!"

"My dear," the old woman said, "I've been to see the clergyman, and he told me I'd better go into the Bastile. 'I've kept my independence,' says I to him, 'by begging and sleeping on doorsteps, and I didn't come to you to be insulted. On threepence a day I'd be quite happy. If your Master was here,' says I to him, 'I'd not be spoken to so scornful.' Then I asked him to let me see his good lady, and he says to me, 'I'm not married.' Now, I couldn't tell him what I wanted, for that was nothing but a nightdress. So I went away just as I came, and here I am with no good advice from him but to go into the Bastile."

"Never mind, granny, we'll pray, and the Lord will send along a nightdress," said the slum lassie.

The labour-mistress whispered to Ruth, " It's time for us to be going," and hurried out of the house before the slum saviour could ask her any more questions.

"A little Salvation goes a long way," she said to herself. "I've no doubt they mean well, and it's impossible to think that those girls are not in earnest. Salvation religion may suit slummers, but it isn't fit for the educated. As to hell, I don't believe in it, any more than do those St. Jude's folks. That's why they don't bother themselves to 'save' the slummers. They think it best to give them a little happiness here, instead of bothering them about a Hereafter."

They left Angel Alley and turned into the Whitechapel Road. When they reached the gaff in which the midget was wont to exhibit, the labour-mistress stood still for a minute.

"No, we will not go in here," she said then. "I will take you to a gaff where they have a Biblical exhibition. I should not like you to see a monstrosity."

So saying, she turned down a side street, and walked quickly on until they reached a small doorway.

"Come in here," she said to Ruth, "and you shall see our Lord's Last Supper, done in waxwork."

"Waxwork Cosmorama and Panorama, programme one penny!" shouted a little girl at the entrance, "giving a description of the East London Palace of Royal Waxworks, containing our most gracious Majesty Queen Victoria, Napoleon the Third, the Shah of Persia, Joan of Arc, and Lady Flora Hastings. Also Sir Moses Montefiore, one of the most remarkable men of a remarkable race; kind Old Daddy of the Lambeth Casual Ward, made popular by a visit from a Lord, who, seeing the kindness of Old Daddy to the paupers, made him a present of a £5 note; the late John Brown, a faithful servant to the Queen; Henry Fuller, mail-driver of Australia, who was murdered at his post defending Post Office property; Johnnie and Maggie, a curious couple, who walked all the way from Land's End to see the Queen, who gave the old lady eight shillings a week for life; and Madame Rachel, the beautifier of London, who obtained £1,500 from Mrs. Barrowdale for making her beautiful forever, and was sentenced to five years' imprisonment at Millbank."

The little girl stopped, out of breath; but began to shout again, in a shrill voice:

"Henry the Eighth and his wives, the beauties of Paris, Moses in the bulrushes, marriage of the Prince of Wales, and Wild Boar Hunt; Old Sarah Blunt, who lived to the age of 114; model of a head of a murdered woman who was murdered in Paris; blunderbuss used in the time of Oliver Cromwell; saddle-bag found on the battle-field after the battle of Waterloo, with black stains of blood on it; and lamp of Queen Anne, said to be the only one in England, very curious, and the Lord's Supper and the Twelve Disciples."

"Where is the Lord's Supper?" inquired the labour-mistress.

"Through the curtain, on the right, just before you come to the Chamber of Horrors," the little girl answered. " Have a programme? only one penny. That will tell you all about everything but the tattooed man; he sells his own programmes, what he's made hisself."

The labour-mistress pushed through the curtain, and entered the East London Palace of Royal Wax works. She was followed by Ruth. The first thing they saw was "a royal group" of wax figures, dressed in satins and silks, with grinning faces, wearing wigs, staring fixedly at one another. The place was dimly lighted, but soon their eyes became accustomed to the semi-darkness, and they were able to see "The Lord's Supper" done in waxwork. A long table, spread with a white cloth, on which were bottles filled with dark liquid, and glasses coloured with the same stuff, stood on some boards to the right of the palace. By the table sat thirteen wax figures, clad in many-coloured garments. In the centre was (according to the catalogue) "the Redeemer, meek and grave, who shows, and almost shades His deep anguish, which does not alter His beauty, greatness, and majesty." He is gazing into the distance, and John, with long yellow hair, leans on His breast. Close by is James, the Just, "who inquires with energy from all who he thinks can inform him;" also Bartholomew, who "is doubtful and uncertain about what he hears;" Andrew, who "is struck with wonder and amazement;" Peter "who interrogates with anger; "James, "who is horror-struck;" Simon, "who doubts;" and Judas, "who, amazed at being discovered, composes himself with an ill-disguised deceit."

"Ain't it life-like!" exclaimed a woman who held a market-basket. "Ain't it a picture!"

"They look as if they'd walked straight out of the New Testament," answered her companion.

Ruth turned away, feeling that the representation of "Our Lord's last Supper" was out of place in this East London Palace of Royal Waxworks. She found the labour-mistress engaged in conversation with the tattooed man, who was exhibiting the calf of his right leg, on which the Immaculate Conception has been depicted.

"A Biblical subject," said the labour-mistress

Then the tattooed man gave a short sketch of his previous existence.

"In the year 188_ I and a friend started for the Black Hills, and then went on to Salt Lake City. Leaving that place, we were surprised by Redskin Indians, disarmed and disrobed, and condemned to die at the stake. While we partook of sage-bush tea, jerked venison, and grasshopper bread, a council of war was held. We were then tied to trees, with our hands upwards, the Indians howling and dancing round us, and gathering dry leaves to burn us. After the war-dance was concluded I was brought before the chief, who conversed about me with a half-breed. I was then tied to a tree, and the painful operation of tattooing commenced. For six and seven hours a day during six months the painful operation was continued, during which time five hundred and seventy designs were tattooed on my body. After the, first five days' working my eyes began to get sore, and five weeks from that time my body was so swollen and sore that I could get no sleep. Still it was a pleasure for those Indians to see me tortured. It was worse than a thousand deaths. After six months I made a most remarkable escape, but I never knew what became of my friend. He was taken to another place."

The tattooed man paused, and the audience crowded nearer to him. Lads of twelve and fourteen stood close by with open mouths, gaping. One small lad crept up to his leg and poked a wet finger into the centre of the Immaculate Conception in order to see if it "was painted." The women wiped their eyes when he spoke of his sufferings, and the little girl who sold the programmes shouted out:

"Come and see Captain Pan Fisher, the tattooed man, and hear him tell about his marvellous escape from the Redskins."

"One night the Indians were greatly fatigued with their day's excursion, and composed themselves to rest as usual. Observing them to be asleep, I tried various ways to see whether it was a scheme to prove my intentions; but after making a noise and walking about, I found there was no fallacy. After a little consideration, and trusting myself to Divine protection, I set forward, naked and defenceless, on my rash and dangerous attempt for freedom. I reached the foot of the mountains, and there I heard the 'wood-cry' which the Indians make when any accidents happen to them. I concealed myself in a hollow tree until the evening, when I renewed my flight, and the next night I slept in a cane brake. The next morning I crossed, and got more leisurely along, returning thanks to Providence. But how shall I describe the fear, terror, and shock that I felt when, on the fourth night, a party of Indians who lay around a fire nearly out, heard the rustling I made, seized their guns and ran towards me. To my great astonishment and joy a parcel of swine made towards the place, and on seeing the hogs the Indians returned to the fire, and lay down to sleep. Bruised, cut, mangled, and terrified as I was, I still, through Divine assistance, was enabled to pursue my journey until daybreak, when I lay down alongside a great log, and slept undisturbed until about noon. On getting up I proceeded to the top of a great mountain. Looking round to see if I could spy any habitations of white people, to my unutterable joy I saw some, which I guessed to be about ten miles distant. I approached a farmhouse, and the farmer gave me a night's shelter and a suit of clothes, also a ticket for Colorado, where I went into a hospital. As soon as I got well I was visited by all the showmen in the country, who wanted to engage me, and since then I have exhibited in the principal American cities."

Captain Dan Fisher then showed the audience the five hundred and seventy devices with which the Indians had embellished his skin, failing, however, to answer the sceptical questions of the labour-mistress, who wanted to know how Redskins could have depicted on him St. George and the Dragon, a man of war, King Sol, and the Immaculate Conception.

"They learn these things from the half-breeds," was the reply. So saying, he turned away to satisfy the curiosity of an old lady, who was poking him with her umbrella, and pointing out his tattooed dress to his admiring audience.

"You're not going away already?" said the little girl with the programmes. "Why, you haven't seen the Chamber of Horrors yet! That's best of all." And she added, "It makes your flesh creep."

The strong-minded spinster looked doubtfully down the wooden ladder that led into a subterranean den, and then went slowly towards it.

"You had better see everything," she told Ruth.

"Our girls come chiefly to places like this, and they don't think that they get their pennyworth unless they feel their flesh creep." Ruth followed her into a cellar lighted by jets of gas, in which there was an earthy smell, and damp air that seemed to fall like lead on the chest of all who came down the ladder. She drew back, for against the wall stood a ghastly row of murderers, made of wax. An old man, bent almost double, was pointing them out with his stick to a number of boys and girls, saying in a sepulchral voice:

"This is Frederick Baker, who murdered little Fanny Adams in the hop-fields, and stuck her head on a hop-pole. He was executed at Newgate, 1871."

"This is Owen Jones, the murderer of the Marshall family, eight in number. The inhuman monster despatched his victims one after the other with a blacksmith's hammer.

"This is Dr. Pickett, who poisoned his patient at Glasgow, and was hung for the crime.

"This is William Cole, who murdered a German sailor on Plaistow Marsh, and hid his head in the reed beds, where it was discovered by a large dog.

"This is George Manning, who, with his wife, murdered a Custom-house officer named O'Connor, and buried his body under the hearthstone in their house.

"This is William Corder, who murdered Maria Martin in the Red Barn, which murder was discovered by a dream, and Corder was hung for it."

The hideous words seemed to fall on Ruth's brain like the heavy thuds of a hammer, and she gazed with fascinated eyes at the speaker and the crowd of boys and girls, whose faces showed that he was making "their flesh creep." Whispers echoed along the sepulchral den, and the audience huddled closely together, as if they were afraid of the murderers' ghosts as well as of the wax likenesses. At the farthest end of the room was a ghastly scene, towards which the cicerone was approaching. The crowd hid it from Ruth's view, but suddenly she saw half a dozen women and men being murdered, or in the act of murdering. A confused mass of wax figures, on the ground, in bed, anywhere and everywhere, met her gaze. Blood was running like water from the throats of victims, and fiends, armed with knives, were attacking women and children.

The cicerone's words were lost in the screams of his audience, but Ruth could hear the word "murder."

She fell against the wall, gasping for air, unable to speak, looking with imploring eyes at the labour-mistress.

The strong-minded spinster lifted her up as though she had been a baby, and carried her up the staircase, past the tattooed man and the little girl with the programmes.

"Now you have witnessed the factory girl's environment," she said, when they were safely outside the East London Palace of Royal Waxworks. "You have seen her work, her home – and her amusements."

CHAPTER XIV

Among the Socialists

The labour-mistress need not have hesitated to take Ruth into the gaff in which Napoleon the midget had been wont to exhibit.

Napoleon was dead. That afternoon Captain Lobe had seen his coffin lowered into a small grave in Bow Churchyard, and had watched the earth fall big on it while a clergyman read the burial service. There had been only one other mourner present – the lady he had wished to see when he was dying. The owner of the gaff had not thought it worth while to follow him to the grave, and he had shaken his head when he was asked, "Have you any relations?"

No one knew where he had come from, and no one could tell where he was going to. He died in his sleep, and he was buried at the expense of an agnostic. No clergyman came to see him while he was ill, only the little Salvation captain. A priest read his burial service; but while he was alive no minister of religion thought it worth while to visit a midget.

After the service was finished Captain Lobe walked away, followed by the lady. They passed through the long lines of tombstones, the hearses, and mourning carriages into the street. For some time both remained silent. Captain Lobe was thinking of the midget's glorified body; his companion's thoughts were with the man who lay in a child's coffin. The Salvationist was glad that the midget had been "fully" converted, and the lady was saying to herself, "At any rate, *his* sorrows are finished."

When they reached High Street their attention was attracted by a man who was talking in a loud voice to a very small audience. They stopped for a minute to listen, and hearing the words "class oppression," passed on with the comment, "A Socialist."

"Are those people doing any good, do you think? Captain Lobe asked his companion. "I believe you know them pretty well. What are they doing?"

"Nothing."

"Nothing?

"Well, next to nothing."

"Why is that?"

"Because they are so jealous. They cannot work together. They split up into small parties, and spend their time in quarrelling. They have a paper called *Justice*, which is in the hands of a few working men, and managed by the chief of the Federation. The same things are repeated in it again and again. Before it leaves the press every one knows exactly what will be said and what will be avoided in it. It is just the same with the lectures. Sunday after Sunday the same things are said to the same people, and there is no change unless the lecturer happens to be an Anarchist,"

"Well – then?"

"Oh, then it is rather amusing. We are told how bad things are for the working classes, and afterwards we are asked to go to sleep and wake up Anarchists. I heard a charming little lady speak to eighty practical working men about Anarchism the other day, and when she was pressed to say *how* the change would come about she told them that she had not come to the lecture-hall with any solution of *that* question, but that she supposed some day every one would rush out into the streets, a revolution would take place, and we should all become Anarchists. The men laughed, of course, for Englishmen like to see the next step, and even then hesitate to take it. They listen rather scornfully to Socialists, because they do not think that the Socialist programme comes within the sphere of practical politics. Anarchism is to them a farce, unless it has dynamite behind it. They look upon English Anarchists as amiable lunatics."

"Are you a Socialist?" inquired Captain Lobe.

"In a way. I believe in the principles of Socialism; but, like every one else, I get tired of seeing so little accomplished. The Federation used to frighten people, I believe, a few years ago, but now it is a mere bogey. Its clubs are like butterflies –

'Born in a bower,
Christened in a tea-cup,
Dead in half an hour.'

Its little papers have their day and cease to be; in fact, are born prematurely. The purpose of these seven-months' children seems to be the abuse of Socialists. Sometimes the abuse is dull, sometimes it is amusing. If these papers do not afford scope enough the quarrels are carried into some Radical journal, and afterwards a meeting is called to decide which party has been the most virulent. I suppose there are five or six little Socialist papers always going on, besides *Justice* and the Socialist League organ. Of course they do not pay their contributors; but Socialists write in them when they have nothing better to do, and so they consume the smoke of the Socialist party."

"What sort of men become Socialists?"

"Enthusiasts, men without much power, but with a great deal of good feeling. These men see the misery of our present social conditions, and throw themselves into Socialism as a forlorn hope, expecting to be worsted. The amusing thing is that these men, who are *all* well-meaning, are so suspicious of one another. You hear them say, 'Oh, So-and-so would be all very well if one could feel quite sure that he is honest.' Or, 'I think his intentions are right enough, but he knows which side of his bread is buttered; one can't help seeing that, and feeling sorry for it.' Can anything be more comical than this? All Socialists must live on bread-and-scrape, and not one of them has a chance of anything but the Union here. Very few of them believe in a Hereafter. So why they do not swallow their petty jealousies and pull together I cannot think. But I suppose they cannot help it."

"How many parties are there at present?"

"The Social Democratic Federation heads the thing, and Mr. Hyndman is at the top of it. It has branches all over the country, and talks very big; but its numbers are few, and its funds are next to nothing. Then there is the Socialist League, under Morris, the grand old poet, and a man who calls himself 'a stalwart Socialist,' but who looks as if a breath would blow him into space. You may have seen his face on some of Morris's papers. He has blue, eyes and pink cheeks; in fact, he looks like a David about to slay our present competitive system with a pebble and sling. But why indulge in personalities? That is a common fault among Socialists, and one that ought to be avoided. I should like to 'take off' the Fabian Society, but I will not do it. They are well-meaning people, who listen to a lecture every fortnight, and when it is done tear the lecturer to bits and flap their little wings over his carcase."

"Are there not some men who call themselves Christian Socialists?"

"Yes, I believe such people exist; but I do not think that they are making much progress."

"You are prejudiced against Christians," Captain Lobe said, reproachfully." Surely you have come across some true followers of Christ?"

They were passing through a back street not far from the London Hospital. A small tavern, with open windows, attracted their attention, and they stood still to look in, while Captain Lobe was speaking. Half a dozen men, half a dozen women, surrounded the bar, laughing and drinking, joking and swearing, dressed in rags – besotted drunkards.

"Perhaps I am," was the reply. "I know that in London one out of every four is at the present time starving; and I see sights that haunt me night and day – little children too weak to move for want of food; mothers groaning over their babies; and fathers coming into a place like this to drown their wretchedness. Why, only the other evening I went into one of these places with a slum lassie, and a man said to her, 'Talk to the guv'nor behind the bar, don't preach to us. He is more to blame than we are, and if you can't do nothing with him, then go to the brewers and give *them* a sermon.' I know that there are many good Christians, but I consider that the state of the London poor gives the lie to our ordinary nineteenth-century Christianity."

She stopped speaking for a minute. Then she said, "Perhaps, after all, it is *au fond* an economic question. Socialists think this, and they say, 'We intend to do away with all this degradation and misery.'"

"Well, how are they going to do it?" inquired Captain Lobe, whose eyes were fixed on the people inside the public-house.

"I cannot tell you. So far as I have seen we should not stand in need of Socialists, if the rule of 'Love thy neighbour as thyself' had ever been, or could even now be put into practice. A few have loved their fellow-men too much, and these have been crucified. Most have loved too little, and the result is our present social condition. Socialists teach combination instead of competition; they demand the land and the means of production for the people, and they say, '*A bas* the individualist.' It is just possible that the Church will have to study economics, if it wishes to hold its own in the struggle that is coming. At any rate, it can no longer put away the problem of poverty; it must scotch the snake, or the snake will coil about the neck of the Church, and strangle it."

"I thought you said the Socialists were doing nothing," Captain Lobe objected.

"So far as their organization is concerned – yes. But Socialism is in the air, it is touching every one, and tingeing everything. Many who abhor the name are greater Socialists than those who hold Socialistic tenets. Some professing Socialists seem to think that a man is orthodox if he wears a red tie and blacks his own boots; that a woman is a sincere believer if she cleans her own grate, and wears a gown tied with a string round her waist. Such people are a poor sort of advertisement. With their help – or in spite of it – Socialism is growing every day, both the sentiment *and* the economic theory. What it will become in time no one can tell. At present its most hopeful sign is an embryonic labour-party. This party is spreading all over the United Kingdom. It is a new Chartist movement, with twice as many points as were contained in the old Charter. I prophecy that in two years' time – say in 1888 – all the most promising Socialists will go into it, leaving the scum to die a lingering death in the League and the Federation."

At that minute a little girl ran screaming out of the public-house, holding both hands to her mouth. Blood streamed through her fingers and down her dirty dress. She stopped, and spat two teeth upon the pavement.

Captain Lobe caught her in his arms, and tried to staunch the blood with his pocket-handkerchief.

"Daddy did it," she said, sobbing; "he kicked my mouth. Oh, I'm killed, I am! Let me go! I lost sixpence, and Daddy's murdered me; let me go! oh, let me go!"

So saying, she tore herself away, and ran down the street, followed by a crowd of ragged children.

"I thank God every day that I am not clever," Captain Lobe said to his companion. "An intellect is a snare of the devil, it seems to me; a misery here, and a stumbling-block in the way of the Hereafter. Why, I should go mad if I did not believe in heaven for these people; their lives would not be worth having if this world ended everything."

"But you believe in hell, too," was his companion's reply, "and that must give you a great deal of anxiety."

"It does," Captain Lobe answered, earnestly. "Sometimes I wake up with the perspiration streaming from my face, trembling all over. I seem to see Satan carrying off my people, and I get up to pray for them. It was a terror of hell that sent me into the Salvation Army. I went through tortures as a boy from fear of it, and when I was fully converted I felt that I must spend all my time in saving sinners from damnation. I was brought up in the Evangelical religion, but that did not satisfy me. Then I became a Methodist. Last of all, I joined the Salvation Army, and I shall leave it directly I find any religious organization that is more in earnest."

"Do you ever doubt the doctrines you preach?"

"Of course not. Why should I? But I suffer all the same," he said in a lower voice. "I seem to feel myself in my people, and I know that, do what I may, I cannot save them all, I cannot get them all fully converted. In heaven we shall not see the damned, or know what they are suffering; but here we are made to realize hell in order that we may not relax our efforts for a single minute. I love my people," he continued, while his face beamed on the wretched men and women through whom they were passing. "I sometimes feel I could leap into the burning pit if only I could save my people from it."

He did not look more than eighteen; but he was older, most likely, for his eyes had a wider range of sympathies than those of boys have, and his voice was strangely gentle and sympathetic. One does not often hear a voice like it, either in the East or the West End of London; but then there is in this world only one such little Salvation captain. If he had not worn an S on his collar he might have been taken for a Volunteer captain, for he was neat from his short-cropped hair to his boots – so spick and span, no corps need have been ashamed to own him. His face was very earnest, and his manner was that of an enthusiast.

"I wish you would tell me your history," the lady said. "Ever since I met you down here, working among the scum of Whitechapel, I have wondered who you are, and where you come from. I know about half a dozen earnest men, and you are one of them."

"Who are the others?" he inquired, laughing.

"One is the labour-master at the London Docks, and another is the head jailer at Bow Street."

"Well, my history is simple enough," he said. "I mean, so far as my outer life is concerned. My inner life has been everything. My father was a village apothecary. He died when I was very young, and I can scarcely remember him. But my mother –" he looked across the road with a wistful expression on his face. Then he went on again, "My father left her just enough to live upon, and we had a little cottage outside the village. I was meant to be a schoolmaster, but I always had a call – I mean a wish – to preach, to teach grown-up people instead of children. My mother used to say that from the way I said my prayers as a boy she knew I was meant for the ministry. But the thing that drove me into it was the terror I went through before my conversion. I mean the fear of eternal damnation. I used to think of hell – nothing but hell; and I could see no escape from it, for sins used to grow up in me, I mean wicked thoughts – blasphemous."

"What sort of thoughts?"

"I remember one. I used to think that the Holy Ghost was the mother of Jesus. That is the unpardonable sin, I said to myself. I was afraid to tell my mother about it. Later on I was troubled about predestination. Lost! lost! lost! I used to hear the devil saying. So it went on for some time, and then –"

"Then?"

"I got fully converted."

"How?"

"Through the Holy Spirit."

"After which you joined the Methodists?"

"Yes."

"How long is it since you went into the Salvation Army? "

"Two years. When my mother died I had no heart to stay down in the country. Some Salvationists came to our place, and they persuaded me to join the Salvation Army."

"Are you satisfied with it?"

"What do you think of it yourself?"

"The Salvationists I have met are very much in earnest, but some of them are dreadfully irreverent."

"We must make ourselves fools to save the foolish," Captain Lobe said. "You have no idea how difficult it is to keep the attention of the people who come to our places of worship. The men and women I get, for instance, never enter a church; and if I did not keep them interested they would not come to another meeting. I never allow any noise at our holiness meetings. If roughs come in then I turn them out, and sometimes I give them in charge of a policeman; but in the streets, and at our ordinary services, I let the people shout and sing. I do all I can to keep them interested."

They reached the little room called "the barracks," and Captain Lobe said, "Come in. It is only a short service!"

The place was almost empty. A few roughs in flannel neckties and fustian, half a dozen girls with rough hair and dirty faces, were gathered near a table. Behind the table, on a raised platform, sat some men and women. It was a holiness meeting. Hearing this, the roughs and the girls went away, leaving the forms almost empty. But Ruth was there, also old Hester. A smile came over Captain Lobe's face when he caught sight of Ruth's golden hair, and the lady noticed it.

"I wonder," she said to herself, "if this little Salvation captain has time to make love; and if so, how he does it?"

CHAPTER XV

Captain Lobe on "Worldliness"

That evening Captain Lobe took for his text, "Love not the world." He said, "Our godfathers and godmothers promise for us at our baptism that we shall fight valiantly against the world, the flesh, and the devil. The flesh we can see, the devil we can imagine – but the world, what is it? We talk of its pomps and vanities," the little captain said, "and we call men and women who indulge in them worldly. We would not be seen at a theatre, in a ball-room, or on a race-course. But we sometimes forget that other things come under the title of 'Worldliness.' When we read the history of the Church, we find its leaders struggling for power, trampling weaker brethren under foot, asserting themselves in high places. At the present time there are bishops and archbishops in the Church, who live in state, who wear robes, and keep large numbers of servants, who expect the inferior clergy to call them 'my Lord' and to kneel for their blessing. I once belonged to the Church; and while I was a member of it, I often asked myself, 'Can such men really be followers of that Jesus Who preached self-abasement and abstinence?' No, they look for a King Who will come in the clouds of heaven; they have forgotten the Son of the carpenter who preached the doctrine of self-sacrifice. I left the Church, and joined the Methodists. Among them I found the same spirit of emulation which is so contrary to the doctrines of Christ, who said, 'If any man desire to be first, the same shall be last of all and servant of all.' Children outside, as well as inside, the Church are taught to win prizes, to get to the top of the class, and parents forget that such lessons contradict all Christ says about love, humility, and meekness. Young men are told to 'get on,' and no one points out to them the evils of ambition; no one says to them, 'If you succeed in the race of life it will be at the cost of others; they must be humiliated if you are to triumph.' Believe me, my brothers and sisters, the world. is no outside thing which displays itself in pomps and vanities – it is within us, it is *the lust of the spirit*. We talk of the lust of the flesh – those carnal appetites which the devil tempts us to indulge in – and we forget the lust of the spirit – those spiritual appetites of rivalry, ambition, jealousy, and emulation which kill the soul, just as the carnal appetites kill the body. Now I fear to see in the Salvation Army this lust of the spirit. A few years ago there was no such thing as a Salvation Army; but at the present time our numbers are increasing – we are becoming powerful. Our power comes from the fact that as yet we have kept under this lust of the spirit, and men who do not believe in the doctrines we preach recognize that we are in earnest. Directly we forget the words of St. Ignatius – 'It is better for a man to hold his peace, and be, than to say he is a Christian, and not to be. It is good to preach, *if* what he says he does likewise' – our power will die, we shall cease to be a reality. There are men and women at the present time who put aside all except Christ's moral precepts, but who accept these sayings of His, and base upon them their conduct. Such people are severe critics. They read the text, 'Blessed are the meek; for they shall inherit the earth,' and they laugh to see the professed followers of Christ compromising as our clergymen of the present day compromise, murdering as our soldiers murder, cheating as our merchants cheat, lying as our statesmen lie, in order to succeed in life, to make money, or to become famous. They say, 'All this is against the example and teaching of Christ. Why do those who practise these things call themselves Christians?' My brothers and sisters, as yet the Salvation Army is free, except in isolated instances, from worldliness. Let us be on our guard against it. We fight against the lust of the flesh, and the devil who tempts us to indulge in it. Let us remember that Satan is still more on the alert to tempt us to indulge in the lust of the spirit."

After the holiness meeting was over the people went home; the place was locked up, and Captain Lobe put the key, in his pocket. Then he followed Hester and Ruth towards ____ Square, where they sometimes spent summer evenings.

Captain Lobe on "Wordliness"

The old woman had drawn Ruth's hand through her arm, and when Captain Lobe came up he was struck by the wonderful look of peace that had settled on her face. Some people have a genius for unselfishness. It is a mistake to think that genius can only manifest itself in art, science, and politics. There are also moral geniuses.

Hester was one of these, and those who believe in spirits would say that a good genius animated her moral faculty. She looked fondly down on her adopted daughter. If she had been Ruth's mother according to the flesh she would probably have been less indulgent. But love like hers can do no mischief, for it is purged from all things low and sordid; it is without the dross of selfishness. There is no love on earth so free from stain as that which a nurse lavishes on another woman's children.

Captain Lobe came up singing –

"We shall meet beyond the river,"

and this made Hester draw Ruth still closer. She thought of the girl's mother, and, thinking, she became conscious of a vague fear about Ruth's future. If only she could see the girl safe in the Salvation Army! Something might happen to herself; she might die, perhaps, and then what would become of Ruth? The story of the interview in Mr. Pember's room, which Ruth had told her, made her tremble for the factory's mistress, supposing that she should be taken away before Ruth joined the Salvation Army.

Then she looked at Captain Lobe, and she seemed to see a way out of her difficulty. She had thought of it before, but that night the idea took hold of her. He must marry Ruth. General Booth could not object to that. Ruth must marry Captain Lobe. That was it.

The moon was full, and in its soft light even the dirty streets and the broken-down houses looked picturesque, as they passed under a bridge in Leman Street. There they met the labour-mistress. She was, hurrying along, with a book under her arm, towards the room she shared with her invalid mother. Her whole soul was athirst, poor thing, for knowledge. In her was a bitter rebellion against the present state of society; for that state forced her to work so hard all day that her brain ached when she tried to read in the evening. She stopped to look at Ruth, and for the first time she felt jealous. The girl was talking to Captain Lobe in the shy

123

way which sometimes comes about when the other sex happens to be religious. Ruth's face wore the expression which the faces of girls often wear while talking to curates. A young clergyman is to them something above the ordinary run of men; they invest him with a garb of holiness because he happens to wear a white surplice. They are like plants in dark rooms struggling towards the light, and they fancy that the light shines for them on the faces of young clergymen. If the curate is a married man the charm is broken, but they think that a celibate can understand their yearnings after holiness, those aspirations which make nuns flee from the world, and throw themselves into the arms of Jesus. It is the habit of strong-minded spinsters to laugh at these things because they cannot fathom their meaning; consequently, when the labour-mistress saw Ruth looking at the little Salvation captain as if he were a superior sort of creature, she felt angry with her sex – angry and jealous. For it was easy to see that Hester's wish might be accomplished. Captain Lobe took no trouble to hide his feelings, not even in the presence of the labour-mistress.

She walked with them a little way, but soon she wished them "Good-evening," and turned her face homewards. The bitterness in her heart was increased by what she had witnessed. She asked herself *why* Ruth was surrounded by all this affection, while she, Jane Hardy, lived with a grumbling old woman. "Force," "the survival of the fittest," "surplus value," all the names that puzzled her so much, that stood for things she could not grasp, she would have bartered at that minute for half an ounce of love, for a few grains of affection.

Presently she reached Tower Hill. There she leant her head against the railings, and watched the moonlight playing on the old walls of the Tower. She thought of all that had happened in that place, the prisoners she had read about.

"Ah, well," she said to herself, "it is something to be able to read. Reading makes one feel of so little consequence. Soon I shall be dead, and it will not matter then if I have been happy or miserable, learned or ignorant. But I wish I had more time for reading."

A bugle sounded in the moat, and the sound carried her thoughts back to the days when she had been young, like Ruth – ah! then it had been different. She had not thought then that she would have to spend all her life as a labour-mistress. She had loved some one then very much, and he – what had he done?

He had robbed her of children.

She raised her head and looked at the passers-by as if they could guess her thoughts. But they went their way, they were altogether oblivious. So she rested her forehead again on the cold railings, and confessed to herself that perhaps after all she had made a mistake.

"I might have married," she said to herself, "only I could not love the men who wanted to marry me. I never could care for any one but Mr. Pember. I do not care for him now, I hate him – he is a capitalist. He has robbed me of children. I shall never feel a child's little arms round my neck; I shall never, never hear the word 'Mother.' It is all his fault. He gave me no peace until he could see how dear he was to me, then, because I would not give in to him, he went away. He never meant to marry me. I kept my virtue, as they call it, and here I am, a withered-up woman, with this hunger for children. It will not, die till I am dead; books and work will not kill it. I hate him – the capitalist!"

A self-educating woman is very pathetic, much more pathetic than a self-educating man; for a man generally falls back on his masculine dignity, and asserts that a thing is as he thinks it to be, while a woman worries herself and every one else with her consciousness of ignorance. The East End is full of people who seek to educate themselves with the help of secularist and socialist lectures, Sunday discussions in the parks, and circulating libraries. They pore over the stalls of second-hand books in the Lane, and finger old volumes outside the shops of literary merchants. They are afraid to speak of their difficulties because they think that better-educated people will laugh at their ignorance; so they muddle on, and die regretting their inability to grasp that interpretation of the universe which our learned men call science. The pain these men and women suffer from mental indigestion can be witnessed in lecture-halls on Sunday evenings, while they listen to things that are beyond their understanding. They carry away words and phrases to puzzle over during the week, and sometimes they give the things they have heard quite a wrong interpretation, or use them in an exaggerated sense that takes away their meaning.

It was thus with the labour-mistress. She had heard the capitalist abused by socialists, and she looked upon him as her natural enemy. It did not occur to her that Ruth was a capitalist, but she used the term to express her wrath against the man who had "robbed her of children."

The abusive epithet did not exorcise her bitterness, however; it only made her feel more wretched than before by adding fuel to her angry feelings. She left Tower Hill, and instead of going home to her invalid mother, she turned her steps to _____ Square, thinking as she went about her daily life, and wondering if she could possibly alter it. "No," she said to herself, "while mother lives I must go on slaving in that place; work is difficult to get, and if I give it up we shall very likely have to go into the workhouse. Slave all day, that is my life, with no time to learn, and no hope to see what the world is like, unless I take a stewardess's place on a boat, and then I just go to the other side of the water and back, without seeing anything but sick folks."

She reached the square through the Thieves' Alley, passing by a public-house outside which were loafers and sailors, also girls dressed in beads and gaudy petticoats. The square lay like an oasis in the midst of East End degradation and wretchedness. It was closed to all people except those who could afford to pay the clergyman of the neighbouring church a yearly fee of two guineas; consequently Ruth and Hester were almost the only women who made use of it during the week, although on Sundays business men smoked there, and talked politics. Tall trees hid the grass-plot in the centre, but the labour-mistress could see the leaves moving in the night breeze as she came close up to the iron railings. Then she heard voices; and presently she caught sight of the Salvationists sitting on a bench near the entrance. Ruth had taken off her hat, and had laid her golden head on Hester's knee. The old woman was looking fondly down on her. Close by sat Captain Lobe. He was talking in an earnest voice, and his eyes were fixed on the factory's mistress. Jane Hardy could not hear what he was saying, although she put her ear to the railings, and listened for at least five minutes.

"Why should a weak little thing like that have so much love, a girl made of wax, that any one can twist into any shape they like?" she asked herself. "He's talking to her about religion, I expect, and she's looking at him so admiring, just as if *he* was anything to worship."

She turned away. Just then the bells of a neighbouring church sent their music floating over the square. The music smote the heart of the labour-mistress. It brought back the old religion, and spoke of the dead Christ. Overcome by her loneliness, the poor thing did not think where she was walking until the coarse laughter of gaudy girls and drunken men forced her to realize her surroundings. Still the bells rang out their sweet music, speaking to the lonely woman of the things she had lost in the course of her mental and moral development.

"Better be a silly little girl with golden hair than a strong-minded spinster," she said to herself. "I might have married over and over again – if I had not had such a contempt for the men about this place – if I had not cared for Mr. Pember."

She disappeared in the dark streets.

The little group of Salvationists talked on, quite unconscious of all the passion and pain they had been causing. Hester's face showed placid contentment, for she seemed to see her wishes accomplished. "Then," she said to herself, "my work on earth will be done, and I can join Ruth's mother in heaven!" She passed her hand thoughtfully over the girl's white forehead and listened to Captain Lobe, who was pouring forth his hopes for Whitechapel, saying how he meant to get the slummers fully converted.

The bells stopped ringing, and Hester said that it was time to go into the house. But Captain Lobe talked on, and Ruth seemed glad to listen.

So they lingered in the little oasis, feeling far away from the trouble and sin of Whitechapel, talking of all that must be done before they left earth for heaven.

While they were sitting there in the moonlight, Mr. Pember came into the square. His appearance showed that he had come from a class above the one he worked amongst. Why he lived in the East End, and contented himself with his surroundings, it is not possible to say in this story. Perhaps the taint of paralysis in his blood made him lazy. He had not troubled himself about Ruth since the day on which she had screamed in his office.

But the voices of the Salvationists attracted his notice, and he walked up to the iron railings. He stood still for a few minutes with an amused smile on his face. Then he said to himself:

"Sweet innocence!"

CHAPTER XVI

The Police Court

Captain Lobe continued his daily work. The following morning he went to the London Docks soon after six o'clock to look for a man who had come to him for advice and assistance a few days previously. He arrived before the gates were thrown open to the mob who go there to "pick up a living," and stood in the crowd talking to his acquaintances until the bell commenced ringing. Then a dash was made by the ragged crew for the entrance, and he was lifted off his feet by the men. They bore him along with them to the place where the contractors take on hands, and set him down near the policemen whose business it is to keep order among the applicants for tickets.

He stood by the bell looking for the man he wanted, jostled by the dock-labourers, and hustled by the policemen. Some of the contractors had taken possession of the little wooden pulpits, others had ensconced themselves behind iron railings.*

The marks of a dock-labourer's fist embellished the countenance of one contractor, and he seemed to have a wholesome dread of brickbats, for he threw anxious glances at the hands of the men while he distributed his tickets; another looked down on the herd that swarmed about his pulpit, and listened to the angry growling of the men with apparent indifference; a third took on his "preference" men, and let the rest scramble for his remaining tickets. And all this time the bell twanged

---

* These iron railings have now been replaced by wooden bars, because some of the men were, according to the words of the labour-master, "nearly cut in two" in their attempts to get the tickets.

dismally above Captain Lobe's head, and it seemed to say, "Hungry! hungry! hungry!"

It was a dull morning. A heavy mist hid the ships in the harbour, so Captain Lobe could only see the unskilled labour-market, and hear the roar of the dock-labourers' voices until the bell stopped ringing. Then those men who were "not wanted" went sulkily away, and left him alone with the policemen.

"You had better have a look for your man in the warehouses," they told him. "Perhaps he has been on night duty; if so, you will find him among the woolsacks."

Captain Lobe made his way to the warehouses, listening as he went to the water that rippled against the wall, and looking at the tall masts of the ships that appeared like the trunks of trees in the white mist. Men passed him carrying food tied up in coloured pocket-handkerchiefs, and they nodded in a friendly way when he put two fingers to his cap. His face was familiar to most of them, for during the winter months he had stood at the dock gates distributing food-tickets, and he had accompanied many of them to their miserable homes after they had made his acquaintance in Lockhart's shop. He had a wonderful way of winning their confidence. He did not talk much, but his voice was strangely sympathetic, and the little he said came from his heart – it was not made-up conversation. So they trusted him with their secrets, and he knew that their struggles were often sharp and fierce before they tried to drown their misery in gin-shops.

"It's just no good, Salvation," they sometimes said to him. "I can't get no work, so I may as well make a beast of myself, and forget God made a man of me at the beginning."

They did not sink all at once into the scum of London. Again and again they came to him penitent, asking him to help them. Then, one day, they visited him in the maudlin condition, and he knew that it was "all up" with them – that is to say, that the craving for drink had been established – and that the publican could henceforth claim them as his most faithful servants."

He often puzzled over these drunkards; and at last he came to the conclusion that they were possessed by evil spirits. It remained for a greater spiritualist than himself to give utterance to his theory of drunkenness. That one* tells us the drunkard is possessed by a spirit of a man who died from drinking, and that if he resists his craving for drink he saves himself, and at the same time he liberates the spirit; but if he drinks himself to death, his spirit passes into the body of some other man, and establishes in his victim a craving for intoxicating liquors in order that he may imbibe their essence. These things are fables in the ears of materialists, but for men like Captain Lobe they have a deep meaning.

He passed slowly through the warehouses looking in vain for the man he wanted, and at last he stepped into a lift, and let it take him up to the top of "the new building." There he discovered the man behind a mountain of woolsacks, sharing a friend's "brick," namely, two pieces of bread with cold bacon in the middle. The friend had brought the brick with him that morning, and had taken compassion on his "pal," who had been busy all night among the woolsacks. When Captain Lobe came up the brick had already been cut in two, and the men were eating it with considerable relish, while they discussed the business that had brought the little Salvation captain to the docks so long before breakfast.

"I'd just tell the magistrate how it is," the man was saying, "and if he likes to send me to prison I'd offer no objection. I've not got five shillings a week to spend on my missus; and if the parish won't keep her, I can't. It was a bad day for me when she became a lunatic; but they do say as lunatics are increasing, and I've no doubt myself but they're right, for where I go to visit my missus I see women that think theirselves John the Baptist, and others that say they're the Prince of Wales' relations, and a lot that have the queerest notions you've ever heard of, let alone my missus. Last time I went a young woman came smirking up to me with a rose in her hand, and they told me she was waiting for her sweetheart. My missus is one of the melancholy sort of lunatics, but they've all sorts in that place; and I've heard it said that they'll have to add to the buildings, because so many folks is going crazy. Ulloa, captain!"

With this salutation the man swallowed the last bit of the brick, and

---

* See "Scientific Religion" by Lawrence Oliphant.

grasped Captain Lobe's hand in his grimy fingers. He had a lean face, grey hair, and a powerful figure, but he had aged prematurely; and his sunken chest showed that he had seen a good deal of illness. The friend moved away, and then he continued his complaint against the parish.

"They've summonsed me to pay this five shillings a week," he said, "and I'm not going to do it. I've been on the parish myself, and they know I can't get regular work, and that I've got three girls to keep; so what do they mean by wanting to make me support my wife what is a lunatic? She's no good to me. I've had to father and mother her offspring, so why should I pay for her? Besides, I've no money to do it, and that's what I'll tell the magistrate."

Captain Lobe did not stop to remonstrate. He merely said that he would be in court that morning to give the man a character; and that he hoped to get the aggrieved husband off with half a crown a week instead of five shillings. Then he left the new building, and went to interview the parish authorities on the subject of the poor lunatic.

"It's a hard case," he said to himself. "Here's a man whose wife is no use to him, and the parish expects him to pay twice as much as it costs him to have her at home; they ask five shillings a week for her maintenance. If he had her at home she would throw herself into the fire or out of the window. He is obliged to send her back every time he fetches her from the asylum. He is put to a double expense by her illness, for he must pay some one to look after his room and the children; besides which, he has been on the parish himself, and has lost his regular work through illness."

It was ten o'clock when the little Salvation captain reached Lower Thames Street Police Station. For a few minutes he stood in the passage listening to the witnesses and their friends; then he went into court, and took a place in the reporters' box, which was, as usual, empty.

The magistrate had fixed his spectacles on the tip of his nose, and was ready to commence the day's operations. Why are London magistrates allowed to sit on the Bench until they grow blind, deaf, and otherwise incapacitated? Two or three younger men would clean out and white-wash the cells of the police stations, which are now a disgrace to both law and justice. But these old men are past doing anything; they can merely hear what goes on through clerks and solicitors, and this seems to make them irritable. Occasionally a feeble joke on the part of some limb of the Bar puts them in a good temper, and then the prisoners get easy sentences; but deaf magistrates are the curse of police-courts. The magistrate who sat on the Bench that morning in Lower Thames Street Police Court had snow-white hair, a beaked nose, and an irascible voice; his smile might have been described as benevolent, but his lips were firmly set, and he did not relax his features more then once in thirty minutes; a fixed scowl was on his face, and he had an unpleasant way of asking short, abrupt questions when a witness became at all prolix. This upset the gentler sex, and confused their utterance. The men did not appear to be afraid of him; but the women seemed to feel that tears were useless, and as they had come provided with pocket-handkerchiefs, he made them stammer, blush, and fidget with their "bits of calico." Possibly these women were the cause of his irascibility; for if there is a sight on earth prone to move a man to wrath, it is an East End woman in the witness-box. The female witness has not changed her character since the days of the famous Mrs. Cluppins; she still enters into a dissertation on her domestic affairs, and informs the court about the decease of her late beloved, the illness of her last baby, and the wickedness of people in general. It is impossible to make her stick to business; and when the magistrate says:

"Now look at me, Mrs. Whatever-your-name-is," she curtsies, and says

'Yes, sir."

"*Will* you attend to me, Mrs. What's-your-name?"

"Please, sir, I was just a-saying –"

"Be quiet," roars the magistrate.

That morning the court was full of women who had taken out warrants against their husbands, and the magistrate's temper was tried to the uttermost.

A young woman stepped forward, dragging two miserable children after her, and kissed the dirty Bible. She planted herself with her back to the individual she had taken "for better, for worse," and produced some torn papers.

"These is my lines, your worship; I'm properly married to him, and he goes on at me something shameful. He's hit me, and kicked my children – just look at my little girl's mouth, your worship – and I can't stay with him any more; the policeman's my witness."

All this the woman said without pausing to take breath; and then she looked for a minute at her husband, who scowled at her from his place in the dock.

"You want a separation, I suppose," said the magistrate. "I shall order him to pay you ten shillings a week."

"I can't do it, your worship," the man objected. "I've been separated from her once, and I had to take her back because I had no money to keep her away. She drinks; I've never hit her or the children. She tell lies, your worship."

"Call the witness."

A tall policeman stepped into the witness-box, and delivered his evidence in a sing-song voice, while gazing hard at the ceiling.

"It's a cat-and-dog life they lead, your worship. He's the worst, but she's bad enough. I saw him hit her Saturday night. She was calling murder, and the neighbours fetched me in to stop them fighting. I've known them this six years, and it's a bad case – incompatibility of temper, your worship."

"I shall order you a separation," the magistrate told the husband, "and you must pay your wife ten shillings a week or go to prison. Next case."

The pair left the court glaring into each other's faces. The woman looked triumphant, and the man seemed to be inwardly swearing that she should not have the money; but she had her "lines" in her pocket, so go where he would she could claim her maintenance, and throw him into prison if he refused to support herself and her children.

Then another woman mumbled some words over the dirty Bible, the cover of which was flabby with tears and kisses.

"I can't get my separation money, your worship. He's only paid me five shillings, and he owes me a pound at least."

"What do you mean by this?" the magistrate asked a miserable little man before him. "You know I ordered you to pay her ten shillings a week."

"Your worship, I ain't got it. She goes to every place where I get work; she's been to Hawkins', and Benson's, and all the other shops with such lies, your worship, that I'm turned away. Do what you like with me, your worship, but don't send her home again."

The fatal lines were produced, and although the man had made a devil's bargain on the altar steps, he was bound to pay for his wife's maintenance.

"My good man, I'm very sorry for you," the magistrate said, " but you must try to find the money. I will give you until next week."

The third case was about an old bedstead, which the landlady had distrained for rent, and which her lodger wanted to have back again.

"I've just come out of the union," the complainant said, taking a pauper's cap off the head of the baby in her arms, "and I thought I'd pawn the bedstead to get along. I'll pay her the rent, but the bed's mine, and you can't take away my bedstead; it's all I've got in the world, your worship. My husband left me after this blessed infant was born, and we've both been in the union. I must have my bedstead."

"You can't have it," the magistrate said; "it's distrained for rent."

"Then send me to prison!" cried the woman. I've had nothing to eat all day. Send me to prison!"

She was hauled down by two policemen, who hustled her out of court. A minute later screams were heard in the adjoining passage, and she was led back again, followed by the landlady, whose face was bleeding.

"She fell on her like a tiger, your worship," said one of the policemen; "she wasn't outside before she flew at the other woman, and if I hadn't been close by she'd have dropped the infant."

"I shall send you to prison for two days for contempt of court," growled the magistrate. "You're an incorrigible woman. Next case."

"That's just what I wanted," said the prisoner, wiping away her tears. "I'm much obliged, your worship; now I'll get something to eat."

She followed the policeman to the cells, carrying the baby in its pauper dress. It slept soundly, for its mother had pawned an old shawl to buy drink, and she had drugged it. Its white, sickly face contrasted strangely with the red cheeks of its angry parent. She wore a short ragged dress, and a hat adorned with a gaudy feather. The expression of her face was both angry and defiant, for much of her life had been spent in fierce feuds with landladies, and she did not like to be "worsted." In the cell she would go to sleep, and when released she would travel on from casual ward to casual ward, dragging her infant with her until Death – whose merciful sickle cuts down so many slum babies – came to release the child from earth.

Captain Lobe's eyes followed the mother and the child until the door closed after them, and for a minute he felt the sickening pain which makes so many turn away from the blains of society and bury their consciences in the sands of good wishes. But Captain Lobe believed that angels hovered about that East End police-court, and that their mission was to carry slum children to "other worlds than ours." "There is room for them all," he used to say to himself, while he looked up from his attic window in the Whitechapel Road at the innumerable lamps of the universe.

There is a pretty conceit that such children change into butterflies, and bask for a few brief hours in the sunshine, thus enjoying the elixir of life before passing into nothingness. For those who cannot console themselves with fairy stories these children are like arrows in the flesh, sent there by the bow of human selfishness. The arrows have poisoned tips (over-sensitiveness), and each wizened child-face, with its mute suffering and its helplessness, takes an hour out of the life of these men and women.

"Eighteen hundred years ago," Captain Lobe thought, Christ said, 'Suffer little children to come unto Me, and forbid them not, for of such is the kingdom of heaven.' Perhaps that is why so many of these children die. They could not come to Christ through all the sin they inherit and the misery of their surroundings, so the angels fetch them young to heaven." He seemed to hear the white wings, and to see the silver garments in the police-court; for angels were to him no fairy stories, but quite as real as invisible molecules are to materialists. Then the voice of the magistrate brought his thoughts back to this mundane existence, and he saw the dock-labourer standing under the dock, facing the solicitor employed by the parish.

"Now what have you got to say to this?" inquired the magistrate.

"Nothing, sir, except it ain't my fault that my wife's a melancholy lunatic; and I don't see why I've got to pay twice as much as when she had the blessing of her right reason; and what's more, I can't do it, sir, for I'm only a casual worker myself, and as that gentleman there knows, I've been myself on the parish."

"Is there any witness?"

"Salvation, speak up," said the dock-labourer; "tell him how it is, and about the children!"

Captain Lobe gave his evidence, and asked the magistrate to make it half a crown a week instead of five shillings.

The magistrate blinked at him as he stood in the witness-box, and the clerks stared at the S on his collar until he had finished speaking. Then followed a period of silence, during which the dock-labourer, twisted an old felt hat nervously in his fingers, the solicitor woke up a neighbour who had gone to sleep, the policemen yawned and coughed, and the audience whispered behind the dock.

The silence was broken at last by the magistrate, "Half a crown a week, and costs."

The dock-labourer mumbled his thanks, and threw a grateful look at Captain Lobe, who escaped through a side door, leaving the magistrate to deal with three or four School Board visitors. (These people are said to have taken out three thousand summonses within twelve months in that one police-court.)

He went home thinking about the woman who had left the union that morning with her baby, whose worldly goods consisted of an old bedstead, and he wondered what would become of the sickly-looking infant. Suddenly he remembered that he had had no breakfast.

"I don't know how it is," he said to himself, "but I always lose my appetite if I go among those dock-labourers while they are being taken on in the morning. I think it's that bell; it seems to say, 'Hungry! hungry! hungry!'"

CHAPTER XVII

The Bastile

"Who are you talking to?" inquired a voice. He looked up, and saw the modern Prometheus towering above him.

The parish doctor had overheard him say, "Hungry! hungry! hungry!" for he had a habit of talking aloud, also of whistling hymns in the street, regardless of passers-by, who sometimes stood still to listen.

"I was talking to myself," he answered. "The truth is, I have had no breakfast; the bell at the London Docks took away my appetite; and since then I have been in Lower Thames Street Police Court, which place does not act as a tonic. Now I am on my way to the Bastile."

"Then we will go together," the doctor said, "for I am going to blow up the officials there about an old woman they have sent into the infirmary; they ought to have kept her in the workhouse."

"I told you," the doctor continued, as they walked on, "that the whole of the East End is starving. The West End is bad, or mad; not to see that if things go on like this we must have a revolution. One fine day the people about here will grow desperate; and they will walk westwards, cutting throats and hurling brickbats, until they are shot down by the military. I know perfectly well that my ideas would be called exaggerated if I put them into print – people prefer to read the pretty stories about the East End made up by Walter Besant; but truth is truth, and if people will insist on hearing smooth things it serves them right to walk straight over the precipice."

It was a beautiful July day, and the sun shone upon the East End streets as it shines on the gardens of rich men and the parks of princes. The sun is no respecter of persons, although some people think that he is afraid to frown on crowned heads, and that queens can always command fine weather. But in this year of grace 1888 old ladies still sally forth on fine days with an umbrella "to keep off the rain," young women consult swallows and flowers to see if they may venture out in a new bonnet, and old men look learned over watery moons and mackerel skies, while young men scan the weather-forecasts in the daily papers. Nothing sells so well as Mother Seigel's almanack, which is a godsend to poor women just before Christmas.

The sun lighted up the Salvation S on Captain Lobe's collar, and the rim of his cap. He did not reach far above the elbow of the modern Prometheus, whose tall figure and big head made the little boys call out "giant." The doctor stalked along heedless of inquiries as to whether it was "warm up there," talking to his companion about the disease that had taken hold of him after, he was bowled over by the loss of so many relations, rattling the chains which bound him to his half-starved patients.

"There is *one* advantage in my life, at any rate," he said, as they passed by a hospital. "I am out of the rut, so I can go my own way without bothering my head about professional etiquette, I am free as air in my parish work, I am not hemmed in by money-making. Those West End physicians are the veriest slaves on the face of the earth; directly a man puts up his brass plate in a fashionable street he must join in the race after prestige and wealth, otherwise he gets no patients. Bob Sawyerish tricks go on all round Cavendish Square, and the truckling to fashion and the humbugging about religion one sees there are enough to sicken any man who has ever had a single glimpse at science. Science is a stern mistress. She admits no heretics into her temple; she insists on clean hands and pure hearts; and if her votaries have an idol hidden anywhere, she scorches them with a single glance. Some of our great surgeons are scientific men, but our physicians –"

The parish doctor burst into a roar of laughter that shook him from head to foot, and made the stethoscope jump half way out of his breast-coat pocket.

"They are very little better than leeches; only instead of sucking blood they suck money," he said. "Really I don't blame them. If people *will* persist in throwing guineas at their heads they may as well pick the money up. But oh! the professional manner, the rubbing of the hands and the blinking of the eyelids that go on among the great guns who sit at the top of the medical tree, are enough to make man ill-physically ill, I say – if he has ever had a glimpse at science."

"All this," said Captain Lobe, gravely, "is the lust of the spirit!'

"What do you mean?" inquired the doctor.

"Well," Captain Lobe replied, "I have thought a great deal on the subject of worldliness, and I have christened it 'the lust of the spirit.' Your West End physicians – great guns, as you call them – want to appear better off than their neighbours."

"They must, if they are to get on," interrupted the doctor.

"That's just it," said the little captain. "At school they are taught to get on, no one tells them anything about the evils of ambition. Their parents never speak to them about the spiritual appetites of rivalry, jealousy, and emulation, which kill the soul just as the carnal appetites kill the body. I have been told that some of the great guns you speak about call themselves Christians. How do they reconcile the teachings of Christ with their mode of life? What do they mean by having grand houses, and carriages when the great Physician went on foot, and had nowhere to lay His head? I wish that they would attend some of our holiness meetings, and listen to what we have to say about the lust of the spirit."

"They would go away like the young man in the Bible who sorrowed over his great possessions," replied the modern Prometheus smiling. "You see their practice depends upon keeping up an appearances and some of them spend as much on the rent of a house as they earn all the year round from their patients. When once they step into the fashionable treadmill, they are obliged to go round with it; it will not stop for them. Their only chance is to keep away from temptation, to follow Science instead of Fashion. Many of them stint in bread and cheese in order to have a carriage, and all they get for their trouble are snubs from grand ladies, who speak of a doctor as a sort of upper servant. I believe that some of them are forcing their way into Society; but the upper ten will never receive them as equals; they will always be sent in to dinner with the wife of the family solicitor. I despise social climbing myself; but

I know that West End doctors must practise it if they are to get on. They dub it ambition; but it is merely a phase of that commercial spirit which makes foreigners call us 'a nation of shop-keepers.' The worst of trying to get on in my profession is that men are obliged to be, or to appear to be, religious, in order to become rich and fashionable. So they mix up 'the Lord' and 'my lord' until it is impossible to tell the difference between religion and humbug. The only sort of ambition that does not degrade a man is the determination to do some real work in the world, to leave his mark, although he may never be talked about. Social climbing, or getting on, always ends in moral degradation.

"I might have been in the treadmill myself," he continued. "I wonder how I should have liked it? It is hard work down here; but I would rather be fettered to the people with iron chains, than wear the gilded livery of a West End physician. I have still some hope left, for I am face to face with nature's secrets. I have seen so many medical students begin life with a keen appreciation of science, and have watched them deteriorating under the influence of ambition, or the love of money-making. Here I am free, I am a law to myself, no one can compel me to do one thing or to leave another undone. Sometimes I spend whole nights prowling about the streets, and stand for hours on the city bridges thinking over scientific subjects, and then I go back to my little laboratory, and work on until it is time to see my patients. Every lover of science is a bit of an alchemist; he wants to discover some secret, and in order to make a discovery one must concentrate all one's efforts upon a single object. "Tell me," he said, looking earnestly at the little captain, "atoms move in something, what do they move in?"

"God," said Captain Lobe, without any hesitation.

The doctor smiled from his superior altitude, and said, as if to himself: "They move in something; they never touch, they never touch."

Captain-Lobe had not studied any book but the Bible, so he could throw no light on the problems that perplexed the modern Prometheus. His one wish, the passion of his life, was to save people from the hell of fire and brimstone that existed somewhere in the universe. He possessed the faith that can move mountains, consequently he did not worry himself with questions as to *how* or *why*, he accepted all that was contained in the Sacred Book, and strove to make others accept "the saving truths of the Gospel." But he had the gift of tolerance, so he could listen to opponents, and sympathize with those who held different views from himself. The modern Prometheus was an agnostic. Captain Lobe had met many men and women like him in the East End, people with a small amount of faith and a large amount of practice; consequently the way in which he treated the theory that in God men "live, move, and have their being" did not seem very astonishing. The little captain thanked God every day that he was not cursed with an intellect. Nothing could shake his faith, for that was made of adamant, and all he had to do was to preach the Gospel; he was not called upon to follow people into the labyrinths of their mental difficulties.

"Have you seen that little girl in _____ Square lately?" the doctor asked, as they came in sight of the workhouse. "Has she joined the Salvation Army?"

Captain Lobe explained all that had taken place in the superintendent's office, and said that Ruth was working in the factory under the care of the labour-mistress.

"I am glad she has someone to look after her," the doctor said. "I daresay you know her better than I do; but I attended her mother, and I remember the sort of temperament she has inherited. Hester has brought her up like a hot-house plant, and the best thing that can happen to her is an early marriage."

The doctor looked kindly at Captain Lobe while he said this, and then he turned the black ring round his finger. He wore no gloves, and his large hands were quite unfit to handle delicate West End patients. But at night those hands busied themselves with nature's secrets; and the parish doctor may yet become famous.

Captain Lobe rang the workhouse bell, which was immediately answered by an official, who said, "The master is in the garden, near the cabbages."

They proceeded to look for him, passing by neat flower-beds, closely shaven grass plots, smooth paths, and trees which had been pruned until their branches had reached the legitimate amount of foliage. The Bastile stretched further than the eye could see, and seemed a standing rebuke to its poverty-stricken surroundings, for it was clean – so clean that it made Captain Lobe shiver; not a spot was on it, not a stain, nothing to show a trace of sympathy with the misery and sin of the people who lived in the neighbourhood.

The Whitechapel Union is a model workhouse; that is to say, it is the Poor Law incarnate in stone and brick. The men are not allowed to smoke in it, not even when they are in their dotage; the young women never taste tea, and the old ones may not indulge in a cup during the long afternoons, only at half-past six o'clock morning and night, when they receive a small hunch of bread with butter scraped over the surface, and a mug of that beverage which is so dear to their hearts as well as their stomachs. The young people never go out, never see a visitor, and the old ones only get one holiday in the month. Then the aged paupers may be seen skipping like lambkins outside the doors of the Bastile, while they jabber to their friends and relations. A little gruel morning and night, meat twice a week, that is the food of the grown-up people, seasoned with hard work and prison discipline. Doubtless this Bastile offers no premium to idle and improvident habits; but what shall we say of the woman, or man, maimed by misfortune, who must come there or die in the street? Why should old people be punished for their existence?

They passed an ancient pauper on their way to find the master, and the doctor stopped to speak to him. He was standing beside two black, upright coffins. His Bastile dress hung loosely on his old limbs, and the cap showed white hair hanging about his neck. He was peering at the coffins, and rubbing his finger up and down them. They were made of coarse wood, and roughly smeared with black paint; there was nothing attractive about them, and yet the old man seemed to be fascinated by these grim coffins.

"How old are you?" inquired the modern Prometheus.

"I be eighty-six."

"What are you doing?

"I be just a-thinking that I'd like to make my own coffin. I've been making coffins here this ten years, mister; I've made 'em for a many, and I'd like to make one for meself."

The old man's tone was so hopeless!

Presently they came in sight of the master. He was an orthodox Poor Law servant, but he found it difficult to keep up the *rôle* of a disciplinarian, for nature had made him tender-hearted; and although his attempts at severity had hardened into a sort of second nature, he was constantly trespassing against Poor Law discipline. For instance, when the doctor and Captain Lobe reached him, he was counting his cabbages in order to see if he could give the old people "a feed" the following Sunday, and thinking that he would root up sundry currant bushes to make room for more vegetables; and a few minutes before that he had paid his pigs a visit, thinking on the way how trying it was to live in a London union after years spent in a lax country workhouse. But when he opened his mouth to speak, behold! a eulogy of the Poor Law came out of it, and he said that "discipline is discipline;" which sentence, of course, needs no interpretation. He was a man of about forty, tall, strongly built, with a pleasant voice, and possessed of the *sine quâ non* of his office, invincible courage, although he had nothing more dangerous to deal with than paupers and lunatics.

After the doctor had told him about the old woman in the infirmary, he conducted his visitors over the labour-yard, which, he told them, received visits from all people interested in the poor of London.

"We are almost self-supporting," he remarked, looking proudly about him; "we grind our own corn, we make our own clothes, boots, and coffins; in fact, meat, grain, and clothes-stuff are all that we take from the outside public. But paupers are so lazy; upon my word, I don't wonder that these people come to the workhouse; they won't work if they can possibly help it."

"I've heard men say they would rather go to prison than enter the Bastile," Captain Lobe suggested.

"They tell me that every day," answered the master, "yet we get the same paupers here again and again. If it's so bad why do they come back to us? We don't want them. But," he added, "I wish the old folks could have alms-houses – I mean those who have become paupers through no fault of their own; it's hard to enforce discipline with old people."

The workshops lay close together, and in each of them men were redeeming the time by making something for the use of the workhouse. Tailors squatted on tables, bootmakers cobbled and patched, men plaited mats; each pauper had his task, and each knew that the morrow would bring the same work, that as surely as the sun rises and sets, his task would be the same tomorrow as it was at that moment. Six o'clock would set him free for tea, but after that he would be handed over to an instructor until bed-time.

The Whitechapel Union allows no man to remain idle from the time he gets up until he goes to bed again. A sodden look had settled on the faces of the older men, and they apparently thought little of what they were doing. The younger paupers seemed to take more interest in their work, for hope was not quite dead in them. But not a voice was to be heard in the workshops; the men did not whistle or sing; they looked like schoolboys in disgrace rather than free-born English citizens.

Captain Lobe, who was hyper-sensitive, felt a strong sympathy for these men. The atmosphere of the Bastile seemed to stifle him. He longed to preach, or to pray, to do something for these hopeless-looking creatures; but he was told that the paupers' souls were well provided for by the parish.

General Booth has stormed many places, but he has not gained admittance for his red vests and poke bonnets into the metropolitan workhouses. These places remain closed to him. The Salvationists hold meetings and sing hymns at the gates, and they seem to think the time is coming when their drum will be heard even in the Bastile. But at present workhouse religion is carried on to order, and pauper souls are as strictly watched as pauper bodies. Paupers pass from the Bastile into the infirmary when too old for work, and before they go there the routine of their lives makes them into automatons. At last death snaps the chain of Poor Law discipline, and they are buried in coffins made on the premises. Little wonder, then, that poor men and women have a wholesome dread of the parish!

CHAPTER XVIII

A Confession

Captain Lobe said goodbye to the parish doctor outside the doors of the Bastile, and walked home along Mile End Waste. He passed the London Hospital, the Pavilion Theatre, and the other Whitechapel landmarks; and then he unlocked the door of his lodging-house. The sun was shining through the open window into his little sitting-room, dancing in beams upon the rules of the Salvation Army, which were framed, and hung upon the wall facing the window. Its rays had killed the fire in the grate.

He threw himself down on the old horse-hair sofa, tired out, without any appetite; and while lying there he began to think about the hopeless mass of sin and suffering he had that day witnessed. His thoughts wandered on in disorderly fashion from the doctor to the police-court, from the police-court to the workhouse. Sometimes he recalled an act of devotion on the part of some man or woman, and this sent a thrill through him; nothing else seemed to lift the spell of hopelessness which had been thrown over him by physical exhaustion, for the amusements of the people appeared to him bestial, and their ideas of happiness mere brute instincts.

Mechanically he rose from the sofa, and proceeded to light a fire, breaking the sticks for it across his knee, and stuffing underneath the lowest bar of the grate old bits of paper. The sun shone on his closely-cropped hair and his face, showing the lines that marked his forehead. He was very young, but the sorrows of the people had taken hold of him, and the terrors of hell haunted him day and night. He set light to the sticks, and placed upon them a kettle to make some tea. There was one thing about him which all must have noticed, namely, he could not sit or stand in one position for many consecutive minutes. He was nervous; that is to say, hypersensitive. He could not harden his heart and toughen his skin; his flesh remained tender like that of little children.

This is metaphorical language, but some things can only be expressed in metaphors. Captain Lobe would remain young all his life; for those experiences which make people old would be softened for him by his faith in a beneficent Providence. But he was delicate, and, like all delicate people, he suffered from low spirits. Sitting there by the grate he thought about the Salvation Army, about the interior working of it. "No one can be connected with an organization, religious, political, or philanthropic, without feeling from time to time disheartened and depressed. The truth is, we expect the wire-pullers to act like bits of machinery, we forget that they are human beings. We flatter them one day and abuse them the next, and yet we expect them to remain perfect. We give them power, that most dangerous. gift, and we are surprised to see it inflaming their passions, and helping their ambition to run riot. We preach against the lust of the flesh, and we quite forget the lust of the spirit. Our cathedrals are full of monuments to men who have shed blood or burnt ships, our churches hang up flags as trophies. We are a nation of hypocrites."

Such were Captain Lobe's meditations while he watched the steam lifting the lid of the kettle, and the flames licking the black sides of the grate. "Those young Booths," he said to himself, "expect every one to bow down before them. It's all very well for the Chief and his wife, but those young Booths –"

He was interrupted by a violent knock on the door, followed by a kick. Before he could say "Come in," a gaunt, untidy woman pushed the door open, and stood looking at him. She wore a shawl over her grey, matted hair, and this she held under her chin; a short brown dress showed her old boots. It was easy to see that she was a Jewess; for her dark eyes shone with the Hebrew fire which has consumed its own smoke ever since the chosen people became vagabonds on the face of the earth, and her beaked nose was a facsimile of the Hebrew noses which ornament the stone monuments in the British Museum.

"Who are you?" Captain Lobe asked.

"I'm a Death Watch."

"What do you want?"

"You."

"Why?"

"I've come to fetch you to a man that's dying."

"Where?"

"Spitalfields, near the Market."

"Is he a Gentile?"

"No; but he's been to your place once or twice, and he wants to see you. He's got something on his mind. Come quick! I must be back to watch him die; and he says you are the only one he'll talk to. Come along, don't bother about your tea. I'll give you a swig of this!"

She produced a bottle out of her pocket, and proceeded to uncork it.

"Gin," she said, smacking her lips; "I've had a little brandy, and a little whisky, and now I'm finishing up with a little gin. I take a sip as I sit by the bed. It's habit!"

Captain Lobe shook his head.

"You won't?"

"No, thank you."

"You're going to drink that muck?"

"Yes," Captain Lobe said, while he poured the boiling water into an old tin teapot. "I've been on the go all day; I've had no dinner and no breakfast. But I'll come if you wait a minute."

The Jewess refused to take a seat. She stood waiting for Captain Lobe, and occasionally she lifted the bottle to her lips, while her dark eyes wandered over the furniture of the room, and into the adjoining bedroom. One wizened hand grasped the shawl under her chin, the other, held the glass bottle.

As a rule, Jewesses are very temperate. It is rare to see an intoxicated Jew in the East End, and still rarer to meet a drunken Jewess. But a Death Watch may be excused for having such proclivities, since her work is to sit day and night by dying people, to hear those groans and watch those gasps which will always make life tragic, even when everything has been done for humanity that science and art can suggest, and love has

148

become a religion.

"I'm ready," Captain Lobe said, after he had gulped down the tea and looked at the bread and butter.

"Then come along, Salvation."

Not a word was said on the way to Spitalfields. Captain Lobe followed the woman through the Jews' quarter, looking up sometimes at the long windows where the weavers used to sit, and noting the foreign names of the streets. Buxom Jewish matrons sat on doorsteps, watching the little dark children who tumbled at their feet. Young Hebrews smoked short pipes, and talked their own lingo. Now and then a young girl with jet-black hair and flashing eyes ran by, carrying a loaf of German bread under her arm, singing a foreign song, or joedelling. There was nothing English about the place, only foreign faces, foreign shops, foreign talk. The Jews looked happy, although they were in a strange land, exiles as their fathers were, crowded into the narrow compass of the East End Ghetto. They had not the down-trodden look of our Gentile population, which, seems to enjoy crouching and whining instead of asserting itself with sturdy independence. The Jews have, it is true, long-suffering faces, but they have hope written on their features, instead of that despair which seems to sodden English East End men and women. Perhaps their habit of looking towards Jerusalem accounts for this, for the synagogues of the East End show men and women full of religious purpose. The down-trodden Gentiles seem to have lost their faith; they speak of death as "the great secret," while the Jew calls death "God's kiss," even when it comes to him in the crowded dens of sweaters or the filthy rooms which he shares with new-comers from the Continent. Moreover, he knows how to grow rich. He leaves the East End to settle in Bayswater; he does not content himself with husks, like our Gentile swine who fill the public-houses. Charity offers him no premium for idleness; so the chosen people hang together, the rich help the poor, and every Jew finds a friend on the Jewish Board of Guardians.

At last the woman stopped before a small house in Gold Eagle Street. "He lies in here," she said. "Follow me; he's not dead, for they said if he died while I went for you they'd lower the blinds. Come along, Salvation."

"Hush!" whispered a voice inside the house. "Don't talk so loud. He'll hear you."

Captain Lobe looked down the passage, and at the further end he saw a room, the door of which was half open. He followed the woman, who walked on tiptoe, to see the dying man. A clock ticked loudly in an adjoining room : all else was silenced by the presence of death; for the man was really dying – any one could see that at a glance. The laboured breath, the ashy colour of the face, the damp flesh, said plainly enough that he had not many hours, perhaps not many minutes, to live. His head lay on the pillow, and when Captain Lobe came into the room he tried to raise it, but all power seemed to have left his muscles, and it fell back.

In an instant the little captain was by the bed, with the dying man's head resting on his shoulder. "I thought you'd come," the man said. "I knew you'd not shrink from me. Tell her to go away," he continued, pointing to the Death Watch.

The woman disappeared, shutting the door of the room after her.

"Don't pray," he whispered then. "Listen."

Captain Lobe bent down his head, and the words fell on his ear one by one, between gasps which seemed to draw the life out of the speaker.

"At first it was horrible to me, Salvation! I used to hear the lambs bleating in my sleep, I couldn't bear to drive them into that place. But I grew accustomed. I could eat my food in it, and I went so far as to fall asleep in the butcher's cart. Then it seemed to grow on me, and I liked it. I wanted to see the blood, and feel it all warm on my fingers. I could wash my hands in it."

He raised his head to look at Captain Lobe, with momentary strength, but it fell heavily back again, and he went on:

"I thought when I heard you talking at your place you would not turn away from me, and I can't die with this sin on my conscience. It grew, that thirst did. People must eat meat, and someone must kill beasts; but to kill and kill makes a man like a cannibal, it gives him a thirst for blood, and I got to feel at last that nothing would quench my thirst but human blood, human flesh."

Captain Lobe felt a cold shudder creeping over him, and for a moment his arms shook. But the dying man lifted imploring eyes to his face, while the terrible words began to fall on his ear again in thick, husky language, half-choked by the approach of death.

"One morning I was standing at the door of the slaughter-house, waiting for the butcher's boy to bring me my work. I had the knife in my hand, and the blade was sharp. No one was there, only me, alone by the long dark passage. I was by myself. Suddenly there came along a miserable-looking woman who had been sleeping there; she was the worse for drink, and as she tottered up the passage that thirst for blood seemed to come over me like a flash of lightning. I wanted to feel her throat, to toss her head back, to see her blood captain. It wasn't me, it was a fiend that did it; but I found myself standing over her and the thirst all gone out of me. I was alone in the passage with that dead woman. I knew I was not a maniac, only a man that had whetted his thirst for blood, till he was no better than a savage. I went back to my work; and no one guessed who did the murder. But I could not go on butchering. I left the place, and I hid myself here among the Jews, who hate blood and never spill it. I'm not a Jew, I'm a Gentile. Lay me back, Salvation; don't shrink away. I couldn't tell nobody else. Pray now; but don't talk of blood, I can't –"

His tongue stopped, and a glassy film came over his eyes.

"He'll not speak again," said the Death Watch.

She had come into the room unnoticed, and now took her place beside the bed, laying her wizened fingers on the man's pulse.

"Dying, dying," Captain Lobe heard her say. "One, two, three, four; he dies hard, but he dies fast."

For a minute Captain Lobe stood looking at the wretched man, then he left the house.

"He dies hard, but he dies fast," muttered the Death Watch.

CHAPTER XIX

With the Hop-Pickers in Kent

A vist to the docks before breakfast, a police-court in the afternoon, a murder in the evening: in this way Captain Lobe's days were spent, unless he was preaching in the Whitechapel Barracks, or listening to the Chief at Exeter Hall. He did not care very much for the public gatherings which rejoice the hearts and cheer the spirits of most Salvationists.

"Drums and processions are all very well in their way," he said; "in fact, I don't know how we could get on without them, considering the class of men and women we have to deal with; but I like to hear my own people singing. I feel at home then; it makes me happiest."

In this respect he resembled a parish priest. To such a one the most beautiful anthem in Westminster Abbey does not sound half so sweet, half so sacred, as the hymns sung by his own choir far away in some country village. The music may inspire him with greater thoughts than those which come to him in the parish church; the voices may fall much more melodiously on his ear than the untrained voices of the villagers; but while he stands in Westminster Abbey his heart is with his parishioners, and he thinks of summer evenings when they sing his favourite hymn in the twilight, when the evening breeze steals in through the open door, when the night shadows fall on the altar steps and the crucifix.

The strain of living day after day in the midst of degradation and misery must tell upon any human being, more especially upon one who believes in fire and brimstone. With Captain Lobe it sometimes amounted to torment, for he said to himself, "No happiness here, no hope hereafter; nothing behind but sin, and nothing before but everlasting punishment!"

He could not see that the people take pleasure in their filthy existence, he could not understand the satisfaction they get by fuddling their brains in public-houses and by coarse love-making; he could only put himself in their place, and think what his own feelings would be in their circumstances. So day by day his environment told on his health and spirits, and at last he was reported to the Chief as ill. Then he received orders to go away for six weeks, to follow his people into Kent, where some thousands of them had already gone hop-picking.

It was 2 a.m. when he stood on the platform of London Bridge Station one Monday morning, waiting for the hop-pickers' train, surrounded by a herd of people – mothers carrying babies, fathers loaded with bedding, girls, boys, old women, and children. He held a canvas bag and a thick coat. Cries of "Ulloa, Salvation!" greeted him everywhere; and "You must and shall come in our carriage!" was said by dozens of people directly he showed his ticket. The station was almost dark; it does not require much light to pack a train with hop-pickers, for they tumble in by themselves; they do not need to be driven in like cattle. They are, in fact, cheaper to carry about than dumb beasts, for they can be packed closer together, and if one or two are suffocated on the journey no one claims damages. The loss of a sheep is serious; but the death of a hop-picker matters to no one, unless he happens to have relations; and these people seem to realize the fact that he is better out of the world than in it, otherwise they would not turn funerals into merry meetings.

"We won't go home till morning," the girls were singing. A tremor of excitement ran through the herd of hop-pickers. They were going away for a holiday into Kent, hop-picking. Some of them had been there before, but not a few had never seen the outside of London. They talked and laughed, sang and chaffed, until the train was ready to carry them out of London Bridge Station. Then they tumbled into the carriages. The mothers scolded the children, the babies cried, the men swore, the girls and boys fought for places. "It was all confusion, worry, and strife," until the porters banged the doors and the guard gave the signal. Afterwards the train crept slowly away, carrying its human freight through the tunnel, and the hop-pickers grew quiet, for all uncommon things set such people trembling.

They feel as masses, not as individuals just as a herd of sheep will run if driven, these people will act if once possessed by the emotion of fear, grief, or happiness. They have no confidence in themselves, no power of forming their own opinions. It is said that a shepherd can distinguish between one sheep and another, that each lamb is born with a different countenance. So it is with these people. Those who know them well can recognize their individuality; but for all political or social purposes they are like a herd of sheep; only, of course, they are of less value than sheep in the money market.

"Do you know what girls do down in the country?" Captain Lobe heard a girl whisper to a friend. "They go for walks with their sweethearts in the dark, all up and down roads that haven't any lamps, and they aren't a bit afraid. I went a little way once with a chap – a country chap, I mean – and I fell into the ditch. My! how I hollered! He had to pull me out, and I wouldn't go again with him not for love or money. Those country girls aren't afraid of nothing."

Captain Lobe stood in the centre of the carriage, tightly wedged in between a loafer, who insisted on keeping both hands deep down in his fustian trousers pockets, which fixed purpose made him occasionally lose his balance and fall against a woman in front, who treated him to "the universal adjective." Captain Lobe was like a sandwich between this loafer and an old woman who had tied round her neck a tin tea-pot (the most valuable thing she possessed), and who carried a bird-cage covered over with a pocket-handkerchief. The old woman had locked up her room in Whitechapel, and had the key in her pocket; so no one could get in while she was away, except the landlady. The landlady had lent her the fare into Kent; consequently she had no fear of losing her pewter teaspoons; but the tin teapot and the canary were too valuable to be left in the charge of a neighbour.

"Och! and the air'll do him good," she said, pointing to the cage; "he's asleep like ony infant."

"It's wonderful how the children *do* sleep down there," remarked another woman. "It's the hops, I expect. I've heard say they make 'em into pillows for people that can't sleep, and sell 'em at big prices."

"It's wonderful how the children *do* eat down there," growled a man beside her. "It's the nutriment in the hops that gets into their fingers, seems to me and makes 'em so hungry. They're always sucking their fingers, and that sets them on for bread. No need of hop bitters to give 'em an appetite at 18*s*. a bottle! I hear the hops is all mildewy this year, but we'll soon tell how they are by the sort of appetite the children get. If I'd my way I'd stop children from coming hop-picking; they spoil the trade, and eat twice as much as they do down in Whitechapel."

The people began to recover their spirits as the train passed through some dimly lighted stations. The lamp spluttered in Captain Lobe's carriage, so he could scarcely see the faces of his companions, but he recognized many voices in the semi-darkness.

He was unable to look out of the window, for the loafer's shoulders reached above his head, and if he turned round he came closely in contact with the old woman's tin teapot. Suddenly the canary in the cage gave a faint chirrup, and the people laughed, as if it were a joke to hear a bird chirping in a railway carriage. Someone produced a bottle of gin, and this was upset in the darkness. "The Miller's Daughter," and "We won't go home, till morning," were sung; and then Salvation was requested to "tune up," after which they sang something about "going up in a chariot in the morning," until they reached their destination, a little station about five miles distant from the hop-gardens.

It was still very dark. Looking east, one could see signs of daylight, but a few yards ahead all seemed black as night. The people huddled together on the platform, afraid to set out on a road that had no lamps, that led through the fields to Squire _____'s place. The little station possessed a small waiting-room, but the ticket-collector, who was in charge, declared that he had no power to unlock it.

"Come along," a man said; "I know the way; but look after the young 'uns when we come to the river. It's deep, it is. There's nothing else to be afraid of."

He set out, having borrowed a lantern from the ticket-collector, and the people followed him in a string, keeping close together, and "hollering" if a bat flew in their faces, or a stone rolled from under their feet. The men were heavily laden with bedding and cooking utensils, the women carried babies or bundles; only the girls and boys were free to enjoy themselves. The people seemed to recognize that the "young 'uns" had come down for a holiday, and that they must be allowed to make the most of it; work was a mere pretext for their country visit. But the "young 'uns" were awful cowards, both girls and boys; they crept along almost in silence, close to their parents. The road led first of all through a village. Not a light was in the windows of the cottages. The villagers were fast asleep, having barred their doors, and locked up their chickens, fearing that the hop-pickers might feel hungry. A red flame burst out sometimes from a kiln where men were drying hops over sulphur fires; but these kilns were much further away in the valley. Leaving the village, the man with the lantern led the way along a broad road, until he reached a bridge.

"Here's the river," he said, "now be careful, it's to the right-hand side, and goes on for half a mile. If a young 'un falls in, I won't pick him out, remember. Look! there's a barge down yonder, waiting to be towed up the river. They keep horses at the inn opposite."

"Just to think the country girls will come all along these lonesome roads at night with their sweethearts," remarked a girl at Captain Lobe's elbow.

The children took good care not to fall into the river They held on to their mothers' dresses, and clung to their fathers' legs, much to the disgust of their parents, whose conversation collapsed into "the universal adjective!" At last a halt was made, in order that bundles might be opened and children might be fed. The little herd sank down by the roadside opposite the river, and the man with the lantern walked up and down, throwing a light where it was most wanted. Then the bundles were tied up again, and they continued their pilgrimage towards Squire _____'s place in better spirits.

As they passed a long common the grey light of dawn showed them the trees, and they groped their way carefully across a wooden bridge, holding on to the barriers. They could see the water indistinctly beneath their feet; someone had courage to drop a stone into it. The splash set the women " hollering," but it was too dark to catch the culprit, the man with the lantern being on in front. Soon the guiding light was no longer wanted, for the dawn showed the grass covered with thick dew and the boughs of the trees laden with dewdrops. They passed through a second village, where all the people lay asleep, and walked on into a wood that had hop-gardens to the right and the left. Words will not express the astonishment, the delight, of the cockneys who had never before seen the hops growing, who had only heard about the gardens from friends and relations. The first thing they did was to taste the hops, in order to see if the green things were like the beer sold in Whitechapel.

"To think," said an old man to Captain Lobe, we come down here to gather our own damnation, to help make the stuff that ruins us!"

"Well, if we didn't pick 'em, some one else would," remarked a woman. "The beer would be made all the same, and we're not obliged to drink it."

"These here green softies what look so innocent," said the philosopher, taking some hops in his fingers, "is full of the evil spirit."

At last they reached a belt of fir trees leading to a village church. It was a very modest little church, covered by lichen and moss, with shoots of trees growing in the ledges of the roof, planted there by the rooks. The cawing above and around it made one think that these birds used it as a place of worship, for no cottage was anywhere near, no house. The rooks looked at the hop-pickers in a wise way, as though they recognized friends amongst them, and cawed a loud welcome.

Far off was a sound of sheep bells; nothing else broke the stillness. Long grass grew over the graves, such as Walt Whitman calls "the hair of the dead," and wild rose bushes straggled over the tombstones. Such wild rose trees are seldom found in our carefully-kept English churchyards, but they grow in, a never-to-be-forgotten place in Paris. A visitor to the Cemetery of Père la Chaise, who leaves the well-known footpaths, may stray to the spot where the leaders of the Commune are buried. Long grass, wild flowers, and straggling wild rose trees grow there, above the uneven mounds of earth. Wreaths are fastened to the wall opposite, and in the centre of the wreaths is a crown of immortelles, draped with crape, upon which the one word "Vaincu" is written. It is the most desolate spot on the face of the earth, and standing there the visitor may see pilgrims picking the wild roses with sad faces, while their eyes are fixed upon Paris. There are few sights so painful as a church-yard covered with wild flowers and long grass, because it seems to say that the dead are forgotten. The melancholy of the place crept over the hop-pickers, who were accustomed to Bow Churchyard, which is always full of people, and where the graves have a holiday aspect. The clock in the tower pointed to six.

"I wouldn't be buried in this place for summut," a woman remarked; "it gives me the creeps."

Afterwards they hurried on to the huts which Squire _____ provides for his hop-pickers, which he uses for pigs or calves during the winter months, but which are white-washed and filled with straw before the advent of the scum from Whitechapel. The huts lay at the back of a farm, not far from the churchyard. Passing under some trees the people emerged in the granary plot, where they found the bailiff ready to receive them.

"Not more than ten in one place, if you please," he said politely, pointing to the huts, which were guiltless of ventilation save for a few holes bored in the wooden doors. "All cooking and washing must be done outside, ladies and gentlemen, and in the open space to the side under the roof. Now you can go to bed, but the Squire will call you over at ten o'clock, and read the rules to you himself, just under the biggest rick of hay there in the right-hand corner. And the Squire says, ladies and gentlemen, he won' have the children eating green apples, but they're welcome to the boluses (small blue plums) they can find on the trees, as the preserving is just finished."

The bailiff wore a velveteen jacket with gun straps, fustian knicker-bockers, and thick boots. He had a good-natured face, ornamented by whiskers a trifle less red than his cheeks, and a heavy moustache of the same hue hid his lips.

"A tidy little thousand altogether," he said complacently, while the people stowed away their babies and bundles, "and a Salvation captain to help 'em pick hops. Our parson's no more fit to preach than an old apple-woman, so maybe Salvation will give us a sermon."

Then he went away to his breakfast. Some faggots had been placed outside the huts, and soon the women had made fires of them to boil kettles, while the men lighted their pipes. The children fell asleep on the clean straw, with their heads and legs mixed up, looking like human centipedes. Their mothers would sort them out later on, meanwhile they snored like the little pigs that inhabited the same huts during the winter. They dreamt, no doubt, about the green apples which they must not touch, and the blue plums which had ornamented the trees before they left London; also about the blackberries, which had a provoking way of getting ripe just after the hops were all picked, when they had to leave the country.

Captain Lobe wandered away into the hop-garden. The sun was rising in a red ball out of the east. He had not seen it thus for a long time, rising without a house on the horizon, behind hills that looked blue in the distance. That purple mist which satisfies the eye by a promise of infinity, without wearying the brain by a glimpse of what we call the infinite, acted like balm on the tired mind of the little Salvationist. Nature is a good nurse; a very, very bad physician. If we come to her convalescent, or victims of some slow disease, she takes us into her arms, and sings to us the "lullabies of the universe." But woe to the man who comes to nature for comfort while under the influence of some strong emotion, while swayed by passion. Our emotions, our passions are to her puny things, of which she cannot deign to take notice, any more than she vouchsafes to notice tempests and earth-quakes. She works on just the same, if waves have closed over a ship full of emigrants, and lava has covered a village. Is it likely, then, that she will stoop to calm little lords of the universe, whose hot blood requires the leech's lance before they can get any benefit from her cold compress?

Captain Lobe stood still, breathing the fresh morning air, listening to the birds, looking at the hops that festooned on either side of him; and he felt the sorrows of the great city a less heavy burden, the conversion of the slummers a less hopeless task.

"They will listen to me here," thought the little enthusiast; "I shall win many souls in this place. It is so beautiful here that they will see the hatefulness of sin as they cannot see it in Whitechapel."

Then he looked at the hops, and remembered the words of the old man: "We come down here to gather our own damnation." He sighed heavily, and said to himself: "The serpent is more subtle than any beast of the field; he is here just as much as in the East End of London."

CHAPTER XX

Captain Lobe's Dream

At ten o'clock the Squire read his rules to the hop-pickers; but work was not to begin until the following morning, for the people were tired, and it was then too late to do a good day's business. The men strolled down to have a look at the hops, and rubbed them in their hands to discover if they had much "nutriment;" the women settled into the huts, making beds of straw, and stowing away cooking utensils; the children examined the hedges, in order to see if the blackberries would change colour before the hop-picking was finished.

But the following day, before the sun was up, men, women, and children sallied forth, after a hasty breakfast, carrying bins with them. These bins they placed between the rows of hops; and then the work began in good earnest. The men cut the stalks and pulled up the poles of the hops; the women put the babies to sleep; the children scampered all over the place, but were caught and forced to work like the grown-up people until breakfast. Then an old man came along with a cart full of home-made bread, and the boys and girls "struck." They hade come down holiday-making, and they did not mean to work. Off they went in batches to the cornfields, leaving their fathers and mothers to fill the bins and look after the babies.

Some natives of the place arrived after breakfast, wheeling antediluvian carriages full of children. These people looked askance at the scum of London, and set up their bins at a respectful distance. The country children came to have a look at the cockney infants who lay on old coats and shawls near the bins of their parents, and then returned to their own bins whispering, with their heads close together and their fingers between their lips. A cockney baby really looked very much like a country infant! The hops had a blessed somnific influence, without which the mothers would have been heavily handicapped. No sooner did the babies smell the hops than they resigned themselves to sleep, and fell into a drowsy state, out of which they only roused themselves to eat and drink. Not a few died of sunstroke; for, owing to the smell of the hops, they grew so quiet that their mothers forgot to cover their heads up. Sol thought it a pity to let them return to London, so he smote them dead, and they were buried.

Captain Lobe was quite in his element. He could sit on the side of a bin and swing his legs (his favourite attitude), while he pretended to help the hop-pickers. The poles lay across the bin, covered with thick green leaves, and what the people called "the little softies." His hands were quickly stained black by the "nutriment." It was a good year. The hops were large and soon filled the bins, so the people did not grumble when the bailiff and his staff came round to measure their work and docket it. Overhead was a blue sky, and all around the sun was shining. The hop-pickers were in the best of spirits. They laughed, they sang, they talked, all day long, they even forgot to scold the children. But their conversation was about the last East End murder, and their songs had the filthiest choruses; nature did not purify their thoughts, as Captain Lobe had expected, and he had no more influence there than in the Whitechapel Barracks. Sometimes towards evening a Salvation hymn might be heard echoing down the long lines of hop-pickers, dying away among the festooning green leaves and "little softies." But when the hymn was finished, and the bins had been carried back to the Squire's yard, the hop-pickers set off to "The Partridge," the village inn, where they drank until midnight. He met them sometimes reeling back to the huts through the hop-gardens, while the moon was full; and in its calm light their faces looked to him more degraded than they did in the Whitechapel streets. Effects are produced by contrast. In the East End, where everything is hideous, these men and women seemed to fit in with their surroundings; but here, with nature, they appeared to him out of place, as if the devil had spat forth human beings to mar the beauty of nature, because he and his demoniacal crew could not bear to see this earth clothed with so much beauty.

"The Partridge" was a terrible place on Sunday. It possessed a long, low room, the floor of which was covered with sawdust. This room had tables in it, and forms for the use of hop-pickers. There they drank all afternoon and all evening. The women were as bad as the men and one evening he picked up a child dead drunk halfway between "The Partridge" and the huts. It was no uncommon thing to see the children intoxicated.

These things lay on his heart, for the General had said to him not long before he came into Kent, "Your time in Whitechapel is nearly up, we shall send you somewhere else – to America most likely. Anyhow, you will be moved on soon, for you are too popular in Whitechapel."

He had no great affection for the Salvation Army. But he did not know any other organization that worked so hard, that fought so manfully against the world, the flesh, and the devil, that so fully put its precepts into practice. To go away, to leave his slummers in their sins, to bear with him into a strange land the heavy burdens of their sufferings, these things were hard to put up with. More than once he had felt inclined to hand in his resignation, and work single-handed in Whitechapel. But who was he? What could he do by himself? Was not this wish the lust of the spirit?

One Sunday afternoon he left the huts, and went into the wood that overlooked the Squire's garden. The sun was blazing down on the smooth grass and the red geraniums; the air was heavy with the scent of heliotrope. Butterflies fluttered across the flower-beds; bees hung lazily to the mignonette; insects basked on the cedar trees. Captain Lobe turned away with a heavy sigh towards the little churchyard.

"I must go down and see my mother's grave," he said to himself; "then I shall be ready to start."

He remembered how she had laid her hand on his head one evening after he had been preaching, and had said to him, "Remember, my son, you can do nothing by yourself; you are but a blessed instrument."

"Perhaps, after all," he thought, "I have gone the wrong way to work; some one else is better suited to the slummers than I am. But I love my people so much, it is so hard to leave them, to go away to a strange country."

He wandered on into the hop-garden. There all was quiet. The shadows of the hops lay on the rough earth, and through the vistas made by their overhanging leaves he could see cornfields stretching far into the distance. A purple mist hung over the hills above the cornfields, and into this mist the white fleecy clouds seemed to be sinking. The hops made him feel sleepy. But he walked on until he came to the foot of the hop-garden. A cornfield was there; and part of the corn had been cut already. He could see the red poppies and the convolvuli growing in between the corn, and hear the ceaseless hum of harvest insects. A corn wain stood close by, and he threw himself down beside it, for the sun was very hot, and the shadows looked to him cool and refreshing.

He fell asleep, with his hands under his neck, and his Salvation cap at his feet. One by one the lines across his forehead grew less, and then a look of peace came over his face, which presently changed to an expression of wonder and happiness. He moved towards the sun, and moving, he heard some one say, "Whither thou goest, I will go; and where thou lodgest, I will lodge: thy people shall be my people, and thy God my God. Where thou diest will I die and there will I be buried."

Coming across the cornfield was a figure he knew, tall and slight, with golden hair that seemed to set her face in a halo of holiness. She carried something in her arms, he could not see what, but she stepped towards him carefully, as though she were afraid to drop it. As she drew nearer he recognized Ruth. He had been thinking about her when he fell asleep. The name meant beauty in the Hebrew language, but he had seen another interpretation of it. He moved again towards the sun, and a smile broke over his boyish face, for it was really Ruth – he could see her clear white forehead, that looked like an ivory tablet, and her slight bending figure. She came nearer and nearer, until she reached his feet. He tried to raise himself, but she put her finger on her lips and pointed to the thing she was carrying. It was a little golden-haired infant. He could not move towards her, but she seemed to understand, and presently he felt the child's arms round his neck. It nestled closely to him, and Ruth watched him, with a smile on her face. Then he woke up.

He was alone, all but for an old rook that had perched itself close by on the top of a pole. The rook had a grey head, and stared at him with one eye open and the other shut, much as an old cynical bachelor looks on when he sees some domestic scene enacted. The rook cawed and flew away, leaving Captain Lobe alone in the cornfield.

CHAPTER XXI

A Letter

"'Tis the unforeseen that always occurs," says Lord Beaconsfield, or something to that effect; which means that we are scarcely conscious of our own and wholly ignorant of our neighbour's environment.

Captain Lobe returned to London much better for country air, and almost reconciled to the idea of going to America. It would be a wrench, he said to himself – he would feel it very much; but he must do his duty, and leave the rest to Providence. He thought about Ruth. After that dream in the cornfield she seemed to be always present with him, and almost unconsciously he began to fill in the future with scenes in which she took an active part. Between the Ruth he had left in London and the one who had come to him that Sunday evening lay a great gulf; but somehow or other that would be bridged over, and then – He did not stop to consider the rest. He turned away to comfort a child who had sucked the "nutriment" of the hops off its dirty fingers until it had grown ravenous, or to help an old woman pick hops.

"I have it!" he said aloud once, while he was sitting on a bin. "I have it!"

"What?" inquired a loafer; "what 'ave you got?"

"Nothing," he said. Then he added to himself, "I will tell Hester, and she can tell Ruth."

He ran up the steps of his lodging-house when he reached Whitechapel, and threw open the door leading into his little sitting-room. The first thing he saw there was a letter. He took it up and carefully examined the envelope, as all people do who are blessed with a limited correspondence.

"Homerton" he said, looking at the postmark. "Who lives at Homerton?"

Then he opened the letter, and looked for the signature. But no name was there; only some blotted words that he could scarcely read – letters that had been written by someone whose fingers trembled and whose arm shook. At the end, on the outside sheet, was written: "P.S. – Erysipelas has set in, and the doctors do not think she will live till the morning. This letter has been disinfected. She wishes me to say she is perfectly happy, and 'I leave you Ruth.'"

"Signed for Hester Meadows by Nurse Clayton, of the ____ Hospital for Smallpox."

He stood with the letter in his hand, staring at the blotted words, unable to make out anything except the nurse's postscript. Evidently the writer had been blinded by erysipelas and crippled by smallpox.

"I leave you Ruth."

The nurse must have guided her hand to write that, for the letters were large and crooked, like those in a child's copy-book.

He looked at the date on the envelope. The letter was a week old. Hester was dead, perhaps buried. And where was Ruth?

Slowly he put the letter in his pocket, and went towards the door. He did not see that it was shut, and knocked his head against it. The blow made him conscious of his surroundings, and he stumbled into the passage, down the stairs, out into the street. He was like a man who has suddenly come from a brilliantly lighted gin palace into the outer darkness; he could scarcely see anything. He walked along as if he were tipsy, saying to himself:

"Ruth cannot be dead – perhaps she is not even ill; I think I am dreaming."

But something seemed to tell him that he had not come to the end of his troubles, and he hurried on towards ____ Square, sometimes taking Hester's letter out of his pocket to look at the envelope, saying to himself:

"They might have sent me on this; they had my address. People are so selfish."

At last he reached Ruth's home, and rang the doorbell. But he heard the bell clanging through an empty house, and no one came to let him in. The shutters were up in the first-floor windows, and the area gate was locked. Evidently the place was no longer occupied, or the inhabitants had gone away for a holiday.

Leaves were falling in the square, and naked boughs were beginning to appear above the seat on which he had so often sat with Hester and Ruth. He turned away, and then he felt as if two icy hands had laid hold of his heart and were squeezing all the blood out of it. He started off to find the factory.

It was getting dark, and the men who had left off work were gathering in and outside the public-houses. He took no notice of them, although not a few asked him how he had enjoyed the hop-picking. He quickened his steps, and arrived at the factory door just as Mr. Pember's factotum came out of it, holding a key to lock up.

"Is Mr. Pember in?" he asked.

"He's nowhere about."

"Or the labour-mistress?"

"She's gone to her mother's funeral."

The factotum locked the factory door, and walked off with the key in his pocket.

Captain Lobe felt the words dry up in his mouth. He could not ask for Ruth. He turned away, and went towards the nearest station; but when half-way there he stopped.

"I'll go to Bethnal Green," he said to himself. "The doctor is sure to know what has taken place. They might have sent me on the letter. It was cruel of them! They had my address. It was very selfish!"

While walking towards Bethnal Green there came over him a nausea of the East End and all its surroundings. He had returned to his work full of life and hope after a long absence, and suddenly, without any warning, this blow had been dealt. A slum saviour passed him, and he mechanically raised two fingers to his cap as he heard the Salvation greeting – "Allelujah." He seemed scarcely to see the passers-by, or the street, as he hurried along towards the parish dispensary.

He found the dispensary empty. The door leading into the doctor's consulting-room was ajar, so he knocked. But no one said "Come in." He pushed the door open, and he then saw the modern Prometheus.

The doctor was talking to a woman who held in her arms a puny, wizened-looking infant. It was wrapped in an old shawl, and on its head was a tattered cap. In a moment Captain Lobe recognized it. He had seen it in the police court some months before; and although it resembled many other East End babies, he remembered its careworn little features and its pinched face.

It looked up when he approached, and then half closed its filmy eyelids, while its head dropped forward. It had been wandering from casual ward to common lodging-house, from police court to Bastile, ever since he had seen it last. Now it had arrived in the doctor's consulting-room on its way to the workhouse. It had been born in the Bastile; and at the same place it would die, of course.

"You had better take it to the infirmary," the doctor said. "It will, not live many weeks. They will admit you both, for you must not leave it."

He sat down at his table to write an order for the woman, and Salvation watched him in silence. But directly the woman had left the consulting-room, Captain Lobe asked: "Where is Ruth?"

"Oh," said the doctor, noticing the little man's disturbed expression of countenance, "that's a bad business."

"Is she dead? "Captain Lobe asked, beneath his breath.

"No; but she has been very ill. She has had the smallpox."

Captain Lobe gave a sigh of relief.

"And Hester?" he asked.

"She died about a week ago of erysipelas in the Smallpox Hospital. I was away for a holiday when Ruth fell ill, and only came back after that fellow Pember had carted old Hester off to the hospital. He called in the relieving officer, made the doctor sign the certificate, and telegraphed up to Norfolk House. The whole thing seems to have been done in less than no time. The first I heard of it was from Ruth, who came here half beside herself. Hester nursed her through it, and then fell ill herself. How on earth they got it I can't think, for there is no epidemic; I have not heard of a single case in the neighbourhood. But I blame myself. I ought to have had Ruth vaccinated. The truth is," said the doctor, with a guilty glance towards his little laboratory, "I have been so taken up lately with my investigations, I have not thought enough about my patients."

"Has Ruth been very ill?" inquired Captain Lobe, in a low voice.

"Very. I scarcely knew her when she came in here. She has lost her hair and her colour; in fact, she looks –"

The doctor stopped, and appeared lost in thought.

"I heard a story once," he said, fixing his eyes on the ceiling; "it is a long time ago, when I was a boy. It was told to me by a missionary. There was an old chief somewhere out in heathen parts who became a Christian, and the first thing they made him do was to choose a wife and stick to her. They wouldn't let him go on living with a dozen women. He thought for some time, then he decided to keep a lady whose nose he had bitten off. 'You see,' he said to the missionary, 'the rest can get other men; I've spoilt this one's chances of getting a husband.' That man was what I call a real, thorough-going Christian."

The doctor paused, out of breath, for he had never preached a sermon before, and in this one he felt that he had touched upon the ludicrous.

But Captain Lobe did not seem to hear him.

The room was almost dark; so the doctor lighted the gas, and gave the fire a poke, before he looked at the little Salvation captain; then he asked:

"What are you thinking about?"

"Hester's letter came with such a shock," Captain Lobe said, passing his hand across his forehead. "I have been away a long time in the country, and the last thing I expected was a letter like this."

He took the letter out of his pocket, and handed it to the doctor.

"By Jove," said the modern Prometheus, when he had read it, "that woman was a moral genius."

The dispensary bell began to ring, and the doctor was obliged to leave his consulting room. Captain Lobe stood still, looking at the carpet, worn by the boots of starving patients. A load seemed to have fallen off him. Ruth was evidently well again; she had been in this room not a week previously, so she must have recovered from the smallpox.

Almost unconsciously he made a mental inventory of the furniture.

Then he began to notice the books on the table and the ornaments above the fireplace. Afterwards he took up a likeness which lay beside the bookcase. It was the doctor's sister, no doubt. Her face resembled that of the modern Prometheus; its expression was full of purpose. You may see the same expression on the faces of men and women who live not for themselves or for their families, but for Causes; who are animated by the wish to serve humanity rather than self, or a limited circle of friends or relations. Many of these people never find an outlet for their sympathies and aspirations. Not a few dash themselves upon the rocks, because they seek their ideals in individuals. Some discover a way to serve humanity, and after long years of self-sacrifice are obliged to confess that they have crucified themselves to no purpose.

All are scoffed at and spat upon by realists.

Presently the doctor came back again, and seeing the likeness in Salvation's hand, he said:

"Stay with me, Lobe, tonight. I feel horribly dull. This is the anniversary of my sister's death!"

He stopped.

Sorrow makes us all selfish; unselfishness is only the aftermath of suffering.

"Can you tell me where I shall find Ruth?" Captain Lobe asked.

"No, I can't. She said when she was here that she meant to join the Salvation Army. She had just come back from the Smallpox Hospital. It seems when Pember had old Hester carted off, Ruth was scarcely convalescent. She is angry enough with him, I can tell you, for sending Hester away. When she reached the hospital the nurses told her that Hester was dead and buried. It must have been an awful shock, for Hester has been to her more than a mother. I do wish that I had remembered to have the child vaccinated."

"You say she has gone to the Salvation Army?"

"Well, I don't pretend to understand your Salvation jargon, but what she told me was something to that effect. Some one – a Captain Cooke – had refused to have her in the spring, she said; he had told her that a more decided 'call' would come, or something. I couldn't keep her here, of course, so I put her into a cab and sent her off to Captain Cooke.

"The truth is," he continued, pointing to the laboratory, "there is so little to be done for the starving people of this district, I am so afraid to give them anything but water coloured with some tincture, that I find all my energies going into scientific work. Atoms move in something; they never touch, they never touch."

But Captain Lobe did not feel inclined to listen. He wished the doctor good-evening, and went out into the street just as the dispensary boy was lighting a lamp inside the red shade above the entrance. The night was dark, and a chilly breeze crept round the corners of the houses. He had not eaten anything since the morning, and now that his anxiety about Ruth was relieved he felt hungry and exhausted.

"It is too late to visit Captain Cooke to-night," he said to himself; "I will go tomorrow directly after breakfast."

Then he turned into the familiar Whitechapel Road, and walked on past the flaming gaslights of the costermongers, the public-houses, and the street hawkers. Everything looked as usual. An old woman offered him pigs' feet; a newspaper man shouted the last ghastly details of a murder; tipsy men and women rolled past him singing East End songs set to Salvation music. He caught sight of the slum lassies in a public-house, and listened at the door while one of them argued with an infidel.

"It will be a bad day for you, my friend," he heard the girl say, "when you stand up before the Almighty. Your learning won't count for much on the day of judgment."

Turning away, he stumbled over two half-naked children who were waiting for their drunken parents. A woman with a sickly infant on her breast asked him for money to find a night's lodging. A small boy tried to trip him up, and ran to join some gutter children. All looked as it had done before he went away – as it would look when he came back from America.

At last he was once more in his little sitting-room, gazing out of the window into the street. Below him was the noise of carts and voices; above him was thick darkness.

"I wonder where Ruth is," he said to himself, and what she is doing? I will go to Captain Cooke tomorrow directly after breakfast."

CHAPTER XXII

Ruth

In the slum saviours' little sitting-room, in the worst slum of London, a girl was sitting by the side of a fireplace. Her head was buried in her hands, her elbows rested on her lap. The room was almost dark, for the fire in the grate had been fed with cinders and bits of broken boxes, and the lamp on the table had no oil in it. The slum saviours had gone out to visit the public-houses, and had taken the oil-can with them, promising to get it filled at the nearest oil-shop and bring it back after their evening's work was finished.

The girl was Ruth.

If Captain Lobe had seen her sitting there he would not have recognized her, for her face was completely hidden in her white fingers, and the golden hair was cropped about her head, making her look like a young nun by whom the vows have just been taken.

The night wind rattled the loose panes of glass in the windows, and sang a doleful song in the passage. The streets were unusually quiet, for there had been an attempt to murder a policeman the night before, and this had muffled the oaths of the men and bridled the tongues of the women for nearly twenty-four hours. But the storm would break out again when the public-houses vomited forth their cargoes of misery and vice, and the fact that a policeman had been nearly killed in the street would bring gangs of roughs from various parts of the metropolis to visit the spot, and bevies of women to sing a paean for the benefit of the half-dozen Bow Street men drafted there to keep order during the small hours of the night. The shrill voices of girls and boy could be heard, and occasionally the wail of a baby, although the door of the little sitting-room was locked. The slum saviours had told Ruth not to open it on any account until they returned home to supper. So she sat there in the dark, with her head in her hands and her elbows on her lap.

It was the very evening on which Captain Lobe had received Hester's letter; but so ignorant are we of what is happening to people unless we see them in the flesh, it never occurred to him that Ruth could be in the worst slum of London, he pictured her in a dozen other places, anywhere else.

A little clock stood above the fireplace, ticking the seconds as though glad to get rid of them, and to the right of it was a triangular piece of looking-glass. Slum saviours have not much time to think about their personal appearance, and Salvation uniform gives the "snub direct" to all that is becoming in the way of female dress, while it encourages the stronger sex to strut about like so many small military peacocks. The owners of the room seldom used the mirror unless one girl said to the other " Your hat is not straight," or "You've got a smut on your face."

Presently Ruth rose up. She reached down the triangular piece of looking-glass, and knelt on the floor, close to the grate. The flickering flames showed her pale face. Her golden hair had lost its gloss, her grey eyes had sunk deep down below her forehead, and from brow to chin she was marked by the cruel small-pox. She looked steadily at herself for a minute; then she let the glass fall on the floor, and as it shivered to bits she gave a sob – a sob that had no tears in it.

The little clock ticked above her head, the bits of wood crackled in the grate; they produced soulless sounds, being inanimate objects, but that sob had in it human anguish. There is nothing really great about men or women if we except their powers of suffering.

She crouched down before the fire with her head bent and her hands folded on her black dress. Painful thoughts came so fast that they had no proper sequence. One moment she saw Hester bending over her bed while she tossed from side to side, feverish, restless, crying out for water to quench her thirst; the next she recalled the days when she had felt Hester place the cold compress on her head but had not been able to move or speak, when Hester's voice had sounded faint and far away, when she had cried like a baby. Then she remembered screams, her voice, or the voice of some one else, while she tried to tear the skin off her flesh, and struggled to reach the water she saw in the distance. At last, one day she had found herself lying in bed with a strange doctor and a strange nurse.

How she had managed to reach Hester's room she could not tell; but in the old woman's arms she had fainted. Coming to herself she had heard wheels in the Square, and had dragged herself to the window. Looking out she had seen Hester, after that all had been darkness. But she could still feel Hester's cold tears on her face, Hester's arms round her, she could still hear Hester whispering in her ear, "I am going to your mother!"

She was roused from these painful recollections by a knock at the door, and a loud "Alleluia!" whispered through the key-hole. The slum saviours had come home. Directly the door was opened they hurried in. One girl threw a bundle of *War Crys* on the table, the other proceeded to light the lamp. Ruth remained absorbed in her own thoughts until the two girls noticed the broken bits of looking-glass. That told its own tale, but the slum saviours said nothing. They set to work, and asked Ruth to help them prepare the supper, singing all the time, or relating their experience in the public-houses.

"I hope we shall have a quiet night," one girl suggested.

"So do I," said Ruth.

"Did you sleep last night?" inquired the eldest slum saviour.

"No, not much. Does that man in the next room to me always beat his wife ? It was dreadful to hear him last night. He banged her head against the wall, and she screamed 'murder.' I thought he must be killing her, for I heard her fall on the floor, and he swore that he would kill the baby if she got drunk again. *He* must have been drinking."

"Yes, they both drink," one of the girls answered. "We saw them tonight in the public-house, and they had drugged the baby."

No more was said, for one of the slum saviours had fallen asleep with a basin of gruel on her knee, and the other was nodding. Ruth watched their faces. She wondered how they could work all day, and sometimes all night, amongst people who were more like beasts than human beings. The life they led there made her shiver.

No one knows anything about the slums, who has not spent whole nights in the worst London districts. By day these places put on a veneer of civilization; but at night the slummers show themselves to be worse than savages. They come out of the holes they call homes, and the public-houses, to enjoy themselves in truly bestial fashion. Policemen are afraid to venture into their lairs, so they are free to do all possible mischief. Every day they suck in honest men and women, for work is difficult to get, and want of employment makes people reckless. Girls are their natural prey, because children are the cheapest sort of nineteenth-century labour force. Very rightly does Professor Huxley say that it is better to be born a savage in some heathen land than a slummer in Christian England.

"I was told to-day that the worst part of this slum belongs to the Prime Minister," remarked the girl who was nodding. "Someone, I forget who, said he wanted to sell it. I do wish the General would buy it up. But, then, poor people pay such heavy rents. I suppose he couldn't afford the money."

"If I were Queen Victoria," chimed in the other girl, "I wouldn't rest in my bed until I'd done away with these places. They are a disgrace, I say, and while they are here we cannot call ourselves a Christian nation. But it's no good to talk. Let's go to bed, and try to get some sleep before they shut up the public-houses."

Ruth followed the speaker upstairs to a room called by the girls "the refuge." This was used for visitors, namely, to shelter children deserted by their parents, or women whose husbands had turned them out into the streets. A low bedstead, a chair – these were the furniture. Ruth went to the window, while the slum saviour lighted a dip and placed it in a candlestick. Already she could hear angry voices in the adjoining room, and down in the street was a low roar, as if half of the beasts had escaped from the Zoological Gardens, and had come to visit the worst slum of London.

Her companion was too tired to take much notice of things that happened there every night. She yawned and said,

"Be sure you come to us if you get frightened. Keep the door locked. God bless you. Goodnight."

Ruth listened while the girl went slowly downstairs. Afterwards she locked the door, and returned once more to the window. In the opposite house she could see a light, and she knew that a woman there was dying. She had visited the woman that afternoon with the slum lassies, and she had seen the husband standing by the bed, and the little wondering children watching while the woman swung one arm round and round, murmuring to herself, "My God, I can't keep on. I can't do no more mangling!"

The woman had supported the whole family for months with her mangle, and on the borderland of death, unconscious, she still swung her arm round and round while she said, "My God, I can't keep on. I can't do no more mangling!"

Ruth could see the light in the window, and the shadow of the man whose wife was dying. He had told the girls: "It's bitterer than death to me to watch her like this. I'd better have died than the missus. I can't get work, and now we'll all have to go into the workhouse."

How the slum saviours could spend their days, their nights, among all this misery and sin Ruth could not imagine. She was obliged to confess: "Captain Cooke is right. I am not strong enough for the slum work."

Poor Ruth!

If she could have cried it would not have mattered so much; but all her tears had been wept in the hospital that day when the nurse had said, "Hester is dead and buried!"

In that little dark room, with the dying woman's voice ringing in her car, "My God! I can't keep on. I can't do no more mangling!" she experienced the only thing that raises man above the beasts – human anguish.

Then slowly there rose before her a vision of Captain Lobe, as she had seen him at the last Salvation meeting, while he was giving his farewell address before he went away into the country.

"My hands are clean of your blood," he had said, looking down on the men and women. "I have warned you of hell, and I have spoken to you of heaven, as these things are written in the Bible. Come, then, my people, if there is one among you that is not at peace – come to Jesus." His face had literally shone with benevolence, and he had spoken in the sympathetic way which wins hearts and unlocks secrets. Would she ever see him again, or must she live and die in the Salvation Army?

She remembered how Mr. Pember had come into her room after Hester's death, how he had closed the door and had seated himself close beside her. Trembling, afraid to run away, she had listened to him while he talked of marriage. Fear and distress had then given her almost superhuman strength, and she had said:

"No, I will never marry you! I will never be your wife!"

He had tried to take her on his knee; but seizing his hand, she had bitten it with all her might, and then he had let her fall on the ground, while he said with an oath:

"You will not see that little Salvation chap again now that you have had the smallpox. You will have to marry me, or join the Salvation Army."

It all seemed like a hideous dream, but it was bitter truth. She must live or die in the Salvation Army. And perhaps even then they would not have her, for Captain Cooke had shaken his head when she begged him to let her join the slum saviours, and had said:

"You shall have a fair chance; but I am afraid you are not strong enough for the slum work."

A frightful yell in the street made her forget her own sorrows and rush to the window. She could see by the light of the lamps a confused mass of men and women, also five or six policemen. The latter stood close together and talked loudly, but without effect, while a half-naked woman bawled at the top of her voice from a window almost opposite.

"If you bait me," she said, "I'll come down, I will. I'd like to know what you mean, you ___ ___, shouting up at me! I'm as good as you are, and better!"

Then followed a volley of oaths, which were met by the vilest curses.

It was the favourite slum game – woman-baiting.

Louder and louder grew the voices, and soon bricks, sticks, old cabbage stalks, and rotten eggs were thrown up to exasperate the angry woman. She returned the blows with curses, and grew every minute more furious. In vain the policemen tried to drive the people away; the street swarmed with human beings. They were too strong for the policemen, and nothing would keep them from the fun of woman-baiting. At last, with a yell, the woman flung herself out of the window into the midst of her enemies.

Ruth thought that she must certainly be torn to bits, but at that moment a door opened, and the eldest slum saviour ran quickly into the crowd, separating the people as she went, and reaching the woman just as she was lifted up by her enemies in triumph.

"You are men and women, you are not wild beasts," the girl said, as she stood there in her white night-dress, with bare feet and arms stretched out. "Go home, I say; go home. You shall not kill this woman."

An angry hiss was heard, but the woman was lowered to the ground, and then she was led away by the slum lassie.

Ruth could not believe that this was the end of the woman-baiting; but the people began to disperse, and when once the mob was broken up, the men and women were jostled along by the policemen. She heard the house door slam, and the door of the slum saviour's room shut. Then she lay down on the low bedstead; and in spite of screams and oaths she fell into a troubled sleep, which lasted until the sun shone into the little room and fell on her face, which was so cruelly marked by the smallpox.

CHAPTER XXIII

Another Letter

Ignorant of all this, Captain Lobe slept the sleep of the just, and did not wake up until the postman opened his door, and threw a letter at his head, saying:

"Here's something for you, Salvation."

The lodging-house possessed no letter-box, so letters were sometimes left on the staircase, sometimes they found their way to his sitting-room table. That morning the postman walked into his bedroom, and pitched the envelope at his head, laughing when it hit the mark, and then fell on the blanket. He took it up and, recognizing the handwriting, put it aside until he was dressed. Afterwards he placed it unopened in his pocket. He did not attempt to get any breakfast, but hurried off to Stoke Newington, where he found Captain Cooke standing in the midst of chairs, tables, and other household furniture, superintending "a move;" that is to say, preparing to change his place of residence.

"Oh yes, she came here some days ago," said the slum superintendent when he heard who was wanted. "She is not strong enough for us. I let her go to Drury Lane because she seemed so cut up; but we can't make her into a slum saviour, not even now she has had the smallpox."

Captain Lobe did not stop to argue, but ran down the steps and took the train to Charing Cross. He seated himself in a third-class carriage, and while on his way to Drury Lane he tried to frame what he had to say in proper language. First of all he would sympathize with Ruth about Hester, he said to himself; then he would ask her a lot of questions about her illness, and after that he would tell her that he was going to America. That would lead on to further conversation, and – .

The train drew up, and looking out of the window he saw "Charing Cross" written above the platform. He was almost sorry that he had come to the end of his journey; but he nevertheless went quickly up the station steps, and walked towards Drury Lane, without lessening speed until he stood in _____ Street.

"You want the sisters," remarked a woman who was sitting on a doorstep. "Well, you won't find 'em; they've gone out for the day. That's their house, the one with the shutters up. They'll be home tonight, but there's a big Salvation spree on somewhere – I mean a big prayer-meeting. The sisters wanted me to go along with 'em, but I says to 'em, 'You won't catch *me* at your prayer-meeting.'"

Captain Lobe looked up and down the street, and then at the little dark house, the windows of which were covered with sepulchral-looking shutters.

"We tried to burn them shutters down one night," the woman vouch-safed to tell him. "It was after something was put in the *War Cry* about this street, and we'd a mind to make a bonfire of them shutters. But there, you *can't* scare those girls; they've got *that* spirit, they ain't afraid of nothing. It's my belief they wouldn't mind being killed. It's no good to try to scare 'em, they just enjoys it."

A small crowd began to gather round the woman, so Captain Lobe walked away and turned his steps towards the Bank. He thought that it would be best to return in the evening; anyhow, until then he must exercise patience, unless he went to Victoria Street and inquired about the prayer-meeting. But he did not want to meet Ruth in a crowd of people, and until he had seen her he did not care to report himself at headquarters. So he made up his mind to go home, and come back to Drury Lane in the evening.

He passed the Bank and went on to Tower Hill; there he stood still, looking at the soldiers in the moat and listening to the bugle. He knew the place well, for he had often been there with Ruth and old Hester when he had walked home with them from Salvation meetings. It was not far from _____ Square, and the factory lay close by. Should he go to the factory? "No," he said to himself, "that is useless."

Then he put his hand into his pocket, and finding the letter he had received that morning, he broke the envelope. He expected the writer would give him half a dozen commissions, and he was surprised when his eyes fell on the words:

"This is the last thing I shall ask you to do for me."

He had come across many people like her in his work, men and women who had no religion, only a great desire to help their fellow-creatures. They made him thank God that he had not been cursed with an intellect; for they seemed to him to be possessed by the evil spirit. They meant so well, poor things, and they were so deluded.

"When you receive this I shall be dead," the letter said, "for the doctors say I cannot live through this operation. I want you to call on my lawyer, Mr.____, of New Square, Lincoln's Inn; because I have left all my money to the slum saviours. They are our nineteenth-century heroines. I die, as I have lived, an agnostic; and now death is so close I wish I had not that lie on my conscience. A Christian can tell a lie, and believe that his God will forgive him; but an agnostic knows that a lie is a sin that can never be forgiven.

"I think of the night when he stretched out his thin white hand to me and pleaded – 'Tell me you believe in God. I shall meet the others again; but if you do not believe in God, I shall not see you in heaven.' I remember how the lie came to my lips, and I *could* not choke it down, for his happiness was of more value to me than anything else. I felt that for him I could even have a lie on my conscience. But in the church, when my brothers stood with bowed heads by his coffin – those men he had said that he should meet again in heaven – and I heard my youngest brother sobbing, I knew that I had told a lie. Each sob that echoed through the church seemed to brand that lie on my conscience. And he lay dead – he could never tell what I had done for him.

"Last night I had a strange dream, or vision. I had been reading in the paper about a woman who had smothered her baby because she could not bear to think that it must grow up to suffer as she was then suffering. Her husband was out of work, and the whole family were sinking into the lowest depths of starvation and wretchedness. They placed her at the bar, and when the jury heard what she had done, they decided that she must have lost her reason. But I knew why she had smothered her baby, because I had seen so many cases like hers; I mean so many children killed in sheer despair by their parents. In my dream I saw the woman led out of court, and a hoary-headed old man step into her place. I heard him say, 'Is it nothing to you, O nineteenth-century Christians, that men starve and drink, that women in despair kill their infants? Will you still forget all that I said when I came here in the guise of a carpenter? Day and night the outcast and the hungry rail on Me; and see what I have done that you might know the kingdom of heaven is within you. I let you crucify Me on Calvary, and since then I have let you make Me your scapegoat. But you crucify Me again and again, in these your brethren!'

"He bowed His head, and I could see that He was God Almighty. Oh, I am glad to die. I know that this is selfish, but the myths of men are cruel, and Christians pour abuse on us when we try to use our reason. Goodbye, little Salvation captain. Do not forget to hold out the right hand of fellowship to all those who love their fellow-men, for heaven is no far-off country we are to inherit, but love – I mean *the good within us*. I believe that love will grow strong, even down in Whitechapel; but before then there will come to pass all that St. John, the Apostle of Love, foresaw in the Book of Revelation. Perhaps, after all, I shall not die with a lie on my conscience; perhaps, after all, my God, and the God of my father, are not so very different. I send you his Bible as a farewell present. You will see the Book he loved best was written by St. John the Apostle. Be sure my money goes to our nineteenth-century heroines; and give my love to the girl with golden hair, the one I saw at your lecture."

The letter fell from Captain Lobe's hand, and fluttered down to the ground. He picked it up, and put it back in his pocket. Was it to be always like this? Since his return from the country he had heard of nothing but sorrow, and that not in the abstract, but from people, well known to him. Every minute seemed to bring him in closer contact with suffering. But when he looked again at the letter he became aware of the great love the writer must have had for her father; and presently he began to realize that love alone makes life worth living. He remembered Hester's devotion to Ruth, the East End doctor who wore the black ring while he bolstered up half-starved patients, and the nineteenth century heroines. And last of all he thought of a quiet churchyard where his mother lay under the grass, and of the dream he had had that night in the cornfield. He would go to the Square, he said to himself, and have a look at the place in which he had spent so many happy evenings. Then he must return home to do some work, or pay some visits.

So saying he turned away from Tower Hill, and passing by the hungry rows of men who sit on the steps outside the Mint, walked through the streets to the Square. As he passed through Thieves' Alley he could see the leaves falling from the trees, whirling round and round before they dropped to the earth. The place looked to him very desolate. He cast a glance at the house he had so often visited, and noticed that the shutters were up. The leaves had gathered in heaps on the doorstep, and a black cat stalked slowly up and down like a mute waiting for a funeral.

Presently he caught sight of two little children who were standing, hand in hand, by the railings, and peering through the bars, while their naked feet touched the edge of the iron partition. He wondered what they were looking at. When he came to them they pointed to a girl on one of the seats, and said in a bewildered way:

"She's been a-crying, captain."

To the great astonishment of the children he, jurnped over the railings and went straight to the seat on which the girl was sitting. They saw the slight black-clad figure rise up, and two hands stretched out towards the little man, whose face they had so often watched smiling down on them when they ventured in to his meetings. After that they ran home, so they did not hear Captain Lobe say, "Ruth, you belong to me; you are Hester's legacy."

CHAPTER XXIV

Jane Hardy

It was growing dark when Captain Lobe left the Square with Ruth.

"I will take you to Miss Hardy's house," he said. "Then I will call on Mr. Pember. If I find him in I will let you know what he says. Anyhow, stay with Miss Hardy until I come back again. Have you seen her since your illness?"

"No," answered Ruth. "She lost her mother, and I hear she sent a note to Mr. Pember then, saying she would not work any longer in the factory. She always told me she would not stay there a single day if it were not for her mother. One of her relations – an aunt, I think – died in the workhouse, and she used to say, 'A pauper funeral is enough to make any woman an infidel.' I have seen her stamp her foot when she spoke of it. You see, she could not keep both her mother and her aunt; she was obliged to let one of them go into the union."

Captain Lobe called to mind the Whitechapel Workhouse, and the master's eulogy on Poor Law discipline. But just then he did not care to let his thoughts drift into unpleasant subjects, so he turned the conversation away from Jane Hardy and talked about his experiences down in Kent until they reached the house of the labour-mistress.

"I shall be back in an hour," he told Ruth; "in half an hour if I cannot find Mr. Pember. Anyhow, stay with Miss Hardy until I come back."

Ruth went up the steep, dark staircase, and knocked.

"Come in," said a voice.

She went in, and there she found the labour-mistress. The strong-minded proletarian spinster was sitting in a rocking-chair, swaying herself backwards and forwards while she read a book. A small lamp stood beside her on a table, also a tin teapot. The room was large, and very dark. It had a low ceiling and two narrow windows. At one end of the place stood an enormous bedstead. Some boxes and chairs were arranged against the walls, but these Ruth could scarcely see as she made her way to the fireplace, because the room was so dimly lighted.

"It's me," said Ruth.

"You!" ejaculated Jane Hardy, letting the book fall from her hands. "Why, I've hunted for you up and down; I've been to the Square, and the factory, and the hospital, and the place in Queen Victoria Street. Wherever *do* you come from?"

All this time she was examining Ruth's face by the light of the little lamp, and when the last question left her lips she gave a gulp, as if she wanted to choke down some superfluous emotion. Then she put her arm round the girl's waist, and drew her nearer to the fire, remarking:

"It's very cold this evening."

"Is it?" said Ruth. " We walked here fast, and we talked all the time; so I didn't, feel cold."

"Who's we?" inquired Jane Hardy.

"Captain Lobe and me. He's been away in the country."

"He has come back again?"

"Yes; and," Ruth added slowly, "we are going to be married."

She turned her face towards Jane Hardy while she said this, and to her great surprise the strong-minded spinster threw two arms about her and gave her a kiss.

Then Jane Hardy drew back, feeling that she had been too demonstrative, and remarked:

"Well, I always said I would rather have to do with a Salvation captain than a curate."

"You don't like curates?" Ruth suggested.

"No, I don't," replied Miss Hardy with emphasis; "I see them meandering through the streets looking as innocent of what is going on as new-born infants. I always want to tie bibs under their chins, and set them down to bread-and-milk or porridge. One of them came meandering in here after my mother, but I soon sent him about his business."

Ruth cast a glance at the big bedstead, and said:

"You must miss your mother very much."

"Yes; I had no idea the room would feel so different. She liked you, Ruth. After you went away – I mean last time you paid her a visit – she began to cry. I says to her: 'Why, mother, what are you crying about?' 'Jane,' says she, 'I believe it's all true what you read out of the Book. I mean about things coming down from parents to children.' 'Why, mother,' says I, 'you're talking Darwin.' 'I didn't know he was the gentleman,' says she; 'but you see, Jane, your father was such an overbearing sort of man that before you were born I almost seemed to hate him; and I've been thinking perhaps that's why you hate men. Now, I says to myself, if I'd been more forgiving, I might have had a girl like Ruth. You're not happy, Jane,' says she; 'hating men don't make you happy.' Why, mother,' says I, 'whatever do you mean?' 'Well,' says she, 'it keeps you from getting married.' Then she began to cry again, and it was that very night she fell down and broke her right arm in two places. She'd brittle bones had mother; she was always falling down and breaking something."

"You must feel very lonely now she is gone," said Ruth.

"Yes, I do. But it's a comfort to know she died in her own bed and was properly buried. I went on at the factory because I was afraid of the union for mother; but there, I got a place the very day after I left Mr. Pember."

"I thought I should have to live by myself after I lost Hester," said Ruth. "I didn't expect to see Captain Lobe again. It's very good of him to marry me now I have had the smallpox."

Miss Hardy looked at the girl, and remarked, "I daresay your hair will have grown before the wedding."

"We can't be married for two years," said Ruth. "Two years!"

"People in the Salvation Army are not allowed to get married until they have been engaged two years, Ruth continued. "I think General

Booth will give us leave to be married; but I expect I shall have to go to the Training Home at Clapton while Captain Lobe is in America. He sails before Christmas."

"It's a long time to wait."

"Yes!"

Jane Hardy poured out some tea, and handed a cup to Ruth.

"Do you know if they are *sound* in America on the Woman Question?" she asked presently. "I hear they are very advanced."

"What do you mean?" inquired Ruth.

"Do they believe in the infinite capabilities of woman?"

"For happiness?"

"No," answered Jane Hardy, with gesture of contempt, "for *progress*."

Ruth shook her head, and said that she had not heard Captain Lobe mention the subject.

"I am afraid he has not given his attention to the Woman Question."

"I'm afraid not."

"But he believes in the subjection of man – even *you* must believe in that?"

"What do you mean?" inquired Ruth.

"Well," said Jane Hardy, "this is the truth: Men *will* be subjected. I am sorry for them; they will suffer very much, but they *must* be subjected. They have subjected us, and now we are going to subject them. You see," she continued, "we have risen owing to this subjection – we are more moral than men. Men have sunk below us through self-indulgence. Now we are going to be the superior sex. We shall see them suffering, Ruth; it will be like the hell you Salvation Army people believe in, and the flames will be the passions men have indulged in."

"And what will happen to us?"

"We shall have seats in Parliament, we shall be doctors and judges, not clergymen – we will have no weak young curates. We shall be where men are now, and they will be subjected."

A pause followed, during which Miss Hardy gazed at the red-hot coals in the grate. She forgot Ruth for a few minutes, but presently she asked

"How is Mr. Pember?"

"I have not seen him for nearly a week."

"Where are you living?"

"With the slum saviours in Drury Lane."

"When did you leave the Square?"

"After my illness. I went to the hospital, and when I heard that Hester was dead I could not go back again. You know Mr. Pember sent Hester away. He let her die among strangers. It is hard to forgive him. I do not mind what he has done to me, but he was cruel to Hester, and she was so good! I think she was perfect."

Ruth's eyes filled with tears, consequently she did not see Miss Hardy shaking a fist at the capitalist.

"The last thing Hester did," Ruth continued, "was to dictate a letter about me. She could only write the postscript, for she was quite blind with erysipelas; but the nurse guided her hand to write that. I have the letter in my pocket."

Tears rolled heavily on Ruth's black dress while. she recalled her visit to the hospital, and the words "Hester is dead and buried." The porter had shaken his head when she asked, "Can I see Hester; I mean Hester Meadows?" and he had fetched a woman in uniform into the hall where she was standing. The nurse had said, " Hester is dead and buried."

Then they had given her a glass of water, and had placed her in a cab. She remembered nothing more. Oh yes! The parish doctor had called Hester "a moral genius." What had he meant by that? Hester had been to her both father and mother; and now she lay in the cemetery; nothing would wake her up until "the day of judgement."

A knock on the door interrupted her thoughts, and before she could dry her eyes Captain Lobe came into the room. He wished Miss Hardy "good-evening."

"It's all right," he said to Ruth. "I found Mr. Pember in, and we settled the business. He told me, 'I'm not a blackguard; I'm a gentleman;' and he asked me to shake hands with him. It was on the tip of my tongue to use some strong language; but I thought, 'Who am I that I should refuse to shake hands with the devil himself if he wished it?' So I held out my hand, and afterwards I came away in a hurry. I wonder who the fellow is? I never met any one like him down here in Whitechapel."

"Where did you find him?" inquired Ruth.

"In his office. He was sitting in an easy-chair, drinking whisky and water, and his legs up. He lighted a pipe after I came in, and by the smell of the place I should say he smoked opium. I've been in half a dozen opium dens, so I know what it smells like. Besides, he's got a sleepy, drawling way of speaking, although he is sharp enough about business."

"Sharp!" ejaculated Jane Hardy, "I should rather say he is sharp. I daresay he does smoke opium, for he seems so lazy; but if he takes trouble there is nothing he can't do – nothing."

"You know him pretty well."

"Yes, and I hate him."

Then Jane Hardy abruptly changed the conversation.

"Ruth and I've been talking about America," she said. "I hear you are going there before Christmas?"

"I think I am; that is, I expect to get orders from the General."

"Will you find out for me if they are sound there on the Woman Question? If they are, I will get a place in a ship as a stewardess, and bring Ruth over to America. I'm tired of England. I want to see what the world is made of. It's all very well for people like you, who think they've got leave to visit the planets; but for any one like me, who feels when this life is done they'll be dead for certain, it's a poor look-out to spend all one's time in Whitechapel."

"Sound on the Woman Question!" Captain Lobe said, looking at the labour-mistress. "What do you mean?"

"I've explained to Ruth, and she can tell you all about it. If you see any opening for me in the New World I'll work my way across the big pond as a stewardess; I don't want to live all my life here in Whitechapel; and as to the social revolution they talk about, I don't see any signs of it at present, although I'm sure I've been to all the Socialist lectures anywhere round this place, and I've listened to speeches hours long by Socialists."

Captain Lobe promised that he would keep his eyes open. Then he suggested that it was getting late, and said that he would take Ruth to Drury Lane in an omnibus.

"There's a meeting to-night," he told Jane Hardy; "why don't you come to it? Religion is better for women than politics."

"For some women," she answered, smiling at Ruth. "Good-night. Take care how you go down the staircase."

But when she had closed the door and had heard their retreating steps, she threw herself down on the big bedstead and said:

"Oh, mother! you never guessed that once I cared for a capitalist!"

CHAPTER XXV

Mr. Pember

Not half a mile away from the disconsolate spinster the capitalist lay asleep in his armchair, with his arms folded and his legs up. A smile of contentment played on his face, and his dreams seemed to be pleasant. He had made a comfortable nest for himself, considering that his office was in an East End butter-scotch factory. On the floor was a Turkey carpet, and opposite the writing-table stood a chair which was only a trifle less luxurious than the one in which he was then lying. Heavy red curtains were drawn aside at one end of the place, showing a recess fitted up as a bedroom. A bottle of whisky and a tumbler were within easy reach on the mantelpiece; also a pipe-rack. Above these hung the injunction to visitors, "Know your business, do your business, and go about your business," framed in gilt. A large fire burned in the grate, and its ruddy light showed the capitalist's face, as he turned lazily in his chair, half-opened his eyes, blinked, and stretched himself. Then he sat upright. He looked at his watch, and put it back in his pocket.

"Let me see," he said; "let me see. Oh! I remember," he continued. "I've got to look at the books, and see if I can allow Ruth one pound a week. Well, I rather think I can manage it. I'm glad he doesn't want me to have an interview with the General. Sharp fellow, Booth – a man of business! Just see what Booth's done by trading on the credulity of the people. There's not a man to equal him, unless it's Parnell. Clever fellow, Parnell! Gets all his cash from America. He's a go-ahead chap, but he'd not be where he is but for those American Irish.

"That's a comical little fellow, that little Salvation captain. 'Ruth's goldenhair and beautiful colour were merely symbols to me of something else,' he said, when I congratulated him on marrying a plain woman, 'Symbols of what?' I asked him. The little chap looked as solemn as a judge. and said, 'Of holiness!'"

Mr. Pember laughed for quite two minutes. "He didn't like to shake hands," Mr. Pember continued, holding up a pink-and-white member with almond-shaped nails, and looking critically at it. "'I'm not a black-guard,' I told him; 'I'm a gentleman.' Then he just touched my hand with the tips of his fingers, and let it drop as if it had had a red-hot coal in the middle of it."

Mr. Pember laughed again, but this time the laugh was void of merriment. No man likes to have his hand shied at, not even by a little Salvation captain.

They've a wonderful way of getting hold of money in the Salvation Army," he continued. "One would think that fire and brimstone were the very last things to bring in money. People are mostly fools, as someone says in some book – mostly fools; so it's quite fair to exploit them when one gets the chance. Booth exploits no end of people, and I exploit Ruth. The biggest fool I ever met was her father; an unforgiving, pig-headed idiot. He took me on here without any character, because I gave him my views on women. The man before me had made love to his wife, and, knowing that, I said I hated women. He made me guardian to his daughter; he left me this little place. I've known many fools, but he was the biggest fool of my acquaintance!"

Mr. Pember reached down from the mantelpiece the bottle of whisky and the glass.

"I'm too lazy now to trouble about women; but in my day – in my day – if Ruth's father had seen me then; if he'd known me before I became so lazy!"

He drank some whisky and laughed. "I'll sleep here to-night," he continued, glancing through the red curtain into the recess. "The house in the Square must be sold; it won't let after the smallpox. I'll wait till Lobe is safe out of England; then I'll sell it. So Ruth is going to the Training Home at Clapton, and I am to give her a pound a week. Well, I think I can manage it." He threw a glance at the ledgers on his writing-table, and smiled with complacence.

"Now, if Booth were to look into those books it might be a difficult business. 'It's nothing to the General whom I marry so long as my wife belongs to the Salvation Army,' the little chap said. 'I manage my affairs myself. More fool you,' I thought. 'My mother left me a pound a week, and if Ruth has the same money, we shall be independent,' he told me. 'It's nothing to the General if my wife is poor or rich. I prefer to tell him nothing about it.' 'That's a good thing for me,' I said to myself. 'I wish him joy of his wife.'"

Mr Pember looked at his right hand, and by the light of the fire discovered three small red marks on it. "The vicious little thing," he said, laughing, "I didn't go the right way to work. I couldn't exert myself."

CHAPTER XXVI

The Emigrants' Ship

Three weeks later, one bright December morning, a tender left the Tilbury Docks with Ruth, Captain Lobe, and Miss Hardy on board it. At the last moment Captain Lobe had received orders to go to Australia instead of America, to accompany six hundred emigrants to Queensland.

"I wonder if they're sound there on the Woman Question?" Jane Hardy said. "You must let us know what's going on. Ruth will spend all her holidays with me, and I shall expect to have news of what you're doing. I'm sick and tired of England. If Ruth comes to you in Australia, I shall come along too. I'll look after her while you're away, and bring her to you in Australia, if you don't come back to fetch her. To make you and Ruth wait two years before you get married is great rubbish."

Now that Ruth was shorn of her good looks Miss Hardy did not feel jealous; the golden hair and beautiful colour had disappeared, and with them had vanished every trace of the spinster's jealous feelings. She assured Ruth that beauty is only skin deep, that hair often grows rapidly after an illness. The girl's face, pitted by smallpox, appealed to her sympathies, and she began to treat Ruth like a younger sister.

"You'll be dull at the Training Home," she said, "and I'm lonely, now I've lost my mother; so we'll be friends. When you join Captain Lobe in Australia I'll come with you, if they're sound out there on the Woman Question."

A lady had been lecturing on the rights of women in the neighbourhood, and the ideas expressed by the lecturer had taken hold of Miss Hardy, although she did not quite understand Women's Rights language. She painted the hell into which men must sink in vivid colours, and seemed to gloat over the destruction of her enemies. Captain Lobe could not conceive what she was driving at; but he recognized in her a tower of strength, and confided Ruth to her care, in case anything should go wrong at Clapton.

"If she is ill, I will nurse her; if she dies, I'll see she is properly buried," Miss Hardy told him. "I've quite a respect for you, Salvation. 'Tisn't many men would act like this. You're too good to be a man; in fact, I think you're a woman."

Captain Lobe laughed.

"I don't go in for religion myself," she continued but I like your sort: it's not all talk and no practice."

"Do you really think," he asked "that women are better than men?"

She hesitated, and then said: "They are much less selfish."

This conversation took place on board the tender while it was slowly making its way towards the big ship full of emigrants. Jane Hardy had taken a holiday at Captain Lobe's request, in order that she might accompany Ruth to the ship and return with the girl to London. They had the tender to themselves, for the emigrants had been conveyed from Blackwall to the vessel, and the captain had joined them in a private steamer, with the officers, and the officials of the Queensland Government. The first-class passengers had not arrived yet, but they would come later on, in time for a champagne luncheon. A steamer passed them full of girls, and began to embark its cargo just as they arrived alongside of the vessel.

"Who are those girls?" inquired Miss Hardy,

"Emigrants!" Captain Lobe answered. "I saw them at Blackwall last night, two hundred and fifty young women without encumbrances."

"And you mean to tell me that all those strong young women are leaving England while we are getting in the scum of Europe?" Jane Hardy said. "What will they do in Queensland?"

"I don't know," replied Captain Lobe, "unless they get married. The Queensland Government wants good material. I was told last night any girl with sound health can get a free passage."

Directly Miss Hardy reached the ship she started off to find the girl emigrants. She came first of all to the quarters of the married people, which was fitted up with an economy of space that seemed to her really marvellous. Tables disappeared to the ceiling when not wanted, berths formed Box and Cox arrangements, cupboards served as chairs: the whole place resembled a rabbit warren.

Miss Hardy looked round for a few minutes, and then hurried to the quarters of the unmarried women. There she seated herself on a kit, and began to moralise.

"To send away all these strong, healthy girls, and get in their place the scum of Europe, is a great mistake," she said to herself. "The country will have to suffer for it. A free country, they call it; freedom to starve, I say, and the people who starve easiest are young women. I saw a picture the other day of an English port, and over it was written, 'Rubbish shot here by order of Prince Bismarck.' I don't know what he's got to do with it, but the picture showed a lot of those miserable foreigners being shot out of ships to take the bread out of the mouths of us English. And all the time there are too many Englishwomen! I remember when I was a girl I read at school that the Chinese killed a lot of their girl babies. Wicked, the book called them; wicked heathen. Wicked indeed! they're much better than we are. A leetle pressure of the finger and thumb on the windpipes of the girls, when they don't feel no more than young kittens, would be better, much better, I say, than to let them grow up and starve, and to live lives worse than starving as they do now in London."

She got up, and walked about among the girls, with a heavy frown on her face. "It's no good," she said, aloud, " it's no good for you girls to emigrate."

"Why not?" inquired some of the emigrants.

"Because foreigners come in to take your places – girls that will work for less money than you, and that makes it bad for the men, it lowers wages all round. You ought to stay here and help us fight; you oughtn't to go to Queensland."

She left the girls to unpack their kits, and proceeded up the stairs, without taking any notice of the shouts of laughter that followed her. She wanted to find Captain Lobe and Ruth, and to do this she was obliged to pass by the place in which the first-class passengers were partaking of a champagne luncheon. A foreign servant stood behind the captain's chair, and half a dozen men in turbans waited on the passengers.

"Try this curry," she heard the captain say to a gentleman. "It is made by my foreign cook. You cannot get anything like it in England."

The red velvet chairs and sofas, the silver, the coloured glass, gave an air of luxury to the place that contrasted strangely with the quarters of the emigrants. Jane Hardy looked at it all, and asked herself, "Why should these people enjoy velvet cushions, while the emigrants have only hard planks? Why should they have air and space, while the emigrants are packed closely together in a stench of sea-sickness?"

"It is all very hard, very unjust," she thought it and the social revolution seems no nearer than when I first began to study these questions. Look at that clergyman on the right hand of the captain! A first-class passenger, indeed! And the fellow pretends to follow One that had no place to lay His head on when He was here on earth, the carpenter's son – Jesus."

She hurried away, for she was losing her temper and if she disturbed the people at luncheon she would be treated as a mad woman. They believe that their position gave them a right to champagne and red velvet; they thought it just that half of the ship should be fitted up as a palace and the other half as a rabbit warren.

"Where have you been?" inquired Ruth, when she reached her friends.

"Downstairs with the emigrants."

"The girls?"

"Yes. To think that there is a way of getting rid of so many women; I mean that the girls are willing to go to the Colonies, and we fill their places with the scum of Europe!"

Miss Hardy pushed back from her forehead a mountain of crape, with some sepulchral-looking flowers on the top of it. She had not overcome the prejudice that the dead are honoured by weeds, and she would not have considered her mother properly buried if she had not bought some yards of what she called "mourning." Her grey eyes were bright as steel, but her face had a kindly expression; and if her features were strongly marked, one had but to look at her mouth in order to see that she was not wanting in feeling.

Every day one comes across such women; people fighting their way on, suffering from mental indigestion, but full of energy, determined to educate themselves in spite of difficulties. They are the pioneers of their sex in questions connected with female labour – eager to work on equal terms with men, defiant of all special legislation for women, sometimes caricatures of the screaming sisterhood, but oftener setting these people an example by the way in which they refuse to separate the interests of the two sexes.

"I'll walk about a bit," Miss Hardy said, looking at Ruth. "To make you two people wait all that time before you get married is downright wicked. I can't think how you can put up with such nonsense."

She moved away, and then stood looking, sometimes at the ship, sometimes at the water. Sea-gulls were hovering near the vessel, touching the waves with their wings, and mewing. The sun was shining on the sea and on the deck where the foreign crew had been drawn up in a line for examination. Miss Hardy stared at these men, who were jabbering like so many parrots, and afterwards threw a glance at Captain Lobe and Ruth. She did not feel jealous. Ruth had lost so much that some compensation seemed to her to be necessary. She had her own code of justice, and when people were unfortunate she was always generous. She took a paper out of her pocket – the latest periodical published by those who hold advanced views on the Woman Question – and, having found a seat, she began to read an article entitled, "A Man who Thinks Well of Women." She became so deeply interested in the subject she did not notice a tender coming from Tilbury, or see a tall man step from the tender to the ship. He was the parish doctor. He went to the place where Captain Lobe was standing with Ruth, and laid his hand on the shoulder of the little Salvation captain, saying:

"I've come to wish you a pleasant journey."

Then he shook hands with Ruth, and declared that the sea air had given her quite a colour.

"I shall look after the child while you are away," he told Captain Lobe. "You may be sure that she will be well taken care of. But it's hard lines on you both, this two years' engagement. I should have thought that the General would have given you a dispensation. Just come here for a minute; I want to tell you something."

He led Captain Lobe aside, and then he said

"Do you know, I believe that Pember gave Ruth the smallpox."

"No!" exclaimed Captain Lobe, drawing back.

"Yes, I believe I could prove it. Last night I had a visit from the girl who used to help Hester with the house-work; and from what she told me, I have no doubt that Pember gave Ruth the smallpox."

"May God forgive him," murmured the little captain.

"Well," said the doctor, "of all the Christians I ever met, you are the only one that has not turned out to be a hypocrite. I'm going to have a look at the emigrants."

He disappeared down the steps, waving his hand to Ruth, who stood waiting for Captain Lobe by the side of the ship. The poor child felt that she was about to be left alone with Hester's grave in England. She had been talking to Captain Lobe before the arrival of the doctor about her parents, and had told him "My mother was perfect." All her mother's letters had been carefully burned by Hester, there was nothing left to bear witness that her mother had been willing to go away and leave her when she was a baby, and had then died of a broken heart, or as Hester said, "of a broken conscience." She had a dim recollection of her father, a taciturn individual, who had never taken much notice of her; a man she had scarcely missed after he died of smallpox. Hester had been to her both father and mother; the old woman's love had surrounded her like a soft, tender atmosphere until the terrible day on which the cab had driven out of the Square, and she had been told that Hester was gone to the Smallpox Hospital.

She was one of those people who cannot stand alone, who must fall to the earth if they have nothing to keep them upright. "A poor sort of creature," Jane Hardy said, "not much better than a weak young curate."

But Captain Lobe thought differently. He believed that Ruth possessed the qualities he admired most in women, that the golden hair and clear white forehead had been symbols of an old-fashioned quality much appreciated in the Bible. He remembered his dream in the cornfield, and he made a shrine in his heart for the mother and the golden-haired infant. True, the symbols had vanished, but they had left him what they represented. Besides, he was a very loyal little man, and having loved Ruth once, it did not enter his head to give her up because she had had the smallpox.

"Ruth," he said, when he came back again, "I want you to do something for me. I want you to visit my mother's grave sometimes, while I am away. I went down there to say goodbye last night, and I don't like to think that weeds will grow over it."

Then he talked on until the bell rang, and visitors were ordered to leave the ship. His last words were:

"'Two years, Ruth; only two years. After that you will come to me, or I shall return to England."

The doctor had already gone back to Bethnal Green, but Jane Hardy was there, and she put her arm round Ruth after she had shaken hands with the little Salvation captain. She could see that the girl was crying, so she led the way to the tender, pretending to take no notice.

Captain Lobe bent over the side of the ship to call out, "Only two years, Ruth."

The steamer moved towards Tilbury, and when the ship was left behind, Miss Hardy took out her pocket handkerchief. "He quite upsets my theories about men," she said to Ruth; "but there! he isn't a man – he is a woman."

THE END

Children of the Ghetto
Israel Zangwill

ISBN 9781900355629

Israel Zangwill (1864-1926) was born in London's East End, the son of poor Russian-Polish immigrants. A brilliant student at the rigorous Jews' Free School, he turned to writing after a brief and rather misdirected stint teaching there. Zangwill soon established a reputation as a quick-witted journalist wielding a trenchant pen, casting a gently sardonic eye on the colourful lives around him. His talents brought him early fame and catapulted him into the orbit of the new wave of writers based around Jerome K. Jerome's frothy literary magazine, *The Idler*. A prolific author, Zangwill published numerous plays, stories and novels about Jewish life in London at the turn of the century, including *The King of Schnorrers* (1894) and *Ghetto Comedies* (1907). His plays include *The Melting Pot* (1908) and *We Moderns* (1924).

Children of the Ghetto, his best-known book, was published in 1892. It documents the lives of immigrant Jews who lived and worked in the Yiddish-speaking streets and densely packed alleys emptying into Petticoat Lane, the East End bazaar that was both marketplace and communal watering hole. His portrayal of the uncertain situation of 'his people,' which all too often had been painted in dreadfully sombre tones by earnest social reformers and drum-beating evangelists, is insightfully told with affectionate honesty and wryness of humour.

To purchase this book or to find out details of other
Black Apollo Press publications, visit our website at
www.blackapollo.com

The Romance of a Shop
Amy Levy

ISBN 9781900355612

Amy Levy was born in London in 1861 and died in 1889, just a few months short of her 28th birthday. In her brief life she wrote two novels, both well received, and several volumes of poetry which explored the changing role of Victorian women in the closing years of the 19th century.

The Romance of a Shop, her first novel, was published in 1888. Praised by Oscar Wilde who, reviewing it for *Woman's World*, thought it 'admirably done . . . clever and full of quick observation,' her little novel seemed to herald a brilliant career.

Ostensibly the story of four young ladies who, after the death of their father, decide to open a photographic studio in the heart of London's bohemia (to the dismay of their more priggish relatives) the book, like much of Levy's work, is concerned with the contradictions besetting the 'new' Victorian woman who, in her quest for independence finds herself constrained by anachronistic social mores and conflicting values.

Written just two years before her tragic suicide, *The Romance of a Shop*, at times sweet and charming, has a resonance that goes beyond its apparent innocence, echoing an undertone of despair and hunger for a liberation that, to Levy's misfortune, came only some years afterwards.

To purchase this book or to find out details of other Black Apollo Press publications, visit our website at
www.blackapollo.com